An Amish Family

Other Books by Kathleen Fuller

The Amish Letters Novels
Written in Love
The Promise of a Letter
Words from the Heart

The Amish of Birch Creek Novels
A Reluctant Bride
An Unbroken Heart
A Love Made New

The Middlefield Amish Novels
A Faith of Her Own

The Middlefield Family Novels
Treasuring Emma
Faithful to Laura
Letters to Katie

The Hearts of Middlefield Novels
A Man of His Word
An Honest Love
A Hand to Hold

Novellas included in
An Amish Christmas—A Miracle for Miriam
An Amish Gathering—A Place of His Own
An Amish Love—What the Heart Sees
An Amish Wedding—A Perfect Match
An Amish Garden—Flowers for Rachael
An Amish Second Christmas—A Gift for Anne Marie
An Amish Cradle—A Heart Full of Love
An Amish Market—A Bid for Love
An Amish Harvest—A Quiet Love
An Amish Home—Building Faith

ACCLAIM FOR KATHLEEN FULLER

"The incredibly engaging Amish Letters series continues with a third story of perseverance and devotion, making it difficult to put down. Both Ivy and Noah, as well as Noah's great-aunt Cevilla, are so likeable and realistic that readers will want to continue turning pages in search of a happy ending for all three. Returning characters from books one and two in the series offer a glimpse into their continuing stories, as Fuller skillfully knits together the lives within a changing, faithful community that has suffered its share of challenges."

—*RT Book Reviews*, 4½ stars, on *Words from the Heart*

"Fuller's inspirational tale portrays complex characters facing real-world problems and finding love where they least expected or wanted it to be."

—*Booklist*, starred review, on *A Reluctant Bride*

"Fuller has an amazing capacity for creating damaged characters and giving insights into their brokenness. One of the better voices in the Amish fiction genre."

—*CBA Retailers + Resources* on *A Reluctant Bride*

"This promising series debut from Fuller is edgier than most Amish novels, dealing with difficult and dark issues and featuring well-drawn characters who are tougher than the usual gentle souls found in this genre. Recommended for Amish fiction fans who might like a different flavor."

—*Library Journal* on *A Reluctant Bride*

"Sadie and Aden's love is both sweet and hard-won, and Aden's patience is touching as he wrestles not only with Sadie's dilemma, but his own abusive past. Birch Creek is weighed down by the Troyer family's dark secrets, and readers will be interested to see how secondary characters' lives unfold as the series continues."

—*RT Book Reviews*, 4 stars, on *A Reluctant Bride*

"Kathleen Fuller's *A Reluctant Bride* tells the story of two Amish families whose lives have collided through tragedy. Sadie Schrock's stoic resolve will touch and inspire Fuller's fans, as will the story's concluding triumph of redemption."

—SUZANNE WOODS FISHER, BESTSELLING AUTHOR OF *ANNA'S CROSSING*

"Kathleen Fuller's *A Reluctant Bride* is a beautiful story of faith, hope, and second chances. Her characters and descriptions are captivating, bringing the story to life with the turn of every page."

—AMY CLIPSTON, BESTSELLING AUTHOR OF
A SIMPLE PRAYER AND THE KAUFFMAN AMISH BAKERY SERIES

"The latest offering in the Middlefield Family series is a sweet love story, with perfectly crafted characters. Fuller's Amish novels are written with the utmost respect for their way of living. Readers are given a glimpse of what it is like to live the simple life."

—*RT BOOK REVIEWS*, 4 STARS, ON *LETTERS TO KATIE*

"Fuller's second Amish series entry is a sweet romance with a strong sense of place that will attract readers of Wanda Brunstetter and Cindy Woodsmall."

—*LIBRARY JOURNAL* ON *FAITHFUL TO LAURA*

"Well-drawn characters and a homespun feel will make this Amish romance a sure bet for fans of Beverly Lewis and Jerry S. Eicher."

—*LIBRARY JOURNAL* ON *TREASURING EMMA*

"*Treasuring Emma* is a heartwarming story filled with real-life situations and well-developed characters. I rooted for Emma and Adam until the very last page. Fans of Amish fiction and those seeking an endearing romance will enjoy this love story. Highly recommended."

—BETH WISEMAN, BESTSELLING AUTHOR OF *HER BROTHER'S KEEPER* AND THE DAUGHTERS OF THE PROMISE SERIES

"*Treasuring Emma* is a charming, emotionally layered story of the value of friendship in love and discovering the truth of the heart. A true treasure of a read!"

—KELLY LONG, AUTHOR OF THE PATCH OF HEAVEN SERIES

An Amish Family

KATHLEEN FULLER

ZONDERVAN®

ZONDERVAN

An Amish Family

Copyright © 2018 by Kathleen Fuller

This title is also available as a Zondervan e-book. Visit www.zondervan.com.

Requests for information should be addressed to:
Zondervan, *Grand Rapids, Michigan 49546*

Library of Congress Cataloging-in-Publication Data

Library of Congress Cataloging-in-Publication Data
Names: Fuller, Kathleen, author.
Title: An Amish family / Kathleen Fuller.
Description: Grand Rapids, Michigan : Zondervan, [2018]
Identifiers: LCCN 2018002998 | ISBN 9780785217343 (paperback)
Subjects: LCSH: Amish--Fiction. | Domestic fiction. | GSAFD: Christian
fiction.
Classification: LCC PS3606.U553 A83 2018 | DDC 813/.6--dc23 LC record
available at https://lccn.loc.gov/2018002998

Printed in the United States of America
18 19 20 21 22 / LSC / 5 4 3 2 1

To my husband, James. I love you.

CONTENTS

Building Trust. 1

A Heart Full of Love. 75

Surprised by Love. 173

A Gift for Anne Marie. 253

Glossary

ab im kopp: crazy, crazy in the head

ach: oh

aenti: aunt

Amisch: Amish

appeditlich: delicious

bruder: brother

bu/buwe: boy/boys

daag/daags: day/days

daed: father

danki: thank you

dawdi haus: smaller home, attached to or near the main house

Dietsch: Amish language

dochder: daughter

dumm: dumb

dummkopf: idiot

Englisch: non-Amish

familye: family

frau: woman, Mrs.

garten: garden

geh: go

grossmutter: grandmother

grossvatter: grandfather

gut: good

gute nacht: good night

hallo: hello

haus: house

hungerich: hungry

kaffee: coffee

kapp: white hat worn by Amish women

kinn/kinner: child/children

kumme: come

lieb: love

maedel: girl/young woman

mamm: mom

mann: Amish man

mei: my

morgen: morning

mudder/mutter: mother

nee: no

nix: nothing

onkel: uncle

perfekt: perfect

schee: pretty/handsome

schwesters: sisters

sehr: very

seltsam: weird

sohn: son

vatter: father

ya: yes

yer: your

yerself: yourself

Building Trust

CHAPTER 1

*P**link. Plink.*

Grace Miller smiled and slipped out of her bed, still fully dressed even though it was past midnight. She snuck downstairs in her bare feet, opened the kitchen door, and went outside. The balmy night greeted her, and so did Joel King. The moon shone bright in the sky, and by its silvery light she could see his handsome face as he smiled at her. She hurried toward his outstretched hand. He took hers, and they walked to the farthest corner of her backyard.

Before she could take a breath, he pulled her into his arms and kissed her. "What was that for?" she asked, her lips tingling.

"I have to give you a reason for kissing you?" He brushed the back of his hand across her cheek.

"*Nee,*" she said with a soft smile. They had been dating for almost a year, in secret. So secret that no one knew, not even her sisters. Faith of course had no idea, since she had married Silas Graber two years ago and moved to her own house nearby. But Patience and Charity, who were sixteen and fifteen and nosy as they could be, could have found out. She and Joel made sure to be careful, and she liked having something all to herself. Growing up with three sisters, she'd had to share a lot.

He slipped his hands into his pockets and took a step back, which made her concerned. "Joel?" She moved closer to him. "Did I say something wrong?"

He shook his head and smiled. In the moonlight she couldn't discern colors, but Joel's dark-blue eyes, reddish-brown hair, and tanned skin, gained from his work as a lumberjack, were engraved in her mind. At twenty-five he was three years older than she was. He smiled that cute crooked smile of his, the one that had caught her attention last year when they played volleyball after a summer Sunday singing. They had accidentally crashed into each other, and when Joel turned around and said sorry and smiled, Grace was smitten. Turned out Joel had been too.

He took his hands out of his pockets and clasped hers. It felt warm. Safe. Secure. Right. "I just . . . I need to talk to you about something. Actually, I need to ask you, not just talk." He let go of her hands and ran his fingers through his hair. "I, uh . . ."

She touched his cheek. "Whatever it is, you can tell me. I love you, Joel. I don't want you to think you can't tell me something."

He reached for her hand and kissed her palm, then took her tenderly in his arms. "I love you too, Gracie. That's why I want to marry you."

It wasn't a complete surprise that he'd proposed. Still, she was stunned. She'd known she would marry Joel King shortly after they started dating. But now that he'd said the words, she was at a loss. "I . . . I . . ."

"Say yes, Grace." He drew her closer to him. "Say you'll be my wife."

Her heart swelled with joy as she nodded. "Of course I will. I can't wait to marry you, Joel."

He kissed her again, this time lingering, his kiss a promise of their future together. When they parted, he said, "I have to get going. We have a big clearing job in Ashtabula, and I have to be ready in a couple hours." He chuckled. "Not that I'll be able to get any sleep after this."

"Me either." She smiled.

"We need to figure out a wedding date. The sooner the better, I think."

"I'll have to talk to *mei* parents."

He nodded. "I don't care who knows we're engaged. I was getting tired of dating in secret."

"Why don't you come over for supper after work? We can both talk to *mei* parents then."

He nodded. "*Gut* idea." He leaned down and kissed her one more time. "It's harder to leave you than ever."

"I know. But soon we'll be together again." She looked up at him. "And I can't wait."

Joel took off for home, which wasn't too far. He was athletic due to his job, and running the half mile was easy for him. Grace hurried back to her own house and snuck inside. As soon as she shut the kitchen door, the gas light hissed to life. She froze and saw her sister, Charity, standing near the tall gas lamp.

"Where have you been?" Charity said, crossing her arms over her chest.

"Just getting some fresh air." She'd had this excuse planned in case she got caught, but she hadn't expected the person to catch her would be Charity. Patience was the light sleeper. "I couldn't sleep."

"You expect me to believe that? Especially after I saw you kissing Joel King?"

"What?" Grace put her fingers to her lips.

"Don't deny it." Charity dropped her hands and smiled. "You're not the only one who knows how to sneak out of the house."

Grace did know that. Their older sister, Faith, used to do the same thing when she and Silas were first dating. Then they were engaged, then they weren't engaged, then they were . . . It was a bumpy road to their eventual marriage, but they were a happy couple now.

Fortunately, Grace didn't anticipate any problems when it came to her and Joel marrying. But that didn't mean she appreciated Charity's nosiness. "I couldn't sleep—"

"Because you were busy kissing." Charity giggled, her light-blue eyes twinkling. "C'mon, Grace. I'm not a child. I know how dating works. Besides, Joel's a *gut mann*. I'm actually a little jealous."

"You are?"

"*Ya*." She sighed and sat down at the table. "Faith's married and you're dating. Even Patience has a *bu* interested in her, not that she would admit it."

Grace sat next to her. "*Yer* time will come. *Yer* only fifteen."

"*Mamm* was almost married at *mei* age."

"I was eighteen when I got married. And I married too young."

Both Grace's and Charity's heads jerked up as their mother walked into the kitchen. "What are you two doing up at this hour? And why are you talking about marriage?"

Grace and Charity exchanged a look. "We couldn't sleep," they both said at the same time.

"So you decided to come in here and wake me up?"

"Sorry," they both said at the same time again.

Mamm gave them a weary smile. "It's all right. I was having trouble sleeping anyway." She went to the cabinet and got a glass, then filled it halfway with water. She turned and leaned against the sink and took a sip. "So . . . Who's getting married?"

Grace's face heated and she glanced at Charity, who to her credit was busy tracing the lines on the wooden table with her fingertip and not looking up. She was twenty-two. Definitely marrying age, unlike Charity.

Her mother's expression turned solemn. "I didn't mean to pry. Obviously, this is a private conversation." She set the glass down and started to leave.

"*Nee*," Grace said, getting up and putting her hand on her mother's arm. "It's not private." *Not anymore.* "Would it be all right if Joel King joined us for supper tomorrow?"

Mamm's eyes grew soft. "*Ya.* That will be fine." She touched Grace's hand. "I should get to bed. Sunrise will be here before we know it. You girls run upstairs too. Quietly," she added. "Even though *yer vatter* can sleep through a tornado."

"We will," Charity said.

"*Gute nacht, Mamm.*" Grace held the back of the kitchen chair.

"Oh," *Mamm* said, turning around. "Let me know what Joel's favorite dishes are. We should prepare something he likes." With another smile, she left the room.

Grace blew out a breath. That wasn't as hard as she thought it would be. Then again, why would it be? Her family knew Joel. Maybe not all that well, since he had left the area and moved to Holmes County when he was a teenager. But there wasn't anything objectionable about him either.

When he first returned and she saw him at church, she knew in her heart he was special. He was broad shouldered, tall, and had a confident air about him, but there was more to him than good looks. He was kind, tender, and devoted to his faith.

And soon he would be her husband.

"Grace?"

She blinked at Charity.

"We shouldn't linger."

"Right." Her mother had been easygoing about being woken up in the middle of the night. Which wasn't surprising since *Mamm* rarely became ruffled. Both of her parents were even-tempered, but they could also get upset when pushed too far, and she wasn't about to push either of them.

She followed Charity upstairs, pausing at the room Charity shared with their sister, Patience. "*Gute nacht*," Charity whispered, then slipped inside, closing the door behind her.

Grace nodded and went to her room. She needed to get to bed, but she was too excited to sleep. Instead she went to the window and looked at the backyard, her gaze landing on the place where Joel proposed. She clasped her hands together. "Thank you for Joel, Lord," she whispered, filled with love and happiness. She couldn't wait to see what the future held for them both.

Joel tugged on the collar of his shirt as he stood on Grace's front porch. He wondered if this was such a good idea. Not about asking Grace to marry him. That was the best idea he'd ever had. He loved her, and if it had been up to him, he would've proposed months ago. But he sensed that Grace liked to be sure about things. She never rushed into anything without thinking. That was his forte. So he was shocked and pleased she had said yes right away.

But now he had no idea what he was going to say to Grace's

parents. He had friends who had gotten married and also dated in secret. They waited to announce the wedding a couple weeks before the ceremony actually happened. But he never talked to them about how they went about getting married or telling the parents. This was new territory for him. He hadn't even told his own folks yet. He figured it would be better to let the bride's parents know first.

He cleared his throat and knocked on the door. Grace answered immediately, and her bright smile made him forget his nervousness. At least mostly.

"Hi," she said as she opened the door wider. She seemed different for some reason tonight. She was still wearing the same white *kapp* she and the rest of the women in the community wore. And he noticed she was wearing a light-green dress. His favorite color. But he'd seen her wear that dress before, so that couldn't be it. Then he looked into her face and saw the rosy cheeks, the sparkling eyes, and realized what else was there. Love. Love was shining, and the connection they had was now stronger because of their promise to each other.

"Hi," he said, wishing he could take her in his arms right now. But he didn't dare. Grace wasn't one for public affection. And besides, he didn't want to get off on the wrong foot with her parents.

"Dinner's almost ready." He stepped inside, and Grace shut the door behind him. "Why don't you have a seat in the living room? *Daed* should be there shortly."

Joel nodded and walked into the living room after he slipped off his shoes. He sat down on a couch that looked like it had seen better days, but was still nice. He glanced around the house. Other than church services, he'd never been inside. It was a smaller, more modest home than his uncle's. Uncle Abner owned a successful logging and lumber business, one that was so prosperous he'd opened up another branch down in Holmes, where Joel had worked before he came back here a year and a half ago. Now he worked for and lived with his uncle while his brother and father and mother stayed in Holmes County. It had been nice to return to Middlefield, but he hadn't crossed paths with Grace's family other than saying a polite hello after a church service or at a community gathering. *I'll get to know them real well now.*

He could smell the delicious dinner wafting through the living room. He tapped his foot on the floor and rubbed his palms over his knees. Where was her father? Unable to sit and wait, he stood up and started pacing a little, feeling a bit better but still filled with nervous energy. He wanted to get this over with.

Grace came back into the living room. "Where did *Daed geh?*"

Joel shrugged. "He never came in here."

"Really? I thought he was going to come talk to you, or at least say hello." She frowned a little, then went up to him. "Come on into the kitchen. I'm sure he'll be here any moment. He's never late for food." She smiled and Joel chuckled, standing close to her but not taking her hand, even though he wanted to.

He went into the kitchen and saw a magnificent spread on the table. They had prepared some of his favorite dishes—pot roast, broccoli salad, and fresh dinner rolls, the tops shiny with melted butter. He and Grace spent a lot of time talking about their favorite things, the future, and what they wanted in their dreams. He shouldn't be surprised she had prepared some of the foods he really liked. He looked at her and smiled, mouthing the words *thank you.*

She sat down and he sat next to her. Patience and Charity sat across from them. All the Miller sisters looked similar, but there was something special about Grace.

"Everything looks *appenditclich*," he said to Grace's mother, Ruby.

"*Danki*, but Grace made most of the meal."

"I made the dessert," Patience piped up. "Blueberry Buckle. Ever had that before?"

"Can't say that I have."

"It's like a cobbler," Grace said, leaning close to him.

He nodded and at that moment her father walked into the kitchen. "Hope you weren't waiting too long," he said. "I had to help the neighbors next door move some furniture—" He stopped and stared at Joel.

"*Daed*," Grace said with a smile. "You know Joel King. He's eating supper with us tonight."

Vernon didn't move, and Joel withered beneath his agitated gaze. He wasn't sure why Grace's father seemed upset, but he would do everything he could to make a good impression.

"*Danki* for having me." He offered a smile.

"I didn't know you were coming."

Joel glanced at Grace, who looked as puzzled as he felt. Vernon was a friendly man, at least from what Joel had observed. But right now he looked like he wanted to kick Joel out of his house.

"Vernon?" *Mamm* said as she went to his side. Her mouth formed a small frown. "We should start on supper, *ya*?"

Vernon moved to the chair at the head of the table, but didn't pull his gaze from Joel until everyone bowed their head for prayer. Wow, this was odd. Joel prayed that things would go smoother than they were right now. He resisted the urge to tug at his shirt collar again.

When he lifted his head, Vernon wasn't looking at him. Whew. Maybe he'd imagined Grace's father's cold reaction to him. He filled his plate with the food as they passed the dishes around. Everyone started eating, but no one said anything. Joel glanced at Vernon again, who was pushing food around on his plate, still not looking up.

Grace's mother cleared her throat. "How was your day, Vernon?"

"Fine." He tore off part of a slice of bread and crammed it into his mouth.

Grace exchanged a look with Joel. He saw confusion in her eyes. He was confused himself. Vernon seemed downright unfriendly.

"*Daed*," she said, her tone cautious. "I'm sure *yer* wondering why Joel joined us for supper tonight."

"*Nee*. I'm not."

That stung, and now Joel knew he hadn't been imagining it. Grace looked stricken, and Patience and Charity seemed to shrink in their chairs.

"Well," Grace said, her voice strained. "He's here because we have an announcement."

"Announcement?" He scowled at Grace. "What kind of announcement?"

"We're getting married." Joel reached for Grace's hand under the table and gave it a squeeze. He had no idea why her father was acting like this, but she didn't have to face him alone. "I want to marry your daughter."

Vernon's hands slammed on the table. "I won't allow it." Before anyone could speak, he shoved away from the table and jumped up from his chair.

"Vernon, your supper—"

"Lost *mei* appetite." He stormed out of the kitchen.

Joel flinched when he heard the front door slam. He looked at Grace. Her lower lip was trembling.

"I don't understand," she whispered. "Why is he so angry?"

Mamm held out her hands as she looked at Vernon's empty chair. "I don't know. I've never seen him like this."

Joel tightened his hold on Grace's hand. He'd had no idea how her family would take the news of their engagement, but he hadn't expected this. From the shocked expressions on the faces of Grace and her sisters, he could see they hadn't either.

"I should *geh* talk to him." Grace pulled her hand out of Joel's and started to get up from the table.

"*Nee.*" He put his hand on her shoulder, stilling her movements. "I'll speak to him."

"Are you sure?"

Joel nodded. He didn't like seeing Grace upset. What was Vernon's problem, anyway? He turned to Grace's mom. "Excuse me," he said, rising from his chair. He paused. "The meal is delicious, Ruby."

Grace's mother nodded, her expression solemn, and Joel left to find Vernon. He checked the barn, a place Joel often went when he was upset or needed to think. Sometimes the physical exertion of cleaning out the barn cleared his head. Vernon wasn't there, though. He looked around the backyard, his gaze pausing at the place where he had asked Grace to marry him. He'd been so happy and full of hope last night. Now he was filled with dread and uncertainty.

He stopped, calming himself. Surely Vernon was a reasonable man. When Joel found him, he would explain how much he loved

Grace, how he would take good care of her the rest of his life. Vernon wouldn't have to worry about his daughter. She would be loved and cherished. What father wouldn't want that?

Yes, he could reason with Vernon. If he could find him.

The door to a medium-size shed was ajar, and he hurried to it. He paused, unsure if he should knock on the open door or walk in. He decided to enter the shed and see if Vernon was actually there. He stifled a sigh of relief when he saw the man there, staring at one of the walls. The building was filled with tools of his trade—shingles, roofing tools, a couple ladders, and a few tool belts. Joel took a deep breath.

"Vernon," he said, the last syllable coming out in a squeak. So much for showing confidence. He cleared his throat. "Can I talk to you for a minute?"

Vernon kept his back to him, long enough for Joel to wonder if he would ever turn around. Finally, he did. "I'm not interested in talking to you."

His words almost made Joel take a step back. "What?" he asked, wondering if he'd heard wrong.

"I'm not interested in talking to you," Grace's father repeated, moving toward Joel. His lips were pressed in a line so tight, they were turning white. His face, tanned and weathered from years spent on rooftops during all seasons, was twisted with anger. "And *yer* not marrying *mei dochder*."

It was as if he'd thrust a knife into Joel's heart. "But—"

Vernon moved in front of him until only inches separated them. "Get off *mei* property."

Joel's mouth dropped open. There was no doubting Vernon's hostility. But why was he so angry?

"What?"

"Leave." Vernon pushed past Joel. "And don't come back."

Joel turned, his mouth still agape. His thoughts were whirring. What had he done to make Vernon so angry? They couldn't get married without her father's blessing. Well, they could, but Joel wouldn't be the cause of strife in their family. His shoulders dropped. What were he and Grace going to do?

Grace paced back and forth on the front porch. She'd never seen her father so angry before. It didn't make sense. His reaction to Joel was irrational, not to mention inhospitable and very un-Amish. *Daed* was normally a calm, friendly man who often liked to have people over, even if he wasn't the most talkative person. Her fists clenched as she waited for him and Joel to come back. Her father had been rude, and he owed Joel an apology.

When neither of them returned, she stopped pacing and clasped her hands together. Their absence wasn't a good sign. Finally, her father came around from the back of the house. Surely Joel wasn't far behind, having made sure everything was all right. But when she saw the fury on her father's face, she knew nothing had been worked out.

"*Daed?*" She flew down the porch steps and met him at the bottom. "Where's Joel?"

"Far away from here, if he knows what's *gut* for him." *Daed* blew past her and started up the porch steps.

"*Daed!*" Grace stiffened. "Why are you so angry?"

He spun around and looked down at her. Then he blew out a breath. "Don't even think about marrying that *mann.* Joel King isn't welcome here, or anywhere near *mei familye.*"

"*Daed*—"

"*Mei* word is final!" His face turned a deep shade of red, then he turned and stormed inside.

Tears streamed down her cheeks. She'd been so excited for tonight's supper, taking extra care not only to make Joel's favorite foods, but also to make sure they had been perfectly prepared. It just so happened that both he and her father loved pot roast. She was sure they would have other things in common and expected the evening to go smoothly. But from the moment her father had seen Joel, something had been off. No, not off. Something was very, very wrong.

"Gracie?"

She turned to see Joel approaching. She hurled herself into his arms, not caring about her father's warning or if anyone saw them together. She buried her face in his shirt.

"I don't know what happened," she said.

"Me either."

She felt his hand stroke her back, and it calmed her nerves. She lifted her head and looked at him. "Were you able to talk to him?"

Joel shook his head. "He's angry with me, that's for sure."

"Any idea why?"

"*Nee.* I've been wracking my brain trying to figure it out, but I can't." He brushed his thumb over her cheek. "But I'll get to the bottom of it."

"*Daed* said you weren't welcome here." She sniffed.

"I know. He told me." Joel gathered her close and rested his chin on the top of her head. "Don't worry. I won't let anything stop us from getting married. Whatever the problem is between *yer vatter* and me, I'll solve it."

"Promise?"

"Promise."

His arms tightened around her, and she breathed in deeply. She trusted him. She loved him, and if he said he would fix everything, she believed him. Because if he didn't . . . she didn't know what she would do.

CHAPTER 2

"Vernon Miller, what in the world is wrong with you?"

Vernon turned around, flinching at his wife's sharp tone. He loved Ruby, but her angry, shrill voice cut into his ears. They were in their bedroom, and he'd known he would eventually face her wrath tonight. And he did, as soon as she shut the bedroom door.

Not that he didn't deserve it. He'd handled tonight badly, and he knew it. He'd been aware of it even while he couldn't stop himself, couldn't stem the blaze of rage rising in him. Even now anger pounded in his ears and made his chest squeeze. Joel King. Of all the men in Middlefield—of all the men in the world—his Grace had to fall for him. Did she have any idea what kind of man he was? She couldn't, or she wouldn't be with him. Of course, he probably had her fooled. He was devious that way.

"Vernon? Did you hear me?"

The whole state of Ohio heard you. He glanced at his hands. They were balled into tight fists. He closed his eyes and prayed for calm. He wasn't like this. He wasn't rude. He wasn't impulsive. And he didn't hurt the people he loved. But he could tell by the pain on Grace's face as he'd left her outside that he'd hurt her deeply. *But it's justified. I'll do anything to protect my girls.*

He felt Ruby's hand on his shoulder. "Vern. Talk to me."

One thing about his wife—and there were many, many amazing things, which was why he'd fallen in love with her practically at first sight—was her level head. He turned, mollified by her calmer tone. But even as he faced her, he couldn't bring himself to talk about *him*. It had taken Vernon a long time to forgive and even longer to forget. Yet all of that disappeared as soon as he saw Joel in his house. He sat on the edge of the bed, his shoulders slumped.

Ruby sat next to him. "What happened to you tonight?"

He ran his hand over his head, feeling the thinning hair on top. He was nearing fifty and showing it. His knees ached when he climbed the ladder, his back cramped when he bent over roof shingles, and his arms strained as he nailed the shingles to the tar paper. He'd weathered blistering temperatures, unexpected downpours, frigid blasts of wind. He'd known what it was like to start over, to worry about feeding a family of six, to have his dreams dashed. And it all paled to the anger and pain he felt right now.

"I don't want to talk about it."

"Well, you need to. Because I'm expecting an explanation."

Vernon turned to her. He owed her an explanation. But no matter how he tried to frame the words in his head, they were clouded by rage. He popped up from the bed. "I said not tonight."

"Vernon—"

He opened the door.

"Where are you going?"

He stopped. "To sleep on the couch."

She got up to stand beside him and shut the door. "You'll do *nee* such thing." She ducked underneath his arm and leaned her back against the door, looking at him. He was only a couple inches taller, which meant she could look him in the eye. And what he saw in her soft, gray gaze nearly undid him. "It's all right," she said, touching his cheek. She brushed her fingers over his beard. "You don't have to say anything tonight."

He slumped with relief.

She held his face in her hands. "But you'll have to fix this tomorrow. Grace is beside herself, and you owe Joel an apology."

Vernon's body tensed again. "*Nee*, I don't."

She opened her mouth, then closed it. "All right. I won't argue with you."

Her kind words made most of his ire dissipate. He gathered her in his arms. "*Danki*," he said in her ear. "*Danki* for not pushing this."

Lying in bed later that night, a single shaft of moonlight coming through the window and his beautiful wife fast asleep beside him, Vernon stared at the ceiling. He didn't imagine anything being different in the morning, but Ruby was right. He had to explain himself to Grace. He wasn't sure how to do it without dredging up the past, or how he would handle her tears when he told her, under no circumstances and over his dead body, would she marry Joel King.

Joel had tossed and turned all night, trying to figure out what he should do. This morning when he woke up he hit his knees, praying that last night had been a big misunderstanding and that today he would be welcomed into the Miller family with open arms. Right now, he would be fine with plain acceptance.

He spent the day working with his uncle in their clear-cutting lumber business. Today's job was short—they were finishing up five acres in Ashtabula County. He was back home by noon. After taking a well-needed shower, he put on fresh clothes and headed for Schlabach's Grocery, where Grace and her sister Patience worked.

When he walked into the store, he was glad to see there weren't many customers. Patience was behind the counter, writing what looked like a list on a narrow white tablet.

"Is Grace around?" Joel asked, approaching the counter. He touched his collar, realizing he was about to tug at it, then dropped his hands.

"She's in the back of the store," Patience said. "Our boss is out for the day and she's doing some accounting for him."

"Think it would be okay to *geh* back there?"

Patience nodded, giving him an encouraging smile. "She'll be happy to see you."

At least her sister was accepting. Joel nodded and walked to the back of the store. He knocked on the door.

"Just a minute," Grace's sweet voice sounded from the other side. When the door opened, her blue eyes lit up. "Joel." She practically pulled him inside the office and shut the door. When she hugged him, he couldn't help but grin. Suddenly his future wife had forgotten her shyness about public affection, since anyone could open the door and walk into the office at any time.

"I was going to come see you after work," she said.

"We finished the job early." He touched her face. "I couldn't wait to see you."

"Thank goodness. I was worried you would take *mei daed* seriously."

"I do, but not about this."

She nodded and leaned against the desk. "He's being unreasonable. I didn't even see him today. He was up before everyone else and left for work extra early. I can tell *Mamm* is confused too."

"Does she know why he's angry?"

Grace shook her head. "She has *nee* idea. She tried talking to him last night, but he wasn't having it." She crossed her arms. "I don't know what to do."

"I'll try talking to him again," Joel said.

"Maybe you should wait a few days." Grace bit her bottom lip. "He might cool down by then."

"And he might get angry at me all over again." He shook his head. "I don't want to wait, Grace. I want us to get married as soon as possible, and right now the only thing standing in our way is *yer daed*. I went ahead and called *mei* parents last night. I know I shouldn't have used the phone. *Onkle* Abner won't be too happy about that. But I couldn't wait until the next time I go back home."

"What did *yer* parents say?"

Lines of worry appeared at the corner of her eyes. He brushed his finger against one of them, wishing he could soothe them away. "They said it was about time."

"*Yer* only twenty-five." Her features relaxed a bit.

"*Ya*, but they didn't think I'd ever find someone to put up with me." He chuckled, but sobered right after. "Seriously, they were happy for us. And I'm sure *yer daed* will be too, once we clear up whatever is going on."

Grace finally smiled, which made Joel feel better. And optimistic. "How about I hang out around here and drive you home after you finish work? Then I can try to talk to *yer daed* again."

"I won't be finished for another hour or so," she said, her brow furrowing. "I don't want you to be bored."

"I won't be." How could he, when he was near Grace? But while he was here, he should find something to do. "Do you have any stocking or cleaning that needs to be done?"

"I know Mr. Furlong has been talking about cleaning out the storage shed in the back. He keeps putting it off. I'm sure he'll be glad for you to do it."

Perfect. He still had some nervous energy left, especially since he hadn't worked eight hours in the woods today. Also, now that he knew he'd be talking to Vernon again in a couple hours, he felt jumpier than usual. "It will be clean as a whistle by the time I get done."

Grace giggled. "I'm sure it will be."

Glad to see his fiancée smiling, he set off for the storage shed. He was finishing up sweeping the floor when Grace walked in after she clocked out. She looked around the shed and whistled. "*Yer* right. It is clean."

Joel hung the broom on the contraption on the wall that held cleaning supplies. "There wasn't that much to do."

"*Ya*, there was. This place was a mess."

It wasn't anymore. This was where the extra groceries were stored, and they had been put in there willy-nilly. Joel had organized them, making room for more supplies and groceries if necessary. He dusted and swept, even shaking out the old mat in front of the door for wiping muddy feet. Yet even after all that physical work, he felt his palms grow damp as he and Grace drove to her house. As much as he wanted to get to the bottom of the problem with Vernon, he wasn't looking forward to seeing him.

He turned into the driveway, and Grace directed him to

the barn, where he hitched his buggy to the post out front. He attached the feed bag he kept in his buggy to Lady's muzzle, and the mare started munching right away.

"Ready?" he said to Grace, trying to keep his nerves steady.

She patted the horse's flanks. Lady was oblivious to the tension, happily eating her feed. "*Ya*," Grace said, giving her one last pat. "Let's *geh* talk to *Daed*."

They held hands on the way to the house, a united front. Grace opened the door. Charity was curled up on the couch, reading a book. When she saw Grace and Joel, she set down the book and jumped up. "*Yer* back," she said to him.

"Of course." He mustered a smile. "Won't let a bad evening keep me away from here."

"*Gut*." Charity grinned, her smile sweet and winsome, but it couldn't hold a candle to Grace's.

"Is *Daed* home?"

Charity nodded, her expression turning serious. "He's been on the back porch sitting in the old swing since he got home. I don't know what's going on with him."

"None of us do." She looked up at Joel.

"To the patio we *geh*." He breathed in deeply and headed for the back porch.

When they walked outside, he saw Vernon still wearing his clothes from work—dirt-crusted boots, broadfall pants that were almost threadbare at the knee, and a shirt still damp with sweat. Joel glanced at Grace. "You should *geh* inside," he whispered.

"*Nee*." She set her chin resolutely. "I'm not leaving *yer* side."

Vernon lifted his head and his eyes narrowed. He pushed his hat back, revealing his creased, tanned forehead. "What are you doing here?"

"We want to talk to you," Grace said.

Vernon turned his gaze to her. "Joel knows he's not wanted here."

"*Daed*," Grace said, her tone tense.

"*Geh* inside, Gracie," Joel said firmly. He could see that her father's position hadn't changed, and he didn't want Grace to witness anything unpleasant between them.

"Joel—"

He turned to her, resolute. "Please, Grace. I can handle this."

She let out a long breath, nodded, and went in the house.

"I made my stance clear yesterday." Vernon crossed his arms, revealing biceps that rivaled Joel's. He was impressed. "I meant what I said. *Yer* not welcome here."

"Why not?" He took a step forward, the image of Grace's nervous face giving him courage. He didn't want her to be worried or stressed any longer. "Why are you saying that to me?"

"Because *yer* not worthy of *mei dochder*."

"That doesn't explain anything."

Vernon's left brow raised slightly. "You know what you did."

"That's the problem." Joel held up his hands. "I don't *know* what I did. I've been wracking *mei* brain trying to figure out why *yer* so mad at me."

Vernon paused. "Think harder."

"Why don't you just tell me?"

The older man's eyes narrowed. "You really don't know?"

Joel shrugged. "I have *nee* idea."

After a long pause, Vernon said, "I wasn't always a roofer. Do you remember that?"

Joel shook his head, a little embarrassed. He probably should have remembered, but when he was a kid, even into his teens, he didn't pay much attention to things. It drove his father crazy, and more than once he'd told Joel he'd have to straighten up or he wouldn't amount to anything. Which was why Joel had decided when he was eighteen he would prove himself to his father and uncle. He would be responsible. In fact, he was the reason his uncle's clear-cutting business had gone through the roof. Joel had tipped off Uncle Abner to a huge clear-cutting job up for grabs and said he should bid on it. He'd gotten that information after church one Sunday, when he'd overheard some men talking . . .

Oh no. His gut dropped to the ground.

"I used to be in the clear-cutting business. Same as *yer onkle* and *vatter*. And *yerself.* Made a decent living at it too."

Memories came flooding back. That day in the backyard, Grace's father and two other men were talking near one of the tables. Joel had been playing catch with a few of the other kids, and one of them had thrown the ball past him. He was retrieving it when he heard the men talking.

"Fifty acres?" one of the men said.

Vernon nodded. "Fifty acres. Biggest opportunity around here."

"I can't believe the old man decided to give in," another man said. "Every lumber company around here has been trying to get Douglas Quartermaine to sell his wood for years."

"And he's finally doing it." Vernon grinned.

Joel bent and picked up the ball, tucking that tidbit of information in his brain before returning to the game. On his way home, he stopped at his uncle's house. Onkel Abner rarely stayed to socialize after church. He was focused on work, so much so that Sunday afternoons were reserved for a well-deserved nap. But Joel had woken him up to tell him about the Quartermaine job.

"Business was slow at that time," Vernon continued, his tone icy. "*Yer onkle* and *vatter* always seemed to outbid me on jobs. They could do it because they had more resources. Money begets money, you know. But I figured I could save *mei* business if I was able to get Douglas Quartermaine to accept *mei* bid for his wood. And I almost did too—until *yer* uncle underbid me."

Joel wanted to crawl in a hole.

Vernon walked toward him. "That was it for me. I had to fold the business. I couldn't keep it and *mei familye* afloat. That's when I started working for a Yankee guy who had his own roofing business. Been doing that for ten years now. I'm even second in charge, despite my aching knees and arthritic hands. But here's the rub—I can't stand roofing. I loved being a lumberjack. And I couldn't figure out how *yer* uncle possibly knew about Quartermaine—until I remembered a conversation where his nephew was nearby, lingering as he fetched a stray ball." He stood in front of Joel, his eyes filled with challenge. "Jogging *yer* memory now?"

Joel gulped. "*Ya*," he croaked.

"I lost almost everything because of you. By the grace of God I was able to get back on *mei* feet and provide for *mei familye*."

"I didn't know." Joel gulped again. "Honest, I had *nee* idea you were going to bid on the job."

"Why else would I be talking about it?"

Joel couldn't respond. He'd only been thinking about how happy his uncle would be to hear about Quartermaine—and he definitely was. It was the opening Joel had needed to prove that he'd matured, that he could be a good and responsible worker. And he had been. After that job, his uncle decided to open another lumber business in Holmes County and sent Joel and his brother and father to run it. Joel decided to move back to Middlefield when his uncle mentioned he'd like to retire soon. Joel was poised to take over the business in a couple years, and it was all because he had told his uncle about an opportunity of a lifetime.

He hadn't realized he'd taken the opportunity away from Grace's father.

"I'm sorry," he said, his words sounding lame to his own ears. How could he apologize for inadvertently ruining the man's business? What could he say that would make up for it?

But he had to say something more. He was Grace's father, and they would be in-laws someday. Joel would make sure of it. But he could see it would be a rocky road ahead.

"What are they saying?"

Grace brushed Charity's hand from her shoulder. They were leaning by the patio door, and Grace was occasionally looking outside, carefully so she wouldn't be caught. "I don't know," she whispered. "I can't hear anything." She couldn't really see anything either, other than Joel's back. He and her father had been out there for a while. That had to be a good sign. Another good sign was that they weren't yelling at each other, although it would have been shocking if they were. Like her father, Joel was even-keeled. But after her father's uncharacteristic behavior yesterday and today, Grace wasn't taking anything for granted.

She saw Joel step back and her father move toward the door. "He's coming." She pushed Charity out of the way and rushed to the sink. She turned on the tap and pretended to be in the middle of washing her hands. A quick glance told her Charity was seated at the table, rubbing off an imaginary spot—their mother always kept the table perfectly clean.

Her father slammed the door behind him and rushed out of the kitchen. Grace turned off the tap, her stomach sinking. That wasn't a good sign. She dried her hands and rushed outside. Joel was just standing there, looking out at the yard.

"Joel?" she said, moving toward him. When he didn't answer or turn around, dread filled her.

"Joel?" she repeated, moving to stand in front of him. She saw the faraway look in his eyes, the tension at his mouth, the jerking of his jaw.

He finally looked at her. "Gracie . . . We have a big problem."

CHAPTER 3

The next morning Vernon showed up for work, his eyes bleary. He hadn't slept a wink last night. After Joel left, Grace ran upstairs to her room. She didn't come down for supper, and Vernon wasn't going to force her to. By now she must know what he and Joel had talked about, although he was sure Joel must have embellished the story to make himself look good. Even as he'd confronted him, the boy didn't look like he really remembered what happened. Then when he did, he turned sickly pale.

Vernon hadn't expected that. He also hadn't expected the feeling of guilt overwhelming him now. But what did he have to feel guilty about? He wasn't in the wrong. Joel had ruined his business. True, the roofing company he worked for was also successful, and his boss was fair and paid well, but he'd rather be working in the woods than on hot slippery rooftops. But he had accepted that disappointment a long time ago, when he realized he'd have to find other work to support his family. He'd even forgiven Joel. At least, he thought he had, until he saw the boy sitting at his kitchen table.

He removed his hat and rubbed his forehead. Grace came down for breakfast, but she didn't eat much, and the usual chatter of an all-female household was nonexistent. His little girl's heart was breaking. He could see that. But sometimes a person had to go through pain to learn the truth about people. He'd found that out firsthand.

The job they were starting today was for a commercial building, so it would take at least a week to get it done. They were also short one worker, a guy who had been injured two weeks ago when he fell off the top rung of the ladder he was climbing to get to the roof. He'd be okay, but he couldn't work with a broken leg. The rest of the crew would have to pick up the slack, and even with them working faster, it would still take a little longer to complete the job.

He had just finished strapping his tool belt around his waist when someone tapped him on the shoulder. Thinking it was Mahlon, the youngest member of their group, who always had a million questions, he was buckling his belt when he turned around.

"Not sure how long this job is going to take," he said before looking up. He secured the belt and lifted his head. "I'm praying we have *gut* weather—" His eyes widened. Not again. Would this kid ever leave him alone?

"Vernon." Joel nodded at him, then started strapping on his own tool belt. A well-worn one, from what Vernon could tell.

"What are you doing here?"

"Reporting for work." He grinned and adjusted his straw hat. "*Here?*"

Joel nodded. "I'm taking Timothy's place until he can get back on his feet."

Vernon gaped. That couldn't be right. "When . . . How . . ."

"I see you've met our substitute." Brian Dawson, the owner of the company, always came by new jobs on the first day. "Called me out of the blue last night and said he could fill in for Timothy. Also said he knew you, and you'd vouch for him. That was *gut* enough for me."

Joel was still smiling, but Vernon caught the trepidation in his eyes. This boy had more nerve than Vernon had expected. He thought about telling his boss he would never vouch for Joel, but he held his tongue. He wasn't going to bring his boss, and an English man to boot, into his private business.

"Everything looks set for the job," Brian said. He pulled down the brim of his baseball cap, the roofing company logo emblazoned on the front. "We'll be done ahead of schedule thanks to the addition of Joel." He clapped Joel on the shoulder. "Be careful. I tell that to all my men. Roofing can be a dangerous business."

Joel nodded, and Brian walked away. Vernon moved to step in front of Joel. "I don't know what you're trying to pull . . . ," he said in a low voice.

"I'm not trying to pull anything." Joel lifted his chin. "I'm here to prove myself to you. I am trustworthy. I'm also sorry for what happened years ago. If I'd known that *yer* business was riding on that bid, I wouldn't have told *mei* uncle about it."

"You had *nee* business eavesdropping in the first place."

"I know. I was wrong." He glanced around the worksite, then looked back at Vernon. "You want the best for Grace. We both do. I love her, and I realize that I have a lot to do to get back in your *gut* stead. I'm willing to do anything to prove it. I figure since you won't speak to me and you won't allow me near your property or *yer dochder*, I'll have to do that proving here."

Several men were already on the roof. Vernon couldn't waste any more time, but that didn't mean he was happy Joel was here. "Keep *yer* distance," he said.

"I will." They started for the building.

"Have you ever done any roofing?" Vernon said, unable to resist asking the question. He didn't like the idea of a complete novice twenty feet off the ground. It wasn't safe for the rest of the crew—or for Joel.

"*Ya*. Barns, a few houses, and I helped expand our current building in Holmes—"

The reminder drove a spike into Vernon, and from Joel's expression he could see the young man knew he'd made a mistake. Joel turned and hurried to the building.

Vernon put his hand on his hammer. This was just another job. He didn't have to pay any attention to Joel. He would do his work, keep his nose to the grindstone like he always did. Joel could try to get back in his good graces all he wanted to—it would never happen. He would never let him marry his daughter.

Joel shimmied up the ladder, not looking back at Vernon. He'd stuck his foot in his mouth by bringing up the business in Holmes. Not a great start. But he was bound to make a mistake with his stomach tied up in knots. He tried to present himself as calm and collected, but inside he was a bundle of nerves. That seemed to be his usual state lately. He'd certainly been nervous when he told his uncle last night that he wanted to take a leave of absence from their business.

"Why?" Uncle Abner had said, setting down the newspaper he was reading.

"I'd like to try *mei* hand at something else." An untruth, because he hated roofing. He had done it before, several times, because he was good with his hands. But being up on a hot roof, bent over, always making sure not to slip or have another kind of accident before the job was done—that was not something he enjoyed. But he would do anything to prove himself to Vernon, including getting up on a roof again. Not only did he owe it to the man, but he owed it to Grace too.

She'd been upset when he told her what had happened between him and her father years ago. And he'd told her everything, not wanting to keep anything from her, even though the whole situation made him look bad. She forgave him right away, understanding that he'd made a foolish mistake.

"I've been so worried about *Daed*. I'm just glad to know what made him so angry," she'd said, taking his hand.

"Turns out it's definitely me."

She squeezed his fingers, then kissed his cheek. "You're not that young *mann* anymore," she said softly. "Today, you're the *mann* I love. I know you'll make everything right in the end."

He'd left her house feeling both boosted and apprehensive. Grace had proven once again that she was an amazing woman, one worth fighting for. Now he had to figure out what to do next. By the time he pulled into his uncle's driveway, the idea of trying to join the roofing crew came to him.

"But our business is doing well," Uncle Abner said. "*Yer* doing well. I couldn't ask for a better employee, and nephew." Despite the kind words, he narrowed his eyes behind his silver-rimmed glasses. Then he lifted his paper in front of his face. "*Nee* need to upset the apple cart."

"Too late," Joel muttered. He'd already upset a few of them in the span of two days.

The paper came down again. "What are you talking about?"

Joel explained the entire situation to his uncle, including his part in Vernon's business failing. "I want to marry Grace. The only way her *vatter* will agree is if I prove he can trust me. I called Dawson's Roofing Company where Vernon works, and they happen to have an injured man they need to replace for the time being."

"You did that without talking to me?"

"I wanted to make sure the opportunity was available."

His uncle shook his head. "I can't believe Vernon's blaming you for what happened to his business years ago. That's all water under the bridge now."

"He blames me because I am at fault." When his uncle started to say something, Joel interrupted him. "Please," he said. "Let me have the time off for a couple of weeks. Hopefully that will be enough time to prove myself. Then I'll come back to work for you."

His uncle scowled. "It doesn't bother you that *yer* leaving me in a lurch?"

Joel held out his hands, palms up. "I realize that. And *ya*, it bothers me. But what else can I do? I have to make this right, and not just because of Grace."

His uncle's eyes narrowed again, and Joel prepared himself for the answer he didn't want to hear. But he would quit his lumberjack job if he had to. He kept his gaze steady as his uncle continued to stare at him, his expression impassive.

Finally, his uncle nodded. "You've never asked me for much, Joel. And you are one of the reasons we've been thriving all these years. Not the only reason, of course." He brought the paper back up again. "Two weeks," he said. "Not an hour more."

Joel had been jubilant after Uncle Abner's agreement, but

now that he was up on the roof, getting ready to do the work he hated, he wondered if he'd made a huge mistake. How exactly was he going to prove himself to Vernon? He hadn't thought that far. Vernon would see he was a good worker, but that wouldn't exactly mean anything, since most all the Amish he knew were hard workers. But at least he was in close proximity to Grace's father. That was a start. He'd figure out the rest later.

"Ow!" He yanked his hand from the roof and looked at his stinging thumb.

"Can't even use a hammer right."

Joel glanced over his shoulder. Vernon was several feet behind him but still within earshot. Joel pressed his thumb to his lips. He was not getting off to a great start.

That evening Grace hurried home from work. They weren't busy and Patience said she would cover for her. Grace had been eager to leave. Her mind hadn't been on her job anyway, but on Joel and her father. After hearing what had happened and why her father was angry, she wasn't even thinking about her wedding anymore. She was just worried about her *daed*.

Joel told her he was going to fix things, and she trusted that he would. She was upset when he told her what he'd done to her father, and by extension, her family. But she also understood that it was a mistake. Joel didn't have a devious bone in his body. She knew that. She trusted him with everything. She loved him.

And she loved her father.

She couldn't believe he'd held on to his anger all these years. What about forgiveness? What about grace? Her father was a devout man who quietly lived his faith but was devoted to it. How could he violate one of the main tenets of his beliefs? Forgiveness wasn't a choice. It was a requirement. And although it could be hard, it benefited everyone. Now because her father hadn't forgiven Joel, their lives were in turmoil.

She went inside and found her mother in the kitchen starting supper. "Is *Daed* home?"

Mamm shook her head. "Not yet. He should be soon, though."

"Oh." She'd have to talk to him a little later then. She should have said something to him at breakfast, especially since she spent the previous evening in her room. But she couldn't bring herself to broach the subject. All day she'd practiced what she would say, and now she'd have to wait longer to say it. "Do you need some help?"

"*Nee*. We're having bacon and tomato sandwiches with the rest of that potato salad left over from Sunday. Charity made apple cinnamon cupcakes for dessert."

Daed's favorite. Seemed like everyone wanted to cheer him up.

"I'll *geh* take care of the horses." *Daed* usually did the barn chores after supper, but it wouldn't hurt for her to help him out.

She'd just finished sweeping the barn floor when her father walked inside. "Looks pretty clean," he said, still holding his lunch cooler in his hand. His gait was a little awkward as he walked toward her, reminding her how hard he worked. Sometimes he grimaced when he got up from the rocking chair, especially in colder weather. It was early fall and the weather was nice, but her father had obviously put in a hard day.

"I'll take this for you." She set aside the broom and took his lunchbox. "*Mamm* has supper ready."

He looked at the cooler as she paused. "Trying to butter me up?"

The words were light, but his expression was weary. She shook her head. "*Nee*. I wouldn't do that. I do want to talk to you, but it can wait until after supper."

"About Joel, *ya*?"

She nodded and held the handle of the cooler with both hands.

Daed turned. "*Ya*. It can wait until after supper."

Grace barely tasted the crisp bacon and fresh tomato as she ate her supper. The garden was still producing a few more tomatoes, and they tasted sweet and delicious. At least they usually did. Everything tasted like sawdust now. She'd been quiet during the meal, but the rest of the family was back to talking. Which eased her mind a little bit, but didn't bring back her appetite.

"Grace."

She looked up as her father pushed back from the table. He didn't say anything else, and she followed him outside. It was a little cool, and she hugged her arms around her body.

"You said you wanted to talk." He put his hands in the pockets of his pants. "I'm listening."

She turned to him, and all her carefully planned dialogue went out the window. "Joel is sorry. Can't you see that? Can't you forgive him for one little mistake?"

Her father was silent for a moment. Then he said, "It wasn't a little mistake." He turned to her. "And I forgave him a long time ago."

"You could have fooled me." At his sharp look she said, "Sorry."

He faced her, his expression relaxing. "Whether I forgive him or not doesn't change what happened. It doesn't make him trustworthy. And working with me on the roofing job—"

"Wait." Her eyes widened. "He's working with you?"

"You didn't know?"

She shook her head. "*Nee.*" But excitement brewed within her. Joel was working with her father. That was perfect. He would see for himself what a great guy Joel was. Although she'd have to talk to him later and find out how he managed to get a job with the roofing company. But the fact that he did meant so much to her.

"He didn't tell you? See, you can't trust him."

"*Daed*, I haven't seen him since last night. Plus you said he couldn't come over here anymore. He's honoring your wishes." She blew out a breath. "How can you get to know him when you keep putting roadblocks in his way?"

"I don't want to get to know him."

"Because if you do, then you'll have to really forgive him. In your heart and soul. You haven't been able to do that yet." She bit her bottom lip. Had she gone too far with her accusations? She'd never spoken so directly to her father. Then again, never had so much been at stake.

Daed rubbed the back of his neck. "You must think you know me pretty well."

"*Daed*, I—"

He held up his hand. "You might be right. Maybe I haven't forgiven him completely."

A little spark of hope ignited. "So *yer* going to give him a chance?"

Turning from her to face the backyard, he said, "I don't know."

Grace knew better than to push him. At least he was contemplating opening his heart and mind to Joel. And that was something, compared to the way he'd been yesterday. She went to him and put her hand on his arm. *"Danki,"* she said, her voice sounding thick. Then she went back in the house. She ran upstairs, got on her knees, and prayed for her father and Joel.

Chapter 4

Vernon stared at the last rays of the sunset in front of him. His daughter's words echoed in his mind, and he knew they were true. He hadn't forgiven Joel. Not completely. But every time he thought about the past, he couldn't let go of the bitterness. He'd kept his distance from Joel, and he wasn't surprised he was a good worker. Better than Mahlon, he had to admit. But that didn't mean he could be trusted with Grace's heart. Being able to nail tar paper to a roof didn't show a man's true integrity.

"Here." Ruby came up beside him and handed him a cup of coffee. Decaf, since he had to get to sleep soon. He took it and looked down at her, smiling his thanks.

"That was a quick conversation you had with Grace."

"Were you eavesdropping too?" He rubbed the corner of his eyebrow.

"Of course not. But I'll admit to peeking out the window a time or two."

He chuckled and took a sip of the hot coffee. "I'm trying," he said.

"I know you are. That's all we can do, other than ask God for help."

Something he hadn't actually done. Since the bitter root had taken hold, he'd shut down communication with God. It felt empty, not talking to him, something he'd done every day of his life since he could remember. But anytime he started to pray, the words would dry up.

Charity poked her head out the back door. "Someone's here to see you," she said. "He's waiting on the front porch."

"Who is it—"

The door shut and Charity disappeared.

Vernon gripped the coffee cup before handing it back to Ruby. He was sure the visitor was Joel. The boy wouldn't take no for an answer. He supposed deep down he appreciated his persistence, but right now he was more annoyed than anything.

When he rounded the corner, it wasn't Joel standing on the front porch. It was Abner King, Joel's uncle. What was he doing here? "Abner," he said, keeping his tone steady. He stopped at the top of the steps, making it clear he didn't want to invite the man in. "What brings you by?"

Abner came up the steps and stood in front of Vernon. He put his thumb underneath one of his suspender straps. "I wanted to talk to you for a few minutes."

"About what?" Vernon put his hands in his pockets, resisting the urge to clench them.

"I think you already know." He glanced over Vernon's shoulder at the front door of the house, but Vernon didn't move. Abner faced him. "Joel told me everything."

"About what?" he repeated. He wasn't about to give away any information.

Abner let out a curt laugh and leaned back on his heels. "Playing it near the vest, I see. I know you and I haven't been close, but we've been cordial over the years. I'd like to think that wouldn't change, seeing as we might become family soon."

Not if I have anything to do with it. "Is that what you wanted to tell me?"

"*Ya*, and I wanted to ask you a question." He stilled and dropped his hand from his suspender. Abner's gaze turned icy. "Are you trying to get back at *mei* nephew for *yer* failure?"

Vernon tensed, but he didn't say anything.

"Because that's what it seems like to me. I didn't think you'd be the kind of man who would blame a *kinn* for *yer* business going under. *Mei* nephew is a *gut mann*. Actually, more than *gut*. He has integrity, he's a hard worker, and he must love *yer dochder* because I can't figure out why else he would put me in a lurch to work with you for two weeks." Abner sniffed and looked around the yard. "You seem to be doing all right for *yerself*."

His jaw clenched. Abner was well known to be the richest man in the district, and while he didn't flaunt his money, he had an attitude about him. And in order for him to be as successful as he was, Vernon's business had to go under. If not, they would be sharing the profits from the jobs in the area. Now he had the entire business to himself. And all because of Joel.

"I don't have any control over *yer* nephew," he said, surprised at the calmness in his voice, since he felt anything but calm. "Except he will not marry *mei dochder*."

"Don't be a fool." Abner shook his head. "I'm surprised at you, Vernon. I've known you a long time. It's not like you to be vengeful." He took a step forward. "It's not Christian of you either."

"Are you finished?"

Abner took a step back. "*Ya*. I can see *yer* not to be reasoned with." He headed for his buggy parked in the driveway. When he reached it, he turned around as if to say something else to Vernon, then shook his head again and got in the buggy.

As he drove away, Ruby came up beside her husband. "What did Abner want?"

"*Nix*." Vernon spun around and charged into the house. He'd get an earful from Ruby about keeping her in the dark again, but right now he didn't care. *"It's not like you to be vengeful."* The words echoed in his mind as he climbed the stairs to the bathroom and splashed cold water on his face. Abner was right about that. He wasn't vengeful. Or bitter. Or nursing a grudge.

He lifted his head and looked in the mirror, water dripping from his salt-and-pepper beard. He hardly recognized the man in the reflection. What was happening to him? He didn't like the knots in his stomach that seemed to grow bigger each day. He didn't want his daughter and wife upset with him. But every time he thought of giving in, he'd imagine Joel sitting at his table. Spending holidays with him. Having him as part of the family. The man who betrayed him. The man who ruined him.

And he couldn't bear it.

He dropped his damp face in his hands. *Lord . . . help me.*

For the next week, Joel and Vernon barely spoke at work. A couple times Joel tried to eat lunch with him, only to have Vernon ignore him and walk off. The man was being childish now. Joel hadn't made much headway in convincing Vernon to let him and Grace marry, and he was growing frustrated.

Then there was Grace. He missed her so much. Although

it had been tricky sometimes to date in secret, they'd managed not to have more than a couple days apart from each other. His heart ached to see her, to hold her. So much so that after he knew everyone in her house had gone to bed, he snuck over and tossed a couple pebbles at her window.

She opened it and waved, her blond hair in a long braid over her shoulder. She pointed down, her signal that she was coming out to meet him. His heart thrummed in his chest.

After a few minutes she came outside, her hair still uncovered, but she was wearing a dress. It was a little askew on her shoulders, as if she'd thrown it on. He straightened it, then took her hand and they ran to the back corner of the yard.

The moon wasn't as bright as it had been when he proposed. In fact, it was almost nonexistent. But that was a good thing, in case her father looked outside for some reason.

"Joel," she said, falling into his arms. "I've missed you so much." She was whispering, even though she didn't have to at this distance.

He rested his chin on the top of her head. "I missed you too."

They held each other in the dark for a few minutes, the crickets and cicadas chirping around them, a lone bullfrog croaking in the distance. Finally, they separated. "Has he said anything to you?" Joel asked.

She shook her head. "He's been more sullen than ever."

"He's like that at work too. Some of the guys were wondering if something was wrong with him."

"Something is." Grace crossed her arms over her chest. "He's stubborn and bullheaded."

"I understand why." He reached out and touched the end of her braid. Her hair was silky soft. "He wants to protect you."

"I don't need protecting." She stepped toward him. "I need to be *yer* wife."

Her words were what he needed to fortify him. "I'm not giving up."

"*Gut*."

He peered down at her. Her expression was hard to see in the dim light, but he could tell she was doubting. "Were you worried I would?"

She turned away. "*Ya*," she said. "A little bit."

"Grace." He tilted her chin toward him. "I love you. I don't care if I have to badger *yer vatter* for the next ten years. I will marry you."

"It better not take that long."

"I'm sure it won't." He drew her into his arms again. "*Yer vatter* will see what a great *mann* I am soon enough."

"A great and modest *mann*," Grace said with a chuckle.

"Of course." He looked up at the house. Somewhere inside Vernon was probably sound asleep. Joel envied him that. He hadn't been able to sleep through the night since he'd proposed to Grace. And he wasn't about to get a decent night's sleep tonight either.

At his bedroom window, Vernon let the curtain fall back in place. He pressed his lips together. He'd heard the noise outside, which sounded like pebbles hitting against the window. He'd crept out of bed and saw Joel standing in his yard. So this was how they had managed to date in secret. Vernon shook his head. He never would have heard the small noise if he hadn't been wide awake, like he had been every night this week.

He turned and saw the dark lump on his bed. Unlike Vernon, Ruby had been able to sleep. He was glad for that. There was no sense in both of them being exhausted come morning.

He looked at the window again. Grace should be outside by now. If he went downstairs he would catch Joel in the act of disobeying him. It would cement his argument to Grace that the boy was untrustworthy. All he had to do was go downstairs, and he would put the final nail in the casket of their relationship.

But he couldn't bring himself to do it. He'd spent more time in prayer, asking God to break him of the bitterness and resentment. But he hadn't. If anything, it had strengthened. Even seeing Joel at work getting along well with his colleagues grated. The boy seemed to come out on top with everything. It wasn't fair.

But he wasn't being fair to his daughter either. Ruby had stopped telling him that, saying that since he wasn't going to listen to her, she wasn't going to waste her words anymore. Patience and Charity acted like everything was normal, but Grace was sullen. His cheerful daughter had lost her spark, and he was the reason for it.

He slipped back in bed and closed his eyes. But sleep didn't come. He had to do something about Joel and Grace. He'd have to give them his blessing. Not because he wanted to. Or even because the bitterness was less. He would have to ignore the pain in his heart, peel his pride away, and put his daughter first. He finally realized he had to think of her before himself.

The next morning Grace left the house early and went to see her sister Faith. She lived a little more than a mile away, and Grace rode her bicycle at top speed. She didn't want to be late for work. As it was, Mr. Furlong had noticed she'd been distracted, and if she didn't get her act together he might let her go. She hadn't planned to tell Faith about her engagement until after *Daed* relented. Patience and Charity had agreed to keep it a secret. But Grace couldn't talk to them about Joel. Neither of them had boyfriends—at least that she knew about. But her older sister was married and had experienced her own difficult journey to the altar. Grace thought if she didn't talk to someone, she would burst.

"Hi," Faith said, looking surprised when she opened the door. "What brings you by so early?"

"Can we talk?"

Her sister's expression turned serious. "Sure. Come on in."

Faith led her to the kitchen, where Silas was putting bread on the table. "Hey, Grace. Nice to have you over for breakfast."

"Breakfast will have to wait." Faith walked over to the table. She put two slices of ham, a fried egg, and some butter between two slices of bread and handed them to Silas.

"Breakfast on the *geh*?" Silas said, lifting a brow.

"Do you mind?"

He shook his head and smiled. "*Nee*. It won't hurt me to get to work early. Might shock *Daed*, though. Bye, Grace." He headed out the back door.

"One day his *vatter* will retire," Faith said as she went to the stove and poured a cup of coffee from the percolator. "In another twenty years."

But Grace couldn't even smile at her sister's lighthearted words. She sat down at the table, a beautiful piece that seated eight. Faith and Silas hadn't started their family yet, but from the size of this table they made together, it looked like they wanted a large one. Like the table, the entire house, built by both of them, was simple yet fine quality. As expected from two master carpenters.

"All right," Faith said, sitting across from her. "What's going on?"

Grace filled her in. Faith's expression went from surprised to annoyed. "And *yer* just telling me this now? Am I the last to know *yer* getting married?"

"The last one in the *familye*, *ya*." She looked down at the table. "I was going to tell you right after we told *Mamm* and *Daed*, but then *Daed* refused to give us his blessing."

"I suppose I can forgive you for that." Faith grinned, but it disappeared quickly. "Grace, I'm joking."

"I can't even joke about it." She leaned forward on the table. "I thought I'd be planning *mei* wedding by now."

Faith took a sip of her coffee. "Maybe you should wait to do that."

Grace's head popped up. "What?"

"Maybe there's a reason *Daed* isn't giving in."

"There is. He's being ridiculous."

"Or maybe he's hurting." Faith put down her mug and took Grace's hand. "I know *yer* in a hurry to get married. I was like that, too, at least the second time Silas proposed. I knew I wanted to be with him for the rest of *mei* life, and I didn't want to wait to make that happen."

"And you didn't wait."

"Didn't I? I broke our first engagement. At the time I had a *gut* reason, but I see now that the timing wasn't right, for either of us. We both had to grow up a bit."

"But Joel and I aren't you and Silas." This wasn't what she'd expected at all. She'd wanted a sympathetic ear. "I can't believe *yer* taking *Daed*'s side."

"I'm not taking anyone's side. I just wonder if you've considered *Daed*'s feelings at all."

"Is he considering mine?"

"Knowing him, I'm sure he is." She let go of Grace's hand. "Remember when all that happened, when the lumber business fell through? We were young back then, but you and I were old enough to remember how down *Daed* was. How tight things were financially until he found another job. He's spent his whole life since then trying to recover. And now the person he feels is responsible wants to marry his daughter."

"But he should forgive Joel." Grace was exasperated. "Isn't that what we've been taught so many times over? Forgive, forgive, forgive."

"Do I really need to bring up *yer* roller skates?"

Grace paused, then slumped in her chair. When they were twelve and thirteen, Faith had borrowed Grace's roller skates, which she had bought with her own money from babysitting an English family's children down the street. It was her first purchase, and she loved those skates. Faith had broken the wheel off one. Grace knew now it was because the skates weren't well made, but at the time she'd been furious. She hadn't even had a chance to skate with them herself.

"Do I need to remind you how you wouldn't speak to me for a week? How I offered to buy you new skates and you refused? How you only forgave me when *Daed* made you?"

"I was twelve, Faith."

"You were angry and hurt, Grace."

Grace knew Faith was right. She hadn't taken *Daed*'s feelings into consideration. She was so eager to get married that she'd only been thinking about her and Joel—and if she was honest, she was mostly thinking about herself. "I've been selfish," she muttered.

"You're in love." Faith smiled. "Sometimes it makes us do selfish things." Faith looked at the clock above the kitchen. "You better hurry to work." She handed Grace a piece of buttered bread. "I know full well how Mr. Furlong feels about tardiness."

"Don't you want to come back to work at the store?" Grace teased.

"You know I don't." She sighed. "I'm actually happy being home and taking care of Silas. I've got some projects going on in the workshop out back too. I have plenty to keep me busy and content."

Grace got up and hugged her sister. "*Danki*, Faith."

"For what?" Faith asked, hugging her back.

"Being honest enough to set me straight."

Faith smiled. "You would have figured it out eventually."

On her way to work, Grace decided to talk to her father tonight. She would tell him that she and Joel wouldn't push the marriage issue right now. She would wait and pray that her father would come around. This time, she would give him the space he needed—something she should have been doing all along.

Chapter 5

That morning on the way to work, Joel made a decision. He wasn't going to wait around for Vernon anymore. He would force the man to talk to him if he had to. Later in the day, of course. He wasn't going to embarrass either of them at work. But things couldn't keep going the way they were right now. Something had to give.

Vernon arrived shortly after Joel, carrying his usual orange-and-white lunch cooler, tool belt slung over his shoulder. His head was lifted, and even from this distance Joel could see he looked tired. That made him second-guess his decision for a moment. Obviously, this hadn't been easy on Vernon either. But the older man was the one who was being unreasonable. If he would just give Joel and Grace his blessing, everything would be fine.

Joel braced himself for Vernon to pass by without saying anything, like he had for the past week. But the man surprised him by stopping in front of him. "I want to talk to you later." Then he walked to the building.

Joel watched him go, stunned. But he didn't have the feeling this would be anything good. Probably another warning to stay away from Grace and to give up trying to prove himself.

They were halfway finished with the roof. Joel found that

he didn't mind the work, although he'd rather be working in the woods. More than once he thought about Vernon's situation. He wasn't doing the job he loved either, but he worked hard. And Joel would be able to go back to the lumber business by the end of this week. Vernon would move on to the next roofing job. It had given Joel pause more than once.

He looked up at the cloudless sky. It would be a warm day, which meant plenty of sweaty work. "Better get started," he mumbled as he strapped on his tool belt. He hurried up to the roof and began laying the large tiles. They were different from residential roof shingles. The good thing about this job was that the roof was flat instead of slanted. Less worry about falling off.

Close to lunchtime Joel climbed down the ladder and went to the drink cooler. He got himself a cup of water. Then he decided to extend an olive branch and filled a second cup. He put the lip of one cup between his teeth and held on to the other one while he climbed back up the ladder. On the opposite end of the roof, Vernon was working, nailing down the graphite. Joel walked toward him.

"Here," he said, holding the drink out to Vernon.

Vernon looked up, then at the cup, then went back to nailing. "Not thirsty," he said.

Joel doubted that, since the back of the man's shirt was soaked with sweat. "Take it anyway," he snapped, past annoyed now. The man could put a mule to shame.

Vernon got to his feet and grabbed the cup, downed the water, and dropped it on the roof. Joel knew he'd pick it up later. It wasn't in Vernon's character to litter. The man could hold a grudge, though.

Suddenly a strong wind kicked up. Joel looked at what had

been clear blue sky only moments ago. It was now dark and stormy. Lightning flickered in the distance. "We need to get off the roof."

Vernon glanced at the sky, then went back to nailing. "There's time to finish this up."

Joel flinched at another lightning strike, this one closer. The clouds were moving fast now, and heavy drops of rain pounded the roof. "Vernon," he said, his tone more firm this time.

"*Geh* on. I'll be right behind you."

Joel started to leave, then stopped. He turned around, knelt, and started helping. "It will *geh* faster this way."

He and Vernon made quick work of the remaining shingles and stood. They were the only ones on the roof now, and a loud thunder boom made Joel jump. "Hurry," he said to Vernon, who was putting his hammer in his tool belt.

A crack of lightning split the sky. But instead of a quick flash in the distance, it came straight toward them. Joel froze as it struck Grace's father and he collapsed mere inches away.

"Vernon!" Another bolt of lightning cracked nearby. Thunder boomed as Joel picked up the lifeless man and put him over his shoulder. Rain poured down as he hurried to the ladder and struggled to carry Grace's father down. The other men had taken shelter in their cars. One of them, Clifton, was getting out when Joel reached the ground. "Call an ambulance!" he yelled, then hurried as fast as he could to Clifton's car, straining under Vernon's dead weight.

He hefted Vernon into the back seat, then put his head to his chest. Nothing. "God, *nee*." He started chest compressions, the way he'd learned in the CPR class his uncle insisted all his employees take. He had no idea if what he was doing was even working, but he couldn't stop. "Don't die," he said. "Don't . . . die."

Grace spent the rest of the day focusing on her work, trying not to think too much about her father. But the guilt was there, humming in the background. The more she thought about how selfish she'd been, the worse she felt. She couldn't wait for tonight to come so she could apologize. Of course, she wasn't going to give up on marrying Joel, but she would be more considerate of *Daed*'s feelings. It was the least she could do.

She was about to head to the back of the store to fill out her time sheet when Patience came dashing through the glass doors, panic in her eyes. "Patience," she said, going straight to her.

"*Daed* . . . ," Patience said, gulping for air. "Joel . . ."

Alarm struck her. "What about *Daed* and Joel?"

"Hospital . . ." Patience grabbed Grace's hand. "Hurry!"

Grace ran out the door with her sister, not thinking about Mr. Furlong or her job. Her father and Joel were in the hospital. "What happened?"

"Don't know. *Mamm* called a taxi."

Tears filled her eyes. *Nee*, she couldn't lose her father. Or her fiancé. She fought to contain herself when she climbed into the taxi. *Mamm* was stoic. Charity and Patience held hands. Grace spent the ride praying with all her might.

Vernon's eyes cracked open. Where was he? What was that pain shooting through his body? He tried to think. Last thing he remembered was drinking the water Joel offered him. No, wait. He had stayed to finish up the last shingles while the others bailed for their cars. A storm was coming, and Joel had pestered him to get off the roof. But Vernon had seen many storms in his life. He could gauge them. And there were only a few more nails left.

"Vernon?"

He opened his eyes fully. His body was jangling, along with everything surrounding him. He saw that he was in an ambulance. An ambulance. "What?" he managed to croak out.

He felt a strong grip on his hand. He turned his head and saw Joel leaning over him, clinging to him. His hair was wet and plastered to his head. What happened to his hat?

"Vernon? Are you with us?"

He tried to nod but was only able to barely move his head. Joel leaned his forehead on his hand, the one that clasped Vernon's. "Thank God."

Vernon started to get up, but his body wouldn't move. "Can't . . . move."

"That happens sometimes." A young English woman wearing a uniform peered over him. "It's called keraunoparalysis, and it's usually temporary."

Paralysis? He looked at Joel again and saw the panic in his eyes. The boy was squeezing his hand so hard, he thought it might break. How could he feel that and not be able to move?

"Good thing you got CPR when you did," the woman continued. She patted Vernon's shoulder. "Getting hit by lightning is no joke."

Lightning? He gasped, then coughed. "You're . . . telling . . . me." He took in a weak breath. He was tired, more tired than he could ever remember being. *But I'm lucky to be alive.* Yet he knew luck had nothing to do with it.

"Where did you learn CPR?"

Vernon realized the woman, the paramedic, was talking to Joel.

"In Holmes County, years ago. I'm in the lumber business, and my uncle made sure that all his employees knew CPR."

"Good idea. The lumber business—and roofing," she added, looking at Vernon again, "can be dangerous."

Vernon knew that. Which was why he'd always been careful. Except this time. Now he remembered Joel was telling him to leave, and he was ignoring him. He also remembered that Joel stayed behind and helped him finish the last of the tar sheets. "Fool," he whispered, not only referring to Joel but also to himself.

"Save *yer* energy," Joel said in *Dietsch*.

He looked at his hand clasped in Joel's. The man had saved his life. The man he had considered untrustworthy. The one person he couldn't bring himself to forgive. "*Danki*," he said, squeezing Joel's hand back.

"*Nee* thanks needed. I'm just glad *yer* okay. You gave us all a scare."

Vernon closed his eyes. His body was stiff and he tried to move again. They all seemed to think he was going to be okay, but he wasn't so sure. What if he could never move again? How would he support his family? How would he live his life?

"Vernon." Joel's voice reached his ears again. "You're going to be all right."

He opened his eyes. He was afraid, but he was also strangely calm. He gripped Joel's hand and nodded the best he could. Because of this kind young man, he was going to be all right.

Grace paced the emergency room waiting area. They had arrived an hour after her father, and so far they hadn't been allowed to see him. She clenched her fists. She hadn't seen Joel either. Was he injured? When she asked, all they said was that he was back with her father.

She stopped pacing and looked at her mother. Patience was sitting on one side, Charity on the other. Faith was at the front desk trying to get more information from the registrar, who insisted she didn't know anything.

The double doors burst open, and Joel walked through. Grace ran to him and in full view of her mother and sisters, hugged him tight. "Thank God *yer* okay," she said into his shirt, which smelled like sweat and rain. He hugged her back, then stepped away. "How's *Daed?*" she asked. Faith, Patience, Charity, and their mother came up beside her.

"They're going to keep him overnight for observation." His face looked tortured and tired. "He's still paralyzed."

"What?" the women all said at the same time.

"Sometimes people who are hit by lightning develop temporary paralysis. The doctor is certain he'll get his feeling back, but he wants to make sure everything is okay before he goes home." He looked at Grace's mother. "He wants to see you."

Mamm nodded, then slipped past everyone and hurried through the doors. Patience, Faith, and Charity went to sit down. Joel pulled Grace to the side and hugged her again. She realized he was shaking.

"Joel?"

"It's okay." He looked down at her. "Just the adrenaline still going through me, I think. I've never seen anyone struck by lightning before. I'm lucky it didn't hit me too."

"Is *Daed* really going to be all right?" Maybe Joel was fudging the truth for her sisters and mother. That would be like him, not wanting to upset them.

He smiled. "*Ya*. It's going to take more than lightning to keep *yer daed* down. You should know that."

She leaned into him and noticed he had stopped shaking. They held each other for a long moment, then parted again. She smoothed the front of her dress. "I was going to talk to *Daed* tonight."

Joel arched a brow. "Oh?"

She nodded. "I was going to tell him we would postpone the wedding."

Joel stilled. "I see."

"It's the right thing to do, especially now." She put her hand on his arm. "You understand, *ya*?"

He looked at her hand and after a moment put his over hers. "*Ya*," he said in a low voice. "I do." He met her gaze. "But it's only a postponement. Not a cancellation."

She was about to answer him when *Mamm* came back through the double doors. "Grace?"

Grace went to her. "*Ya*?"

"*Yer daed* wants to see you." She looked at Grace's sisters. "Of course he wants to see all of you. But he asked for Grace first."

Grace swallowed, gave Joel another look, then went to see her father.

CHAPTER 6

Grace knocked on the door before entering the room. Her father was lying there on a bed, machines beeping around him. He had a tube coming from one arm leading to a machine where a bag of clear fluid hung. His eyes were closed, and he wore a hospital gown. Tears sprang to her eyes.

"*Daed*," she whispered.

His eyes opened. "Grace. Sorry, I can't sit up at the moment. Come here so I can see you."

She hurried to his bedside and sat on the chair next to him. "I'm so sorry, *Daed*," she said, putting her head down.

"For what?"

She looked at him and wiped her tears. For a man who just got struck by lightning, he looked pretty relaxed. In fact, more relaxed than she'd seen him in a long time. "I'm not getting married," she blurted.

"What? Where did that come from?"

Taking his hand, she said, "I've been selfish. I haven't been thinking about your feelings at all, just *mei* own. I already told Joel that we're going to wait."

"And he's all right with that?"

"He has to be." She looked over. Her father was staring at the ceiling now. "We won't marry until you give us permission. And we won't try to force you."

"Is that what you and Joel really want?"

Grace nodded. "That's what we want."

Her father let out a big sigh as a nurse walked in. "He should get some rest," she said. "We'll be moving him to a room soon."

Grace stood. As she walked away she whispered, "I love you, *Daed*." The nurse was already taking his blood pressure, so she headed for the waiting area.

She paused in the hallway and took a deep breath. *Daed* was okay. So was Joel. That's all that mattered right now. Everything else could wait.

Joel returned to his uncle's house later that night. He was beat. The adrenaline had finally left his body, and now that he knew Vernon would be all right, he'd managed to settle a little bit. But he was still on edge. When Grace came back from visiting her father, she'd hardly spoken to Joel. The Miller women were planning on staying until Vernon was settled in his room. Since the hospital was busy and full, the staff wasn't sure when that would happen. Joel said he would stay with them, but Grace insisted he leave.

"We'll be fine," she said. "You need to get some sleep."

But how was he supposed to sleep when she told him she wanted to postpone the wedding? True, he felt like a heel even thinking about his and Grace's future when Vernon was still in the hospital. But everyone was sure he would be okay. And Joel was certain that after today, Vernon would at least give Joel another chance to plead his case. Except now it turned out he didn't have to. Grace had made the decision for him.

He shook his head as he walked into the house. He'd have to sort this out tomorrow. He didn't want to wait, but if Grace insisted, he'd have no choice. He'd honor her wishes.

"Well, if it isn't the hero."

Joel looked at his uncle, who was seated in the rocking chair reading his evening newspaper, as he did every night. He nodded toward the couch. "Have a seat, hero."

Joel frowned as he sat down. His uncle had the most impassive face of any man he knew. It was almost impossible to tell whether he was joking or being serious. "I'm *nee* hero."

"That's not what I heard." He set down the paper and gave Joel a ghost of a smile. "The taxi driver who takes you to the roofing job stopped by earlier tonight. Said you saved Vernon Miller's life."

"It wasn't like that." He explained what happened.

His uncle leaned back in his chair. "That's exactly what it sounds like. I'm glad those CPR lessons were put to *gut* use. Is Vernon all right?"

"They say he will be."

"What about you?"

"Me?" He leaned back and ran his hand through his hair. "I'm fine."

"You look like a wreck."

"Gee, thanks."

His uncle looked at him. "Make any headway with the wedding plans?"

"That's not exactly an appropriate thing to bring up at a time like this."

"*Nee*, but you said Vernon will be all right. Seems to me he owes you one."

Joel's shoulders slumped. He didn't want Vernon's blessing because he saved the man's life. He wanted it freely. Not that it mattered anymore. "I'm heading for bed," Joel said as he stood.

His uncle folded the paper in half. "Seems like Vernon is going to be out of work for a little while until he's fully recovered." He looked up at Joel. "If you decide you need a longer sabbatical, let me know."

Joel nodded, surprised at the offer. He went upstairs, took a shower, then dressed in a T-shirt and shorts and climbed into bed. But he couldn't sleep. Finally, he got up, dropped to his knees, and prayed. He prayed for Vernon, for Grace, for their family, and especially for the patience he would need to wait to marry Grace. That would be the hardest thing he'd ever have to do.

After spending the night and most of the day in the hospital, Vernon finally came home. The paralysis had worn off, thank the good Lord. The only residual effect was a headache, and even that was at a dull roar. The doctor had prescribed painkillers, but Vernon doubted he would fill the prescription. He could handle the pain.

What he couldn't handle was Grace putting off her happiness for him. How had he let this get so far? And how could he have doubted Joel? But he realized the situation had nothing to do with Joel and Grace. It was his own pain, stubbornness, and pride, and he had dragged the two of them into it. Now it was his job to fix it.

"I want to have Joel over for supper tonight," he told Ruby as she forced him to lie down in bed.

"Tonight?" She pulled the quilt over him, even though he wasn't the least bit cold. "Don't you think you should rest instead? I'll have one of the girls bring you supper in bed."

"I've never eaten a meal in bed, and I'm not about to start now." He was about to toss the covers off and stand up, but he didn't want to draw Ruby's ire. "The least I can do is have Joel over for supper, after he saved *mei* life."

She looked down at him. "You can wait to thank him."

But he didn't want to wait. He wanted to settle this marriage issue once and for all. He'd made them suffer too long. "Have Charity run over there and let his uncle know we'll see Joel at supper."

"I don't suppose I can convince you otherwise," Ruby said. At Vernon's headshake she added, "Then at least rest for the next couple of hours."

Somehow, he managed to fall asleep, and he woke up to the delicious smells of supper cooking. He sat up, his body more stiff than usual. The doctor said he had to take a few days off work to rest and heal, but Vernon wasn't sure if he could do that. Each day he didn't work, he lost money. That was reality.

When he walked into the kitchen, Ruby said, "Just in time. I was going to have one of the *maeds* come get you." She took a plate of rolls to the table. Only then did he notice Joel seated next to Grace.

"Joel." He walked over to his chair and sat down.

"Vernon."

The kitchen was quiet, which unnerved him. He missed the constant chatter of his daughters and wife. Since Grace and

Joel's announcement, they had been subdued. Tonight they were downright mute. After Ruby sat, he bowed his head. Instead of asking for blessings on the meal, he asked for forgiveness. *I've been wrong, Lord. I've been so very, very wrong.*

But he was ready to rectify that, and when he lifted his head, he looked at Joel. "I give you *mei* blessing. You and Grace can get married as soon as you want to."

Joel's mouth dropped open and he looked at Grace, who seemed equally confused. "But, *Daed,*" she said. "I told you we were going to wait."

Vernon glanced at Joel and saw a flicker of consternation fly across his face. Clearly the man wasn't in agreement, and Vernon didn't blame him. "You don't have to wait." He picked up his knife and fork, ready to dive in to the thick slice of meat loaf on his plate. "You're free to get married."

"*Nee.*"

Vernon looked at Joel. This time he was shocked. "What?"

"We're not getting married. Not like this." He turned to Vernon. "Can we talk in private?"

Vernon looked at the meat loaf, which was growing colder by the second. But his family was more important than meat loaf. He nodded. "Let's *geh* outside."

Joel followed Vernon out the back door. There was still plenty of light, but the sun was starting to set. Vernon walked slowly to the end of the patio, then turned around. "You wanted to talk, so talk."

Joel gulped. A part of him wondered what he was doing. He

and Grace were free and clear to marry now. Vernon had finally given them his permission and blessing. But it didn't feel right. "You don't owe me anything," Joel said.

The older man's brow lifted. "Owe you?"

Joel swallowed again. "I don't want *yer* permission to marry Grace because I saved *yer* life. I want it to be genuine. I want to earn *mei* place in *yer familye*."

"Don't you think you did that already by saving *mei* life?" Vernon crossed his arms over his chest.

"It's not the same."

"All right." Vernon walked toward him. "What if I told you I want you to be a part of this family, and not because you saved *mei* life or because you work hard? That I was wrong to keep you and Grace from getting married." He paused, his bottom lip trembling slightly. "I shouldn't have denied *mei dochder*—and you—your happiness because of *mei* pride." He looked away. "I thought I had forgiven you for betraying me. But I hadn't. I held on to the bitterness." He shrugged. "I'm not even sure why."

Joel was surprised at the confession. He knew how hard it must be for Vernon to say these words. "I never meant to betray you," he said, his voice laced with emotion. "I was a dumb kid trying to impress *mei onkel* and *vatter*."

"I know. And I should have realized that long before now. But the truth is, I'm not a *gut* businessman. It was easier to blame you than take responsibility for the mistakes I made. *Ya*, the job would have gotten me out of a bad situation, but would it have lasted? I shouldn't have been in that tight of a predicament in the first place." He let out a sigh and put his hand on Joel's shoulder. "*Yer* a *gut mann, sohn*. Grace is blessed to have you as her husband."

Joel's eyes burned as he nodded. This was more than he'd expected. "*Danki.*"

His future father-in-law dropped his hand. "Now, you can *geh* back to work at *yer* business. *Nee* need to work with me anymore."

Joel shook his head. "I told *yer* boss I would stay for two weeks. I intend to do that. Besides, they're short another man now."

"*Nee*, I'm going to work in the morning."

"Does Ruby know that?" Joel thought he saw Vernon pale a little under his tanned skin. Before Vernon could say anything, Joel added, "Take the time off. You deserve it."

Vernon's eyes misted. "We better get back before the meat loaf turns into a cold brick." He looked at Joel. "We have an understanding then?"

"*Ya.*" Joel grinned. "Understood."

Although it was strange not to go to work the next morning, Vernon had to admit it was nice to take things easy for a change. He didn't sleep in, but he did take his time with breakfast, and after his daughters left for their jobs, he and Ruby relocated to the back patio to enjoy another cup of coffee.

"Still feeling all right?" Ruby asked.

Vernon turned to his wife. She was seated close enough that he could see the tiny lines of worry at the corner of her mouth. "I'm fine, *lieb.*" He smiled, then took a sip of his coffee and looked out into his tidy backyard. He was more than fine. He was truly at peace. He hadn't realized until now that the bitterness from his failed business had always been there over the years, humming in the background, keeping him from fully trusting God. Now he felt light, as if a burden he hadn't realized he was carrying had been lifted.

"*Gute morgen.*"

He looked up to see Abner walking toward them. He set his coffee mug on the plastic side table and stood. "Morning," he said, keeping his tone neutral.

"I knocked on the front door, but when no one answered, I thought I'd check back here." He smiled and nodded at Ruby, then looked back at Vernon. "I thought we could talk for a few minutes."

Vernon moved closer to his wife, wary. What did Abner King want now? Hadn't he taken everything from him?

He halted at the thought. Blaming Abner for his troubles had become a habit. One he intended to stop right now.

"I need to get started on *mei* sewing anyway." Ruby placed her hand on Vernon's arm, then turned to Abner. "Can I get you some *kaffee?*"

Abner shook his head. "Had three cups before I came over."

Ruby gave Vernon an encouraging glance, then went inside.

Bolstered a bit by his wife's confidence, Vernon gestured to the now empty seat next to him.

"What do you need to talk to me about?" Vernon said once they were both seated.

Abner leaned back in his chair. "You've got a real nice place here."

Vernon gripped the arms of the plastic patio chair. Was that a dig? But when he turned to look at the man, Vernon saw sincerity in his eyes. And why not? He did have a nice place. Along with a wonderful family, and now that he was seeing things clearer, a great life. Vernon relaxed his grip on the chair and nodded in acknowledgment.

"I've been thinking things over." Abner folded his hands across his belly. "A lot of things. Ever since Joel asked me for the time off to work with you at the roofing company, *mei* mind has been stuck in the past." He turned to Vernon. "It's not pleasant mulling over regrets."

Vernon nodded. "*Nee.* It's not."

Abner let out a long breath. "I've been wondering what would have happened if we'd been partners instead of competitors."

Now that wasn't what Vernon had expected. "Really?"

Abner nodded. "I've been a greedy *mann*, Vernon. I can admit that. Which is why it never would have worked out for us to combine our businesses when I was younger. But now that we're soon to be family, I think it would be a *gut* move for both of us."

Vernon turned in his chair to face Abner. "I haven't been in the lumber business for years."

"That doesn't mean you've forgotten it." He paused. "Surely you'd rather be working with me and Joel than boiling on rooftops in the hot sun."

Hesitating, Vernon looked out at the yard again. Abner was offering him a great opportunity. More importantly, he was giving Vernon a chance to leave the roofing company, something he'd wanted to do but knew he never could. Not if he wanted to support his family.

After a few more thoughtful moments, he turned to Abner. "*Danki* for the offer, but I can't accept it."

Abner frowned. "You and that stubborn pride," he muttered.

"*Nee.* It's not about pride this time." God had given him the roofing job when he was financially desperate. Through that job he'd been able to get back on his feet and take care of his family. And while it was hot, hard work, it was also satisfying. He could see that now. He'd spent so much time being angry over losing his lumber business that he hadn't appreciated the good job he had. Even now he was itching to go back to work, despite the fact he was doing the right thing by taking the time off.

"I've got a job already, Abner. One I'm not interested in leaving."

Abner squinted at him. "*Yer* serious, aren't you?"

"*Ya*," he said. He managed a smile. "I am."

Rising from the chair, Abner hooked his thumbs under his suspenders. "The offer will always stand. Just want you to know that, in case you get tired of climbing those ladders."

Vernon stood and held out his hand. "I appreciate it, Abner. I truly do."

The man grinned back. "We're family, after all."

"*Ya*," he said, shaking Abner's hand. "We are."

Epilogue

Grace looked at her reflection in her bedroom mirror. She touched her white *kapp*, her fingers trembling. "Do I look all right?"

"You look beautiful." Faith handed her the black bonnet that was hanging on its hook on the back of her closet door. "Joel won't be able to take his eyes off you."

She knew it was vain to think that way, but she smiled. It was her wedding day, and she wanted everything to be perfect. The road to get here had been a little bumpy, but also worth it. Since her father had agreed to her and Joel getting married, Vernon had been spending more time with her fiancé, even after Joel finished his two-week stint with the roofing company.

Daed and *Mamm* had also taken a well-deserved vacation, something her father never did in the past. They'd gone to visit family in Kentucky, and when they returned they both looked happy and refreshed. Her father had regained his health and gone back to work, while Joel resumed his job with his uncle, who generously donated the wood to build their new house. Her father and Joel had put on the roof together.

"Ready?" Faith asked, smiling. "You don't want to keep him waiting."

Grace nodded, and they went downstairs. They were marrying in May, which was prime planting season, but they hadn't wanted to wait until November. She walked outside to where the wedding would take place. Every chair they set up in the yard the night before was filled, and Grace felt tears swell in her eyes. As she walked toward Joel and the bishop, she saw Charity and Patience, then Joel's uncle and his wife, who was dabbing at the corner of her eyes. Joel's parents and brother had also come for the wedding, which had made Joel happy. Then she saw her mother, who gave her a trembling smile.

Her gaze landed on her father. His eyes were misty, and while she knew that was the most emotion he was going to show, it was enough for the tears to spill down her cheeks. He smiled, and she wiped them away.

The rest of the ceremony went by in a blur, and before she knew it she was Mrs. Joel King. The wedding meal was delicious, and there was more food than they could eat, so plenty of the guests were able to take some home. By the end of the day, Grace was exhausted. She and Joel would be leaving in the morning to visit the rest of his family in Holmes County, but tonight they would be alone.

They approached the door to their new home. She hadn't been there in more than a week, at Joel's insistence. At the time the walls still needed to be painted and the furniture moved in.

"Close *yer* eyes," he said before opening the front door. When she did, he came up behind her after shutting the door and placed his hands over her eyes.

"You don't trust me?"

"I do," he whispered in her ear. "But this is a chance to get closer to you."

She giggled and tried to push his hand away. He ignored her and together they walked several steps forward, him leading.

"Surprise." He moved his hands away and she opened her eyes. They widened when she saw the beautiful hickory rocker and footstool in their new living room. She also saw an oak coffee table, matching end tables, and a magazine rack.

She whirled around and looked at him. "Where did all this come from?"

"Wedding presents." He grinned. "The rocker is from Silas's parents. The coffee table and end tables are from Faith and Silas."

"They made these?" She sat down on the couch, which was the one piece of furniture she and Joel had picked out together. She thought they would have to wait for more furniture, but her family had come through.

"*Ya.*" He sat down next to her. "Silas's *vatter* made the rocker and stool. Faith and Silas made everything else. The magazine rack is from Patience and Charity. I picked out the wood and the stain."

"They did all this in six weeks?" She ran her hand across the smooth top of the coffee table.

"They were highly motivated." He gathered her in his arms and she leaned her head against his shoulder.

They sat there in silence for a few moments. "I wasn't sure this would ever happen," Joel said, his quiet voice breaking the silence.

She nodded. By God's grace, it had. Joel told her about the discussion with her father that night he had given his blessing. She knew only God could have turned her father's heart. Whether it was Joel himself or the lightning strike, Grace didn't know. It didn't matter.

She lifted her head and kissed her husband. She could hardly wait for the future they would build together.

A Heart Full of Love

CHAPTER 1

A re you ready for this?"

Ellie Miller turned her head toward her husband Christopher's, concerned voice. Their horse, Clyde, whinnied and pranced a bit in his buggy harness, signaling his eagerness to be on his way instead of waiting in their driveway. Ellie put her hand over her swollen abdomen. "Do I have a choice?"

She felt Chris take her hand. "We could wait and let it be a surprise."

"I don't think *Mamm* would appreciate that. She wasn't exactly thrilled when we told her we were expecting."

"That's because she worries too much."

"And you don't think she'll be worried about this?" She touched her belly again. She remembered her mother's tone of voice when she'd announced that she and Chris were having a baby. *How on earth will you manage?* Those were the first words out of her mouth. Not "I'm so happy for you," or "I'm going to be a *grossmutter*!" Had she even congratulated them on the pregnancy? Ellie couldn't remember.

77

Chris squeezed her hand before releasing it. "We can't control how your *mamm* reacts." He kissed her cheek, the softness of his beard tickling her skin. "But we can show her how happy and blessed we are."

She smiled. "*Danki* for reminding me."

During their buggy ride to her parents' house, Ellie's mind wandered. Despite her husband's reassurance, she couldn't stem her growing anxiety. She and Chris had been married for two years now, and they had fallen into a comfortable routine, with Chris working construction jobs in and around Paradise while she had continued her jelly-making business, Ellie's Jellies, which she had put on hold recently. She had never been so happy. When she discovered she was expecting, she could barely contain her joy.

Then she had given *Mamm* the news. Ellie had expected some reservations from her. Since the car accident that had taken Ellie's sight eight years ago, she'd had to prove to her mother that she was capable. She created her own business. She married the most wonderful man in Paradise. She was going to be a mother. Yet with a few words, her *mamm* could make her feel like that inept young woman who wondered if she would ever deal with her blindness, much less accept it.

Ellie clasped her hands together, tamping down her nervousness. Chris was right. She wasn't in control of her mother's reactions or feelings. She wasn't in control of anything. God was.

A short time later they arrived at her parents' house. Ellie stayed in the buggy as Chris settled Clyde in the barn, and then she heard the familiar crunch of his boots on the gravel drive as he came back to assist her. When his hand touched hers, she gripped it as he helped her step down to the ground.

She entwined her fingers with his, the strength of his nearness giving her the courage she needed to walk to the house. Ellie knew her father would be supportive when they told him the news. Maybe *Mamm* would surprise her and be excited too.

"You're cutting off my circulation," Chris said to her, his tone half joking.

"Sorry." She loosened her grip on his hand as they ascended the porch steps. Before they reached the top, Ellie heard the soft squeak of the screen door opening.

"Ellie!"

Her mother's shrill, worried voice made Ellie wince. She flinched when *Mamm* put her hands on her shoulders.

"You look tired. I knew we should have taken supper over to you instead of Chris bringing you here," she said.

"Hello to you, too, *Mamm*." After the accident her mother had been overly protective. Ellie had resented it at first, wanting her independence and working to achieve it. Eventually *Mamm* had realized Ellie could be independent. But now it was as if they were going back in time, when her mother was filled with doubts and worry. When she didn't believe Ellie was capable of anything.

"Let them get in the *haus*, Edna, before you start hovering." Her father's voice came from the direction of the doorway.

Mamm released Ellie's shoulders and stepped aside. Chris still held Ellie's hand as they walked through the front door. The tangy scent of stuffed cabbage mingled with the buttery aroma of fresh, cooked corn made her stomach rumble. Lately she'd been constantly hungry. As Chris liked to remind her, she was eating for two.

Not anymore . . .

"Smells *appeditlich*, Edna." Chris released Ellie's hand.

"Ellie, you have dark circles under your eyes." Ignoring Chris's compliment, *Mamm* stood in front of her so close that Ellie could feel her warm breath against her face. "Christopher, you need to make sure she's getting her rest."

"He is," Ellie said.

"And she shouldn't be out this late at night."

"It's not even seven o'clock." Ellie searched for her mother's hand and took it. "Everything is fine. You don't need to worry."

"That's what I've been trying to tell her," *Daed* said. "Edna, she looks healthy to me. Stop borrowing trouble."

Her mother didn't say anything, and Ellie could feel her intense gaze. "A mother knows her *dochder*," she said. "Something is going on."

"Ellie, didn't you say you were *hungerich*?" Chris said quickly.

"Starving," she said with a nod, grateful for her husband's ability to step in when she needed him to.

"But—"

"You heard them, Edna." *Daed* came up on the other side of Ellie. "They're hungry and so am I. Let's eat."

They all went to the kitchen, but Ellie could still sense her mother's scrutiny, imagining the mix of concern and frustration on her face as she tried to puzzle out what was going on. She should have known her mother would suspect something.

As she sat down at the table, she felt a movement in her belly. "Oh," she blurted, the strong kick taking her off guard.

"What?" Her mother was immediately at her side. "What happened?"

"Just the baby . . ." She felt Chris squeeze her shoulder. She took a deep breath. "Or the other one."

The room grew silent. After a long pause, her mother finally spoke. "What did you say?"

Ellie turned her face toward *Mamm*. "Christopher and I are having twins."

Neither of her parents said anything. As the silence lengthened, she felt a tightening in her chest. She expected her mother to be upset, but her father's silence surprised her. She covered Chris's hands with hers.

"Twins?" her father said at last.

Ellie swallowed and nodded.

He burst into laughter. "Two *bopplis*? That's wonderful news!"

"Ephraim, how can you say that?" Ellie heard the creak of a kitchen chair as her mother plopped down on it. "Twins? How will she ever manage?"

Ellie couldn't help but frown, her mother's words echoing her own thoughts when her midwife, Barbara, had told her she suspected Ellie was carrying twins. Yet when Ellie had told Chris, he'd been ecstatic, his enthusiasm and confidence bolstering hers. But as usual, her mother's words nicked at her, and those feelings of doubt crept back in.

"She'll be fine," *Daed* said, chuckling again. "Twins. Who would have thought?" Ellie heard him slap Chris on the back. "Congratulations, *sohn*. Now let's eat."

"Ephraim—"

"It's time to eat." Her father's tone had turned stern.

Ellie heard her mother rise and mumble something unintelligible under her breath. Chris patted Ellie's shoulder and sat down next to her. "See," he whispered, "that wasn't so bad."

She nodded, even though she disagreed with him. During the meal her mother didn't say anything, letting Chris and her father do most of the talking. Ellie tried to focus on the delicious food, but her earlier, ravenous appetite had disappeared. Why couldn't her mother be happy for them? They should be celebrating. Instead, Ellie just wanted to go home.

After supper, she halfheartedly offered to help with the dishes, knowing her mother would refuse. Would she have to prove herself all over again? How could she fight both her doubts and her mother's?

When Ellie and Chris reached home, he pulled the buggy to a stop but didn't get out. "Don't let your mother get to you."

"I'm not." She frowned. "Well, I'm trying not to."

"You're going to be a great mother. I truly believe that. Your *mamm* will see that too." He patted her knee and jumped out of the buggy.

Ellie touched her belly as the twins moved around inside. She'd already come to notice that one of the babies was more active than the other. "From your mouth to God's ears," she whispered, then said a silent prayer, asking the Lord to help her get through the next few weeks.

Three weeks later Ellie and her mother were spending the early afternoon in Ellie's garden. She couldn't have asked for a prettier spring day. She listened to the soft rustling of the oak leaves as the tree branches swayed in the gentle wind. Her skin soaked up the warmth of the sun, her mind drawing peace from the calm, quiet surroundings.

A spasm went through her, making her catch her breath. She paused, waiting to see if her mother would notice. She'd had a few of them since they had started working in the garden an hour ago, but she'd kept them hidden from *Mamm*. Barbara had told her she would experience pre-labor contractions the closer she came to her due date, so she wasn't too worried. She wasn't supposed to have the babies until June, another two weeks away.

Ellie sat on the ground with her knees bent and her legs to one side, supporting her weight slightly on one hip and one hand flat on the soil as she worked with her other hand to pull weeds. She smiled as she shifted her weight and moved her legs to the other side. She could hardly believe that soon she and Christopher would be parents. Even her mother had seemed to settle down a little bit since they had told her about the twins, although she had insisted on coming over every day this week to help Ellie prepare for their arrival.

She and Chris already had everything ready, though—a cradle for the boppli to share until they were ready to transfer to separate cribs, plenty of clothing, cloth diapers, pins, even a few baby spoons, although it would be awhile before the babies would eat solid food. Ellie thought she had everything under control and taken care of, but her mother kept finding things to do, as if she couldn't keep still for more than a minute. Ellie insisted on being involved in the running of her own household, despite being tired. Her house had never been cleaner, her garden was almost weed free, and it seemed as soon as she and Chris put on fresh clothes for the day, the ones from the day before were washed and hung on the line before breakfast. Her mother seemed to have an endless supply of nervous energy.

Another contraction went through her, catching her off guard. She took in a sharp breath.

"Ellie?" *Mamm* scurried to her from the opposite end of the garden. "What's wrong?"

She clenched her teeth, weary at the panic she heard in her mother's tone. Just when she thought *Mamm* had gotten a handle on her stress, she overreacted once again. "I'm fine," she said, moving her hand from her side.

"Are you sure? There isn't something wrong with the babies, is there?"

"They're fine too." She moved to a kneeling position, not an easy feat considering her belly seemed to have doubled in size in the past month.

"Maybe you should *geh* inside," *Mamm* said. "I can finish up the weeding."

Ellie shook her head. "The *bopplis* are just active today, that's all." She discerned the weeds from the plants in front of her by lightly touching each one. She was near the tomato plants at the edge of the garden. A few minutes earlier her mother had placed wooden stakes next to each tender plant, in anticipation for when they would need to be tied to the stakes for support. She pulled a small tuft of grass that had invaded the tomato row, one of the few weeds she could still find.

"I'd like to finish taking care of this, *Mamm*. It won't take long. Then I'll *geh* inside and start dinner for Chris and me." She searched for another weed, hoping her mother took the hint.

"Nonsense. I'll make supper tonight."

"You don't have to—"

"You've been looking so tired lately." From the direction of her mother's voice, Ellie could tell she'd walked to the other side of the garden. "Exhausted, actually."

Ellie couldn't deny that she'd been more tired lately. But she wouldn't say she was exhausted. She opened her mouth to tell her mother not to worry when another twinge assaulted her belly, this time on the other side, followed by a healthy kick that took her off guard again. *"Ach!"*

Her mother's footsteps came so fast Ellie was certain she'd trampled a few plants. "That's it. You're going inside and putting your feet up. Here's your cane."

Ellie stifled a groan. She knew exactly where her white cane was. She'd made sure to keep it less than a foot away from her, and she didn't appreciate when her mother—or anyone else—assumed she couldn't find it. But she held her tongue as she took the cane from her mother.

"Let me help you up," *Mamm* continued, putting her hands underneath Ellie's arms.

It was no use arguing with her, and this time Ellie accepted her help willingly. Getting up was a lot harder than sitting down, and that had nothing to do with her blindness. To reassure her mother that she was all right, Ellie gave her a smile before turning her face toward the sun, taking in one last sunbeam of warmth before she was banished inside.

At least Chris would be home soon. In his diplomatic way, he would tell her mother that he and Ellie were fine and she could go home, making sure to let her know how much he appreciated her help during the day while he was at work. Then her mother would be on her way. Ellie wished *Mamm* would listen to her the way she did Chris, but she was thankful for small miracles where her mother was concerned.

She angled her cane in front of her, running it lightly in a half arc and making sure the path to the back porch was clear. It usually was. She and Chris kept their house and property neat and organized out of necessity. "You're turning me into a tidy person," he'd joked a few weeks after they had moved into their home two years ago. "*Mei* whole *familye* is shocked."

Ellie smiled at the memory, only to immediately double over in intense pain. She gripped her cane with one hand and cradled her belly with the other while she gasped for breath. *Uh-oh. That wasn't a normal pain.*

Her mother's arm came around her shoulders, and Ellie leaned against her. She could barely hear her mother call her name as another wave of pain came over her.

"I think it's time, Ellie."

For once her mother's tone was calm, comforting, and breaking through the pain. With *Mamm*'s support she continued toward the house, thankful her mother was by her side.

CHAPTER 2

As Sarah Lynne pulled into the Millers' driveway, she saw her brother, Chris, pacing in front of his barn. When he noticed her approaching, he walked to her buggy. She stopped the horse and handed him the reins before climbing out. "What are you doing outside?" she asked him as he looped the reins over a tying post.

"Edna won't let me see Ellie. It's been seven hours since labor started."

Sarah Lynne saw the pain etched on her brother's tanned face. Chris had always been dark, his hair nearly as black as the coal in her stove back home. But since he started working construction soon after he and Ellie married, he had a perpetual tan, even in the winter. She put her hand on his arm. "She will be okay. Barbara is a *gut* midwife. And you know Edna won't let anything happen to Ellie."

Chris nodded, but her words didn't seem to bring him much comfort. "I should be with her. Not out here, doing *nix*." He looked at Sarah Lynne. "She's in so much pain."

"But not lasting pain. Besides, she doesn't need to see that you're worried."

He leaned against the fence post. "You're right. I'm always

the one telling Ellie not to worry. That everything's going to be okay. It wouldn't do for me to give her pause now."

Sarah Lynne tilted her head. "Chris . . . she will be all right. The *bopplis* too. You believe that, *ya?*"

"*Ya.*" He ran his hand over his face, weariness seeping into his brown eyes. "Although I've had a time convincing Edna of that. Don't get me wrong. I am glad she's been here while I'm at work, especially today. If Ellie had been alone when she'd gone into labor . . ." A look of panic entered his eyes.

"But she wasn't."

"Thank God." Chris hung his hat on the corner of the tying post. "Still, Edna continues to drive me *ab im kopp* sometimes. I don't know how Ellie keeps her patience. I've been trying to keep her fretting from affecting Ellie, but it's been difficult."

Confused, Sarah Lynne frowned. "Is there a reason Edna is so worried?"

He shrugged. "I'm not sure. I haven't brought it up with Ellie, but I've noticed how her *mamm* is even more overprotective than usual. She's concerned Ellie can't handle the babies, or that something is going to be wrong with one of them . . . or both. We all know how strong Ellie is, and Barbara has given us only *gut* reports about the pregnancy. Yet Edna can't seem to let her fear *geh.*"

"Have you mentioned it to Ephraim?"

"I don't have to. He sees it too." Chris sighed. "Hopefully after her grandbabies are born she'll be able to relax and enjoy them." He looked at Sarah Lynne, giving her a half smile. "I'm glad you're here. We haven't seen much of you since Ellie started to show."

"I wish I could have visited more. But I've been helping

with the farm now that Isaiah has had to take on extra work."
She had married Ellie's cousin a year before Chris and Ellie had
married. Isaiah had wanted to make a go of the farm, and he
had. But they couldn't ignore the economic realities, and Isaiah
had found work at a local factory. They were saving every
penny for the day they started their family . . . whenever that
would be.

Chris began to pace, and Sarah Lynne could see he'd only
partly heard her. She put her hand on his shoulder, stilling him.
"Why don't we check on Ellie?"

He nodded eagerly and grabbed his hat. As they neared the
house, Sarah Lynne's excitement grew. "Twins," she said glancing at Chris. "I can't wait to meet them. Will they be girls or
boys? Maybe one of each?"

"I just hope they're healthy." He shot a look at Sarah Lynne.
"And maybe one of each."

Sarah Lynne chuckled. "I knew it."

As soon as they entered the house, the midwife came out of
Ellie and Chris's bedroom, a large grin on her small, round face.
"She did it," Barbara said.

"Is she all right?" Chris asked, his tanned face suddenly growing pale. Sarah Lynne realized that for all his talk about being calm
and steady for his wife and mother-in-law, he had been holding a
lot inside. "The *bopplis* . . ."

Barbara put her hand on Chris's shoulder and smiled. "Ellie
and the *bopplis* are fine. Two *maed*, as sweet as can be. And *yer
frau*, she is incredible. There were no complications, although she
is very tired. I expected her to be in labor longer, but those *bopplis*
were ready to be born." She motioned to the bedroom. "*Kumme*
and see *yer dochders*."

Sarah Lynne stayed back as Chris left with the midwife. She briefly touched her own flat stomach. Would she and Isaiah ever have a family of their own? After three years of trying, she was starting to doubt.

She clasped her hands together and forced the thoughts away. Today was her brother and sister-in-law's day to celebrate the miracle of life. Two lives, strong and healthy. She thanked God for the tiny blessings.

Despite the residual pain coursing through her body, Ellie was eager to hold her daughters. When she first heard one tiny cry, then two, she had laughed through the tears pouring down her cheeks. She was exhausted and ecstatic at the same time.

"Where are the *bopplis*?" Ellie asked, her voice sounding weak with weariness.

"Here is the first one." *Mamm* placed a tiny bundle in the crook of Ellie's arm. The baby was clean and wrapped in a soft flannel blanket.

"What does she look like?" Ellie asked, running her fingers over the top of her daughter's downy head.

"Beautiful, like her mother."

Ellie smiled at Chris's voice, turning her head in his direction. "You're a little biased."

"Maybe." She felt the springs of the bed give as he gently sat down next to her. "I'm holding the other one, and they're both *perfekt*." His hand brushed away her damp hair, allowing the breeze from the nearby window, now open, to cool her forehead. "How are you?"

She leaned her cheek against the baby's head and smiled. "Happy," she said. "I'm so happy."

He continued to stroke her hair. "I wanted to be here, by your side," he said, his voice almost a whisper. "But *yer mamm*—"

"It's okay, Chris." Ellie lifted her face. "Tell me what they look like. Are they identical?"

"They look like babies to me." Chris chuckled. "Barbara said they're fraternal. Both have dark hair. The one I'm holding has a little more than the other. She's also got a tiny dimple in her chin."

"I suppose we should name them, *ya?*"

They had discussed many names over the past few weeks, but hadn't come to a conclusion for either boys or girls. "This one is Irene," she said, sliding her finger down the baby's tender cheek and over her tiny chin.

He paused. "After *mei grossmutter?* I thought we had decided not to name either one after members of our families."

"*Ya*. But the name feels right for her, don't you think so?"

"She looks exactly like an Irene."

"What should we name our other daughter?" Ellie said, her eyelids growing heavier.

"Julia," he said.

"After *mei grossmutter*." She smiled. "Can I hold Julia too?"

"Of course."

Ellie opened her other arm and Chris nestled Julia in the crook. She tilted her head toward Chris and smiled. "They're finally here," she whispered, fighting off the weariness that threatened to take over.

"*Ya*," he said, brushing her cheek with the back of his knuckles. "They finally are."

"All right, that's enough."

Ellie's eyes flew open at her mother's voice slicing through the precious moment.

"Ellie needs rest," *Mamm* said, taking Irene from her.

But Ellie wasn't ready to let go. "Christopher?" she cried as Julia was also lifted from her arms. She didn't want to rest. She wanted to hold her babies.

"*Yer mamm's* right," Barbara said. "You do need to rest. Your body has been through a lot. Don't worry, you'll get to spend plenty of time with them soon enough."

Ellie could hear a soft cry from one of the babies. "But they need me now."

Chris rose from the bed and kissed her temple. "I'll bring them to you later. Sleep now, Ellie. You've earned it."

She nodded, her eyes already drifting closed as she heard everyone leave the room. Then silence. After the excitement and pain of giving birth, being able to hold her precious babies, to spend a brief but special moment with her husband and their twins . . . now all she felt was emptiness. And alone.

"Why did you take them away so soon?" she mumbled, her eyes stinging with tears as she closed them, drifting off into a fitful sleep.

Sometime later Ellie's eyes opened. She had no idea how long she'd slept, and she didn't feel refreshed. If anything, she was agitated. She shifted slightly in the bed, ignoring the throbbing in her body. She stilled when she heard low voices right outside her doorway.

"I don't know how she'll handle the babies, Barbara."

Ellie frowned and then sighed. Of course her mother was still worried about how she'd manage. But how was she supposed to figure out how to be a mother when she couldn't hold her own babies for more than a second?

"I'm sure she'll be fine, Edna. Ellie is a smart woman. She does very well considering she's . . ."

"Blind. You can say it. And you're not telling the truth, Barbara. I can see it on your face. You're as concerned as I am."

"I wouldn't say concerned, but realistic, ya," Barbara admitted. "There will be some challenges. There always are with twins."

"And when the mother is blind? Ellie doesn't know anything about taking care of a baby. Now she has two. She and Christopher should have waited until they were more prepared."

"Edna, listen to me. All this worry is going to affect your *dochder*—and the babies. They can pick up on the tension."

Ellie struggled to sit up. Her babies could sense stress?

"Ellie will be a *gut mudder*," Barbara continued. "But she will definitely need help. Has she made arrangements?"

"I don't know." Her mother sounded hurt. "Anytime I tried to talk to her about helping out, she changed the subject."

Ellie's face heated. That was true. But her mother had always made it sound like Ellie wouldn't be able to do anything to care for her own babies. And she didn't want to be a burden to anyone—especially her mother.

"She'll have to talk about it soon. But not now. You and Christopher are here—that will be enough for the time being. I'm going to check on Ellie. She's been asleep for two hours."

Two hours? What about the twins? They had to be hungry by now. When she heard Barbara walk into the room, she asked, "Where are my babies?"

"They're fine." Barbara's voice was soothing, but that didn't keep Ellie from wanting her children. "They're in the cradle in the extra bedroom." Ellie sensed Barbara nearing the bed, and within a few seconds, she felt the woman's hand on her arm. "How are you feeling?"

"I want to see them."

"Are you in a lot of pain? I can get you some herbal tea. That will take the edge off."

"I want to see my babies!" Ellie didn't understand the utter panic going through her, the whirlwind of emotions that churned like a storm inside. She only knew that she needed her twins with her.

"Ellie, listen to Barbara." Now her mother had come in and was walking toward her. "She said the twins are fine."

"They have to be hungry." Ellie's breasts ached to feed them.

"They've already eaten."

"What? How?"

"Barbara and I gave them formula. We thought that was best."

"You thought that was best, Edna," Barbara said quietly.

"You made that decision without me?" Ellie pushed off the covers and felt for her cane. "Where's Christopher?"

"He's outside taking care of the animals," Edna said, her calm infuriating Ellie.

"I need to talk to him." Surely Chris didn't know what had happened. How could her mother have decided how the babies were to be fed without even consulting her?

"Barbara," *Mamm* said evenly. "I think Ellie could use that tea now."

"I don't want any tea!"

"Ellie. Enough." Her mother sat down on the bed near her. "Barbara, please bring the tea."

Once Ellie heard Barbara's footsteps disappear, Ellie said, her voice growing sharp, "Why are you keeping the *bopplis* from me?"

"Because they're sleeping, Ellie. You shouldn't disturb them."

"I'm their mother—don't tell me what to do!" Sobs choked her, a mix of anger and something else she couldn't define. She shouldn't be crying like this. She shouldn't be so weak. Yet she was powerless in the face of the emotions overtaking her.

"You're being irrational." Her mother's voice was stern but soft. "Now listen to me. I talked it over with Christopher while you were sleeping. He agreed with me that it would be easier for you to bottle-feed the babies. They both need to be on the same feeding schedule, and someone else can feed one while you feed the other."

Ellie wiped her eyes, unable to speak. It sounded logical, but she wanted to be consulted. "Where did you get the formula?"

"I bought it a while ago."

"And you never said anything to me?"

"Ellie, anytime I brought up making a plan for the babies, you didn't want to talk about it."

"That's because you always tell me what to do. It wouldn't be my plan. It would be yours!"

Her mother didn't say anything for a moment. Ellie crossed her arms, tears streaming down her cheeks. Was this how she was supposed to feel as a new mother? Her emotions out of control? Her resentment growing toward her own mother—even her husband? This wasn't how she imagined it would be after the babies were born.

"Here's the tea," Barbara said when she returned. "I already had it steeped and ready for when you woke up."

Ellie paused before uncrossing her arms. "Set it on the side table. Please," she added, realizing she had sounded rude.

The soft thud of the ceramic mug touching the wood echoed in the room. Her mother stood. "I'll get supper started. I imagine Christopher is hungry."

Ellie ignored her mother, still resenting how she had taken over. But once she was sure *Mamm* was gone, Ellie slumped and put her head in her hands. "I'm sorry, Barbara. I don't know what's wrong with me."

Barbara sat down on the bed and rubbed Ellie's back, the rounding motions feeling soothing underneath Ellie's thin gown. "It's all right, Ellie. I understand."

Turning her head toward Barbara, Ellie shook her head. "My relationship with my mother is . . . complicated."

"I know. And right now your emotions are fragile. It's the hormones from giving birth. You'll be more settled in a few days. Please drink the tea. It will help you feel better."

"I hope so." Ellie felt for the tea, then cupped her hands around the warm mug. She took a sip, not recognizing the blend of herbs in the lightly flavored tea. "Right now I feel helpless."

"Trust me, Ellie, you're not. But you are tired, and I'm sure in some pain."

Ellie nodded.

"I know you don't want to, but you do need to get as much rest as you can. The *bopplis* will sleep a lot at least during the first week or so, and you need to take advantage of that. Soon enough they'll be keeping you up at all hours." She patted Ellie's hand.

"I know you're upset with your mother right now, but she is here to help. And she's partly right about the bottle-feeding. The twins do need to be on the same feeding schedule. It will be easier on all three of you that way. If not, you'll be feeding one or the other the whole day and you won't have time for anything else."

"You don't think I could manage breastfeeding them."

"I never said that. But you need to do what's best for you and the twins. There will be times when bottle-feeding will be easier."

"Because I'm blind?" Ellie sounded snappish, but she didn't care.

"Because they'll be hungry at the same time. Two babies are hard for anyone to handle. But you can also breastfeed them."

She felt a glimmer of hope. "I can?"

"*Ya.* I'll show you before I leave. I'll also show you how to use the hand breast pump for when you're unable to breastfeed. But regardless of how you feed the *bopplis,* don't be afraid to ask for or accept help." The sheets rustled as Barbara stood and smoothed the bedclothes back over Ellie's legs. "That's not a sign of weakness."

Ellie nodded, but she didn't completely believe Barbara's words. If she could see, would everyone be treating her this way? Would she feel this way, growing more and more doubtful that she could take care of her own children?

"Is it all right to come in?" Chris's voice sounded tentative near the doorway.

"Of course, Chris," Barbara said as she placed pillows behind Ellie's back. "I'll check on the babies. If they're awake, I'll bring them to you, Ellie, and you can try feeding them. They ate a couple of hours ago, so they might be hungry again."

"*Danki,* Barbara." Ellie set down the mug and leaned back against the stack of pillows. Chris sat down beside her. She felt him take her hand, but she turned away from him.

"Ellie?"

Tears stung her eyes, then slid down her cheeks. She didn't

understand. This was supposed to be a happy day, one of the happiest of her life. Instead, she couldn't even face her husband, not wanting him to see her tears . . . her weakness.

He didn't say anything else, only stroked her hand. She felt the familiar roughness of his skin from the past two years of working construction. Her eyelids fluttered as the tea began to take effect, and she shifted her body down so that her head was against the pillows.

"You look sleepy," he said.

"I am. Must be the tea."

"It's also past ten."

"Then you should get to bed," she said, mumbling.

"I love you," he said, his voice sounding far away.

"I'm sorry."

"What?"

But that was all she could bring herself to say.

CHAPTER 3

Chris slid his hand from Ellie's as she drifted off to sleep. He stared at her, worry filling him. This wasn't his Ellie. She thought she'd hid her tears from him. But he knew her well. Those were not tears of joy, but of pain.

He rose from her side. Something had happened while he had been outside finishing up the chores. He left their bedroom, walked to the other side of the house, and found Barbara coming out of the spare bedroom. "What's going on with Ellie?"

Barbara put a finger to her lips and closed the bedroom door. "The babies are still sleeping. Edna is in there keeping an eye on them."

"Why? Is there something wrong with the *bopplis?*"

She shook her head and led him to the living room. "They're fine. She insisted on being in there with them."

"Did she say something to Ellie?"

"Nee." She gave him an odd look. "Why do you ask?"

"Ellie's upset."

"She's tired. And she's apprehensive. New mothers always are." She smirked. "So are new fathers." Then she smiled, her eyes filled with wisdom and understanding. "She's going to be fine. You both are. Keep encouraging her, Christopher." Her smile slipped a little. "Is Edna the only one available to help?"

"*Mei schwester* and *mamm* offered."

"*Gut.*" She paused. "Edna seems very attached to the *maed* already."

He nodded, not adding that he thought Edna might be too attached. But what did he know about any of this? When Edna had insisted the twins be bottle-fed, he agreed. Her argument had made sense. He wanted what was best for his daughters—and his wife. But he wasn't sure what that was anymore.

"Christopher," Barbara said, putting her hand on his arm. "Set aside your worry. Enjoy your new *familye.*"

He took in a deep breath as she walked toward the kitchen. Of course she was right. So many times he had told Ellie not to worry, and now he was doing the same thing. He closed his eyes and prayed for peace in his soul and the strength and wisdom to be the husband and father God wanted him to be. When he opened his eyes, calm had replaced the stress. God was in control. He needed to remember that.

Edna stared at her precious granddaughters as they lay in the cradle next to the bed. They were so beautiful, so perfect. They both had plump cheeks and long fingers, just like Ellie had when she was born. Julia's left hand formed a tight fist while Irene's right hand was similarly closed as they both slept. Edna watched the slight rise and fall of their tiny chests.

She turned at the sound of the door opening. Barbara walked in and motioned for Edna to come into the hall. Edna paused, looked at the babies for a long moment, then reluctantly left their side.

Barbara closed the door behind them. "Edna," she whispered, "are you okay?"

Edna lifted her chin. "Of course I am."

"Just making sure."

"You should be taking care of Ellie, not checking on me." Edna put her hand on the doorknob. "I won't let anything happen to the *bopplis.*"

"I didn't think you would." Barbara tilted her head. "You're hanging on to these babies too tightly, Edna."

Edna scowled. "You're telling me how I should handle *mei* grandchildren?"

"I'm only pointing out what I see."

"Are you finished?"

Barbara folded her arms across her chest. *"Ya."*

"Then let me get back to the *bopplis.*" Edna opened the door and shut it behind her, a little too loudly. One of the babies started to stir. She tiptoed to the cradle and smiled when she saw they were still asleep.

Barbara didn't understand. She didn't have a blind daughter. Her grandchildren weren't at risk.

Deep inside, Edna knew she wasn't being fair to Ellie. But two little lives were at stake here. She would make sure nothing happened to Julia and Irene, just as she had protected Ellie and her son, Wally, when they were infants. She would be as diligent now as she had been back then. Even more so, considering Ellie's disability.

She couldn't—and wouldn't—let history repeat itself.

Three days later Ellie snuggled Julia in the crook of her arm. She searched for her baby's mouth, and once she found it, slipped the nipple of a three-ounce bottle inside. The now-familiar sounds of a baby taking her bottle reached Ellie's ears. She'd only had a chance to breastfeed the babies a couple of times, and she didn't feel confident doing it discreetly in front of company. She sat back in the rocking chair and turned her head toward Chris's mother, who was sitting on the couch opposite her, feeding Irene.

"They are just precious, Ellie." Bertha Miller cooed at Irene. "Absolutely *perfekt*." She paused for a moment. "Irene looks like you."

"She does? Chris thinks she looks like him."

"She has his dark hair, but this round little face and clear blue eyes are all you."

Ellie grinned. "What about Julia?"

Bertha chuckled. "She looks like me, of course."

Ellie laughed. "Obviously."

Sarah Lynne walked into the room. "I brought some sandwiches and iced tea," she said.

"*Danki*." Ellie felt the bottle slip from Julia's mouth. She leaned close to her daughter and listened for her soft, steady breathing. After a few moments, she realized the baby had fallen asleep. "Is Irene still awake?" she asked Bertha.

"*Nee*. They both fell asleep at the same time. Imagine that."

"I'll take them to their cradle," Sarah Lynne said.

"I can do it." Ellie set the bottle down on the small table next to the rocker. She gripped Julia and started to get up.

"I'd like to, if you don't mind."

Ellie caught something in her sister-in-law's tone. "*Danki*, Sarah Lynne."

After Sarah Lynne left with the twins, Ellie turned toward Bertha. "Is Sarah Lynne okay?"

Bertha sighed. "She's fine. But you know *mei dochder*. She's impatient to start her own family."

"Oh. I should have realized—"

"Don't apologize. Sarah Lynne and Isaiah will have children in the Lord's time. Like you and Christopher."

Ellie leaned back in the chair. "I'm glad you're happy about the twins."

"Why wouldn't I be?"

"Not everyone is." She ran her hand along the smooth, curved arm of the hickory chair.

"If you're talking about Edna, you're wrong. She's happy. She just has an unusual way of showing it. Here, let me get you a sandwich. Sarah Lynne made your favorite, chicken salad."

"I'm not really hungry." Ellie's mind was on her mother. She had left earlier when Bertha and Sarah Lynne had arrived, saying she was going home to pick up a few things and would be back in a couple of hours. Ellie dreaded her return. Her mother was so efficient, she never gave the babies a chance to cry. Or Ellie a chance to tend to them, saying that Ellie needed to "heal." But she was healing just fine. What she wasn't doing was taking care of her daughters.

"Are you sure?"

"*Ya*. But you go ahead. I know you like chicken salad too." Ellie rose. "I'll be right back."

"Okay." A few minutes later Bertha said, "Mm, I think Sarah Lynne outdid herself with this chicken salad."

Ellie made her way down the hall to the spare bedroom where her mother was staying. Her mother had also insisted on keeping the cradle in that room, explaining that she could take care of the babies at night while Ellie and Christopher slept. For the first two nights, Ellie didn't argue. Her emotions were still rocky, and doubt about her ability to care for the twins had lingered. To add to that, Chris had been working extra hours and came home the last couple of nights exhausted. But Ellie ached for her babies, and each time she heard them cry, she wanted to rush to them. But with the spare bedroom at the opposite end of the house, she couldn't reach them in time.

She heard Sarah Lynne's sweet, soft singing as she entered the room. Her sister-in-law's voice was just above a whisper as she sang one of the church's popular hymns. Instead of singing it in the chanting voice usually used during church, she had added a lovely melody to the words. Ellie touched the doorjamb before entering the room, then walked toward Sarah Lynne's voice.

The singing stopped. "They're still asleep," Sarah Lynne whispered.

"*Gut.*" Ellie moved to stand beside her. She ran her fingers along the edge of the cradle.

"You are so blessed," Sarah Lynne said quietly. "Such *schee bopplis.*"

Ellie took Sarah Lynne's hand. "Your time will come."

She sighed and squeezed Ellie's fingers. "I know. That's what Isaiah says. I had just thought . . . hoped . . ." She let go of Ellie's hand.

"I'll pray," Ellie said.

"*Danki.*"

Ellie heard the back door slam shut. She tensed. "*Mamm*'s back."

Hurried footsteps sounded down the hall. "Ellie, I have a

surprise. I brought your bibs from when you were a *boppli*." Her mother entered the room.

"Shh," Sarah Lynne said.

"They're sleeping," Ellie added.

"Oh, let me see *mei* precious ones." Her mother sandwiched herself between Ellie and Sarah Lynne. "Are you sure they're all right?"

"Sarah Lynne just put them down."

"*Gut*. I wouldn't want you to have to—"

Ellie turned toward her mother. "Have to what?"

"Never mind." Her mother walked away. "We must leave now. We don't want to wake the *bopplis*."

Sarah Lynne threaded her arm through Ellie's as they left the room. When they were several steps away from the bedroom, she leaned over and whispered, "Has she been this way the whole time?"

Ellie nodded. "Sometimes worse."

Ellie could sense Sarah Lynne shaking her head. "Ellie, I'll be praying for *you*."

CHAPTER 4

A nd just look at what *mei* friend Linda made for you."
Ellie gripped the back of the chair at the kitchen table.
When her mother didn't say anything right away, Ellie snapped,
"Do you want me to guess?"

"Of course not. You didn't give me a chance to explain it."
Her mother sighed. "Honestly, Ellie. Have I ever made light of
your blindness?"

"*Nee*. I'm sorry." The knot in her stomach had tightened since
Bertha and Sarah Lynne had left a few minutes ago. She remembered what Barbara had said about the babies sensing tension. Ellie
took a deep breath and tried to smile.

"Feel this." *Mamm* took Ellie's hand and ran it over something pliable and pillowy. "Isn't it wonderfully soft?"

"*Ya*." She ran her hands over the object, trying to detect
what it was. Some kind of cushion, she guessed. She'd never felt
anything like it before.

"It's quilted with pink-and-white cotton fabric," her mother
added. "*Perfekt* for the *maed*."

"What is it?"

"A specially shaped pillow that will help with feeding the
twins. You can lay them on each side of the pillow and have them

face you. See how the edges are raised and firm? That keeps them from falling off."

Ellie continued to check out the pillow. Her smile grew as the strain between her and *Mamm* eased a bit. "This is nice."

"It will make feeding them at the same time much easier." *Mamm* took the pillow. "I'll *geh* put this in *mei* room."

So much for relaxing around her mother. "*Mamm*, I think it's time the *bopplis* moved to my and Chris's room."

She heard her mother's footsteps stop. "It's too soon."

"*Nee*, it's not—"

"I'll be back in a minute," she said, walking away again. "Then I'll get started on supper. I hope Christopher will be home on time today for once."

"He's had to work—"

Her mother disappeared out of the room.

"—late." Ellie scratched the top of her head through the kerchief she'd taken to wearing since having the twins. When she was ready to leave the house, she would wear her *kapp*, but right now the kerchief would do. She reached in front of her and touched a paper bag with handles on it. Pulling it closer to her, she searched inside.

A thick stack of diapers, which could also be used as burp cloths. Four small baby bottles, plastic and still attached to the cardboard. A couple of cans of formula. Despite being irritated with her mother, Ellie was glad she had brought the supplies. And of course the pillow. That would be a lifesaver. She'd have to dictate a thank-you note to Chris and send it to Linda to express how much she appreciated the wonderful gift.

She found another big bag and started riffling through it. She frowned. The clothing inside wasn't baby clothes, but her mother's. At least a week's worth. How long was she planning on staying?

Ellie heard one of the babies crying. She turned and made her way down the hall, passing her bedroom to reach the spare room. By the time she arrived, both babies were fussing, but she could hear her mother making calm, cooing noises above the din.

"You're both a little wet, that's all," her mother said. One of the cries grew into a screech. "Now, Irene, is that the way a *yung maedel* should behave?"

Ellie approached her. "I'll change Julia," she said.

"Already done."

"That fast? They just started crying."

"Julia was making a bit of noise right before that." Ellie heard the snap of a safety pin. "There you *geh*, all clean and dry."

"Where's Julia?"

"In the cradle. I thought I'd rock them for a little while."

"But you said you were going to start on supper."

The creak from the rocker sounded when her mother sat down. "Why don't you make it tonight?"

Ellie put her hands on her hips. "I have a better idea. How about I rock my *dochders* while you cook?"

"But they're already settled. You don't want to disturb them, do you?"

The rocking chair moved back and forth along with the different sound of the cradle being manipulated by her mother's foot. Ellie listened for the babies, but her mother was right. They did seem settled. She rubbed her forehead. There was no point in starting an argument. "All right. But I'll feed them next time." Ellie turned to go.

"We'll see," her mother murmured.

"What did you say?"

"*Nix*, Ellie. All the ingredients you need to make meat loaf and potatoes are in the bags on the table."

Ellie left the room, her nerves wound tight again. She couldn't go on like this. After supper she was determined to set some ground rules with *Mamm*.

A few hours later Ellie checked her Braille watch. Six thirty. Chris was late from work again. She finished washing the dishes, except for the plate of meat loaf and mashed potatoes that she would heat up for Chris when he got home. She covered that in foil and set it by the oven, which she had on the lowest warm setting.

She went to the spare bedroom to check on the babies. When she walked inside, her mother said, "Shh. They're almost asleep."

"You fed them again?"

"You were busy."

Ellie fisted her hands. "You could have told me they were awake and needed feeding." How was she going to be able to take care of her daughters if her mother wouldn't give her the chance? *Lord, give me the words to say to her.*

She moved toward the cradle. "*Mamm*, I want to spend some time with the twins right now. Just the *three* of us."

"Julia's already in the cradle and Irene's eyes are closing." Her mother's voice sounded tight, defensive. And her words, too overprotective.

"How can that be?" she asked, feeling like her mother was duping her. Were they really asleep, or was *Mamm* just saying that to keep Ellie away from them?

"They're newborns, Ellie. That's what wee ones do. I thought you knew that."

"I knew they slept a lot, just not this much," she admitted.

"In a couple of weeks they'll be up more often. You should enjoy the time you have to rest."

"I don't want to rest!" The words came out in a harsh rush. "I want to be with *mei bopplis*."

A pause. "Don't you raise your voice with me, Ellie Chupp."

"It's Miller, *Mamm*. I've been married for two years." She made her way to the rocker, bumping her shin against the end of the bed. "Ow." One of the babies started to murmur. "Why can't you remember that?"

"Old habits die hard." The baby's murmuring grew into a soft wail. "Look, now you've woken Julia." Ellie heard her mother getting up from the rocker. They met at the cradle, Ellie's hand bumping her mother's as they both reached for the baby.

"*Mamm*, this is ridiculous. You're already holding Irene. Why won't you trust me to get Julia?"

"I do trust you." Her mother paused. "I just don't . . . ," she whispered.

Exasperated, Ellie raised her voice over Julia's louder cries. "Don't what? Don't want me to hurt them? Or drop them?"

"That's not what I said—"

"Ellie? Edna?"

Chris's voice sounded from the back of the house. Ellie heard the heavy tread of his feet as he made his way down the hall.

"Is everything all right?" Chris said as he entered the room.

"*Nee*—" Ellie said.

"*Ya*—" *Mamm* said at the same time.

"Doesn't seem like it." He neared the cradle. "What's wrong with Julia?"

"How did you know it was Julia?" *Mamm* asked.

"Easy. I'd recognize her little squalling anywhere." He inserted himself between the two women. Ellie heard him pick up their daughter. She instantly quieted.

"She's a daddy's girl." He chuckled. "Has she been fed?"

"*Ya*. Diaper changed too." *Mamm* moved away from the cradle and sat down in the rocking chair. "She was asleep until . . ."

Even though she couldn't see her mother's face, Ellie knew she was giving her the usual disapproving look. Her throat burned with the threat of tears. Both her mother and husband were better with the babies than she was. She turned and rushed out of the room, ending up in the kitchen. She grabbed on to the edge of the sink, forcing the tears at bay.

A few moments later Chris came up behind her, just as the tears she tried so hard to stop slipped down her face. Why couldn't she control her emotions anymore? She wiped at her face, retrieved his supper plate from the counter, and put it in the already warmed-up oven. "Your dinner will be ready in a few minutes," she said, trying to keep tears of frustration from falling. She may be a terrible mother, but at least she could fix her husband a decent meal.

"Ellie." Chris put his hands on her shoulders. "Talk to me. What's going on?"

"*Nix*. I know you must be starving, and I want to get your dinner to you."

"Supper can wait." He turned her to face him. "The tension between you and your *mamm* is thicker than a slice of her sourdough bread."

Ellie shrugged, turning away from him. "It's nothing I can't handle." She didn't need him to think she wasn't capable of dealing with her mother. It was enough of a hit to her confidence that her mother didn't think she was able to take care of the babies. "She's been a lot of . . . help."

"Maybe too much?"

Ellie stood like a statue in front of the sink. Although she didn't need to, she washed her hands, letting the water get near to scalding. "She's doing what she thinks is right."

"And what about you?" He reached over, turned off the water, picked up a kitchen towel, and started to dry her hands. "What do you think is right? Having the babies sleep in the same room with her instead of us?"

She didn't realize he'd even thought about that.

"You've been working so hard lately. You need your sleep. *Mamm* said the babies would wake you up in the middle of the night."

"So? I'll fall back to sleep. Or I'll feed them with you." He ran the back of his hand over her damp cheek. "You've been crying. And I haven't seen you smile in days. Honey, I'm worried about you."

His kind words should have brought her comfort. Instead, they burst the brittle dam of emotion inside her. "You're worried I can't take care of the twins. That's what this is all about."

"*Nee.*" He sounded surprised. "That's not it at all."

"Then what?" She backed away from him, wishing she could see his expression. Since they'd been together, she'd touched every inch of his handsome face, and of course she remembered what he looked like as a teenager. But there were times when memories and touch weren't enough. Times when it wasn't fair. Although she tried to stop them, the tears flowed down her cheeks again.

"Ellie, please don't cry." He tried to take her in his arms. "I didn't mean to upset you."

She pulled away from him and threw open the oven door. She reached in to yank out his supper, only to burn her hand because she'd forgotten to use a pot holder. "Ow," she yelped in pain, jumping back. *Stupid, stupid.* She couldn't do anything right.

"Let me see your hand," he said. "Did you burn it?"

She opened her mouth to speak but couldn't find the words to voice her frustration. She rushed out of the room, bumping into walls in the darkness of her world. When she reached her room her chest heaved with sobs. Her hand burned from her mistake with the oven and her self-assurance was in shambles, like it had been when she'd first been blinded.

Her hand throbbing, she went to the bathroom and found a jar of salve in the medicine cabinet. She rubbed the soothing cream on her burn, but it did little to relieve her turmoil. What was happening to her? She couldn't wait to be a mother. When she found out she was pregnant, she'd been thrilled. When the babies were born, she'd been ecstatic and filled with love for the tiny miracles God had blessed her and Chris with. But in only three days everything had changed. Now she was miserable.

Is this what motherhood was? Pain and self-doubt and endless, helpless tears? How could she overcome any of it?

CHAPTER 5

Edna rocked back and forth in the chair, both babies snug and asleep in her arms, resting peacefully. But turmoil ruled her heart. She'd heard Ellie's raised voice, the pain smothering her words, the frantic, familiar footsteps as she fled down the hall. Ellie wasn't the only one in this house with heightened senses.

She should put the babies in their cradle and go talk to her. But what could she say? Her daughter had been so stubborn, unwilling to see that all Edna wanted to do was help care for the twins. She straightened in the rocker. Ellie should be thrilled to have a mother who would drop everything in her life and make so many sacrifices for her granddaughters. But instead Ellie was resentful. Surly. Not appreciative . . . the way she should be.

Yet as Edna held the babies closer, she couldn't ignore the guilt her thoughts triggered. Ellie was capable, the most capable woman she knew. Her daughter had not only overcome a tragic accident and the loss of her best friend and her sight, but she had also become an independent woman who had her own business, one she'd given up in the third trimester of her pregnancy. There wasn't any reason to think she wouldn't be a wonderful mother.

Except that she was blind.

Every time she thought about leaving the tiny babies with

Ellie, Edna panicked. So many things could go wrong with one baby, and that possibility doubled with two. She also couldn't be honest with Ellie. If she told her about her fears, about how she'd lain awake nights wondering if these precious babies would be safe with their own mother, Ellie would be deeply hurt. And her daughter had suffered enough.

A quiet voice sounded in her head. *Aren't you hurting her now? Can't you trust me to watch over those you love?*

Edna breathed in the sweet, baby-powder scent of the babies, resisting what God was speaking to her heart. Yes, she'd heard all her life to let go and let him be in control. But she couldn't do that . . . not yet.

"Edna?"

She glanced up at Christopher as he entered the room, blinking as she cleared her thoughts. He wasn't making things easier by working so late. If she wasn't here, Ellie would be alone with the babies even longer every day, and how would she manage?

Edna held a sigh. She'd been hard on Chris in the past as well. When he'd left the Amish after Ellie's accident, which had taken the life of his fiancée, she had thought him weak-minded and ill-suited for an Amish woman, especially her Ellie. But she hadn't understood the depth of his pain that drove him from Paradise. Her husband, Ephraim, always had to remind her not to judge others, and she had fought to curb that side of her spirit when she joined the church over fifty years ago. Yet despite her prayers and pleas, it reared itself at the worst times. Like now, when she believed he should be more available to his young family instead of working fourteen hours a day, six days a week.

"*Ya?*" she finally said, forcing an even tone. She pulled the babies even closer to her.

Chris raked his hand through his hair. The dirt from work still clung to his clothes. Outside the light had dimmed with dusk approaching. He looked weary. No, he looked plain tired. Still, she didn't move from the chair.

"We need to talk," he said.

"The babies are asleep," she whispered. "I don't want to disturb them."

"Put them in the cradle, Edna."

She lifted her chin. How dare he speak to her like that? Yet he was the head of this home, and she had to respect that.

"Once they're settled," he added, "meet me in the living room."

"I'll be there in a moment."

As Chris turned and left, she stood, balancing the twins, her arms aching from their slight weight. Truth was, she was tired too. Taking care of these two was the hardest job she'd ever done. Raising children was so much easier when she was younger. She carefully laid the babies in the cradle, taking a few seconds to touch Julia's soft hair and stroke Irene's plump cheek before leaving to join her son-in-law.

When she entered the living room, Christopher sat down on a chair. He gestured to the couch across from him. When she sat down, he said, "Ellie's upset."

"She's tired—"

"It's more than that." He scrubbed his hand over his face, stopping to tug at his thick, black beard. "There's a problem between you two, and I aim to find out what it is."

Edna touched her chest, offended by his tone. "I'm only trying to help her with the babies."

"I don't think Ellie sees it that way."

Edna crossed her arms. "Then how does she see it?"

"I'm not sure. She won't talk to me. I just know that when I came home today she was crying, and you seemed very . . . protective."

"I am protective of *mei dochder*. I won't apologize for that."

"I wasn't talking about Ellie. I'm talking about the twins. Edna, I'm sure Ellie appreciates your help. I know I do. But I'm concerned she's not getting a chance to spend enough time with the babies. You feed them at night. You're up with them in the morning. Tonight when I came home you were taking care of them again. When does Ellie . . . you know . . . what's the word? Get close with the babies?"

"You mean bond with them?"

He nodded. "It's like you don't trust her to take care of our *dochders*. Is that true?"

Edna looked away. "You have *nee* idea how difficult it is to manage twins."

"You're right. I don't. I'm gone a lot, and the timing couldn't be worse. I wish things were different, but I have to take the work when it comes. But that doesn't answer *mei* question." He blew out a breath. "Do you trust her to take care of our *kinner*?"

"Of course I do." But she couldn't face him when she spoke.

"If that's the case . . . Then prove it." He took a deep breath.

She looked at him. "What?"

"I think it's time you went back home."

The muscles in her jaw tightened. "You want me to leave Ellie alone?"

"Not completely. But you don't have to spend the night anymore. Give Ellie and me a chance to take care of the twins at night. And *mei schwester* and *mamm* can help out during the day too. They've been wanting to spend more time with Julia and Irene."

Hurt coursed through her. "I see how it is. You'd rather have your family here than me."

"That's not true." The weariness in his eyes seemed to increase. He sighed. "I'm letting you know that Ellie has plenty of help. You don't need to take on the whole job yourself." He leaned forward. "Ellie needs the chance to be a mother. I know you're worried about her and the babies. But you have to trust us, and trust her. With God's help, we will make this work."

His words made sense, but they didn't override the rejection she felt. "So you don't need me. Fine. I'll leave right now."

"Edna, I meant in the morning—"

"Oh *nee*. I don't want to upset you and Ellie further." She shot up off the couch. "And I don't want to be where I'm not wanted." She pulled back her shoulders. "Despite everything I've done, this is how you treat me."

He stood, shaking his head. "That's not what I meant."

"I know exactly what you meant. I'll pack my things and be out of your way in a few minutes. You won't have to worry about me being underfoot at night anymore." She turned to go.

"Edna."

She stopped and turned. Even though she recognized the regret on his face, her own pain wouldn't allow him any sympathy. "What?" she said sharply.

"I didn't mean to hurt your feelings. I think you misunderstood me."

She paused. Maybe she had. Perhaps he realized how important it was for her to remain with the babies as much as possible. "I have?"

Chris walked toward her. "Edna, I want you to know"—he paused to smile—"you're always welcome here during the day."

The day. So he was dictating the hours she could see her daughter and grandchildren. "How generous of you."

"I . . . never mind." He shook his head. "At least say good-bye to Ellie before you leave."

"I don't want to *bother* her." She squared her shoulders again and left her ungrateful son-in-law behind. She went to the spare bedroom, walking straight to the cradle. In the dim light of the gas lamp, she could see the twins' tiny bodies pressed against each other, their delicate fists clenched as they usually were when they were sleeping. Irene's lips moved a bit, as if she were drinking from a bottle. Edna's heart ached. She loved them so much. And now she was being dismissed, as if she were hired help.

She couldn't move, her mind spinning with hurt and worry. When she thought of Ellie taking care of these precious little ones without her help, she remembered the fragile young woman who had discovered she would never see again. The anger that had nearly consumed Ellie in the months afterward. And how difficult it had been for her to learn and master the simplest of tasks, even after she had accepted her blindness.

How easy it would be for Ellie to trip while holding Irene, or for her to poke Julia with a diaper pin. Edna was willing to take care of those things for her. To take care of her babies and keep them safe. Yet Ellie and Christopher didn't want her help. They didn't want her around.

Finally, she was able to pull herself away from the cradle. She quickly packed her belongings and went out the back door. Christopher had already harnessed her horse and was hitching it to the buggy. Obviously he couldn't see her leave fast enough.

He handed her the reins. "I wish it didn't have to be like this."

"You've made your wishes plain, Christopher." Edna climbed into the buggy, bypassing his offer of help. He said something else, but she ignored it as she tapped the reins on the back of the horse and guided him down the driveway.

Chapter 6

In her dreams Ellie heard her babies crying. But she couldn't reach them. They were too far away, and she couldn't find them. She held out her hands, seeking them but finding nothing. Their cries grew louder, feeding the rising panic in her chest.

Her eyes flew open, unseeing, yet she could still hear the twins. She'd struggled to bring herself out of the dream. Once she was completely awake, she realized her daughters' cries were real.

As their wails grew louder and more high-pitched, she reached out to feel for Chris. She touched his side, detecting the slow rise and fall of his chest. He was so deeply asleep, he didn't stir. The babies continued to cry. Confused, Ellie sat up. She'd never heard the twins this upset before.

She carefully got out of bed, not wanting to disturb her husband. She made her way to the spare bedroom. Julia's cry was especially piercing. She entered the room. *"Mamm?"* But there was no answer. She hurried to the bed, to find it was still made from this morning.

She moved to the cradle, alarm going through her. Why wasn't her mother here? She reached inside the cradle and felt one of the diapers. Soaked. She felt the other one, and it was also wet.

"Shh," she said to the girls amid their screeching. "It will be all right." She wanted to look for her mother, but the twins needed tending first. She went to the dresser where *Mamm* had told her she put the extra diapers and cloths, but they weren't there when she opened the drawer.

The babies' cries echoed around the room. Had her mother moved the diapers and not told her? She called out for her again, and once again heard no response.

"Ellie." Chris's sleepy voice sounded behind her. She heard him snap on the battery-powered lamp. "What's wrong with the girls?"

"They need changing." She turned toward him. "Where's *Mamm*?"

"She . . . went home." He sounded alert now—and wary.

That didn't make any sense. "Why?"

"We can talk about it after we get the twins calmed down."

She held up her hands, frustrated. "I can't find the diapers. *Mamm* must have moved them." She heard Chris open a few of the drawers. Then he walked past her and opened the closet. "They're in here."

Ellie picked up one of the babies. She touched the *boppli*'s right ear, searching for the tiny dent at the top. When she felt it, she knew she was holding Julia.

"Do you think they're hungry?" Chris asked.

"I'm sure they are."

"I laid the diapers and pins on the bed," he said. "You take care of changing them and I'll fix their bottles."

He sounded so tired. "I can do it," Ellie said. "You *geh* back to bed."

"*Nee*. I'm up now."

Ellie easily found the diapers. Chris never failed to give her the instructions she needed. Even when they were dating, he was always sure to verbalize everything so she didn't miss a single thing. She took the diapers to the cradle. She quickly changed Julia and Irene before Chris returned. She balanced both babies in her arms and sat down in the rocker just as Chris walked back into the room.

"Midnight snacks are ready," he said. She heard him move toward the rocker, and she knew he was about to take one of the babies.

"I can feed both of them," she said.

"How?"

"There should be a pink-and-white pillow-looking thing in the room somewhere. Maybe in the closet. When you find it, bring it to me."

A few minutes later she had both babies nestled in the pillow.

"Let me know when you're ready for the bottles," Chris said.

But Ellie didn't want the bottles. The urge to nurse was so strong, and it was the first time she'd had the opportunity to try to feed both of them at the same time. She adjusted her nightgown, and with very little effort both babies were feeding. Soon the cacophony of the babies' cries receded, replaced by soft suckling noises. Ellie leaned back in the chair, pleased that she was finally able to feed her babies on her own.

She heard Chris collapse on the bed. "That pillow is a lifesaver," he said, sounding even more exhausted than before. "Where did you get it?"

"*Mamm*'s friend Linda made it."

"Guess we didn't need the bottles after all."

She nodded. "Chris, why did *Mamm geh* home? Is she all right? And why didn't she say anything to me?"

He sighed. "You were so upset last night, I thought I should have a talk with her. I know things have been tense between you."

She couldn't deny that. "What did you say to her?"

"That she should leave. I told her we could take care of the babies at night."

"Oh *nee*." She cringed. "I guess she didn't take that very well."

"Not at all. I thought she'd *geh* home in the morning, but she was so mad she left right away, and I didn't tell you because you were already asleep when I came to bed." He paused. "I wish she would have waited until morning, but I still believe I did the right thing. We need to learn how to take care of them ourselves, Ellie. And she wasn't letting us—especially you."

Ellie closed her eyes, blinking back more tears. This time they came from a different place. Her husband did understand. She opened her eyes, unseeing but sensing he was looking at her, waiting for her to respond. "*Danki*," she said softly.

He let out a weary chuckle. "At least one woman isn't mad at me tonight."

"*Mamm* will be okay. She just needs some time. She's never taken to being told what to do."

"Sounds like someone else I know."

"Ha." Ellie shifted a little in the rocker but didn't disturb the babies. For the first time since they were born, it felt like she could handle being their mother. But that feeling was tempered by reality. "I can't do this alone," she said. "If you hadn't been here I wouldn't have even found the diapers without having to search too long."

"Sarah Lynne said she would come over during the day.

Mamm too. And I told your *mudder* she was welcome here, just not at night. Although I probably could have handled that better."

"You handled it fine." Although Ellie could only imagine how upset her mother was right now. Still, she wanted to encourage her husband. "Don't worry about *Mamm*, Chris."

"I won't. I'm sure your father is glad to have her back home."

"I don't know. He might have welcomed the break."

Chris chuckled. She heard him get up from the bed. He kneeled next to her and kissed her forehead. "I love you, Ellie. Everything is going to be okay. God is watching over us."

She nodded. "I love you too." He was right. Everything would be okay. She'd have help during the day, and Chris would be here at night. She'd make sure tomorrow she knew where everything was so she didn't have to wake him unless she needed his help. She didn't like the idea of him getting up and losing sleep, but he didn't seem to mind. She smiled, enjoying the moment with her sweet babies and wonderful husband. And as long as she had him by her side, everything would be all right.

"Things seem to be going well," Sarah Lynne said a week later. She was in Ellie and Chris's room, and Ellie had given her the task of folding small onesies freshly dried on the line. "How do you like the babies sleeping in the same room with you?"

"I was nervous about it at first," Ellie said. She held Irene while Sarah Lynne's mother was with Julia in the kitchen. "But after a couple of nights I figured out how to feed the babies without waking up Chris. Which is *gut*, because he's still working extra hours."

"Wonderful." Ellie could almost hear Sarah Lynne smiling. "I can hardly believe the change in you since the last time I was here. You seem so much more at ease with everything since . . ."

"*Mamm* left." Ellie rubbed Irene's back.

"I probably shouldn't have said anything."

"It's all right." Besides being related by marriage, the women were also friends.

"Has she been by to see the *bopplis*?"

Ellie paused. *"Nee."*

"Not even once?" Sarah Lynne sounded surprised.

"Nee."

"Ellie, I didn't realize you had been here alone during the day with the *bopplis*. I assumed *yer mamm* was coming by every day."

"Fortunately I've had lots of visitors, so I've had plenty of help during the day." Ellie held Irene against her shoulder as she rocked back and forth in the chair. "Of course, Chris is here with me at night. So we have everything under control."

"But what are you going to do about *yer mamm*?" Sarah Lynne asked.

"I'm not sure. I want to talk to her, but I haven't had time to go see her. I do miss her and wish she was here with me." She lifted her head toward Sarah Lynne. "I'm sure that sounds strange, considering we asked her to leave." Ellie lifted her chin, trying to keep her voice steady. "But if she can't be bothered to visit her grandchildren, that's not *mei* problem."

"Oh. I see."

Ellie didn't miss the note of disapproval in Sarah Lynne's voice. But Ellie didn't care . . . at least not that much. Sarah Lynne didn't understand. Neither did Chris, who had offered to take her and the *bopplis* to her parents more than once. Ellie had refused. She hadn't done anything wrong—she only wanted to have time with her own children. Her mother was being ridiculous. And stubborn.

Like mother, like daughter.

Her father's oft said words echoed in her mind, but did nothing to change it.

"Ellie, are you sure you're doing the right thing?" The floorboards creaked softly as Sarah Lynne stood up and padded across the room. "I know how important independence is to you. But so is family."

"I don't want to talk about it." Ellie knew she sounded childish, but there was nothing more to discuss. Obviously her mother cared more about nursing a grudge than seeing the twins.

"All right." A drawer shut, and Ellie assumed Sarah Lynne had put away the clothes. Sarah Lynne sat back down on the bed. "I'll change the subject. Have you and Chris figured out what you're going to do when the babies get older? Before you know it they'll be scooting around."

"*Ya*," she said, eager to discuss what she had recently learned about taking care of Irene and Julia. "I contacted my rehabilitation teacher, the one who helped me after my accident. She gave me a lot of ideas for what we can do through each stage of life. For example, when they're old enough to crawl I'll tie bells to their shoes—a different one for each *maed*." She put her lips against Irene's cheek.

"Has Barbara been by to check them?"

Ellie nodded. "She came earlier in the week. She said Irene and Julia are doing well. Everything is wonderful right now."

"Except you and *yer mamm*."

"Sarah Lynne—"

"You've got to talk to her, Ellie."

"I will. When she decides to talk to me. And even then, I'm going to have to lay down some ground rules when it comes to the twins. She can't take over like she did before. I know she doesn't think I'm capable of being a *gut mamm* . . ." She turned away, pain pricking at the admission.

"*Yer* a *gut mamm*. Anyone can see that."

"*Danki*, Sarah Lynne." She sighed. "Sometimes it's so overwhelming. But then I get some time to spend with one of the girls, or I'm feeding both of them and they fall asleep in my arms . . . it's so special." She stilled, her face heating as she remembered Sarah Lynne was trying to conceive. "I'm sorry. I wasn't thinking."

"It's okay."

When Sarah Lynne didn't say anything else, Ellie grimaced. How could she be so thoughtless? But Ellie had no idea what she could say to make her feel better.

"Can I hold Irene?" Sarah Lynne suddenly asked.

"Of course." Ellie held Irene out to her. "Do you want to sit down?"

"I can stand." Sarah Lynne took the baby from Ellie. She started to walk back and forth across the room. "I'll have to get used to holding a *boppli*," she said. Then she added, ". . . in about seven months."

Ellie gasped and jumped up from the chair. "Congratulations!" She smirked. "And here I was fretting about hurting your feelings."

Her sister-in-law laughed. "Gotcha."

"I'm so happy for you."

"Me too. And relieved." She lowered her voice. "You can't say anything to anyone, Ellie. Not even Chris. I haven't said anything to *Mamm* . . . or Isaiah."

Ellie nodded. "I won't say a word. But why haven't you told Isaiah?"

"I wasn't sure at first." She stopped in front of Ellie. "I'm seeing Barbara tomorrow. After I talk to her, then I'll tell him. Although he might suspect something since I've been sick for the past week. I didn't realize morning sickness lasted all day."

"You're feeling all right now?" Ellie asked.

"*Ya.* I make sure to keep crackers with me." She laughed again. "I hope you don't mind me asking you to keep the news secret. But I had to tell someone. I was about to burst!"

"I don't mind at all." Ellie hugged her, mindful of Irene. Although she wished she could tell Chris the good news. He would be as thrilled for his sister and brother-in-law as Ellie was. "I'm so happy for you both."

Five hours later happiness was the furthest thing from Ellie's mind. She was at her wit's end. Chris was late coming home from work again. It was well past suppertime, and the babies hadn't stopped crying for over an hour.

She was seated in the rocker, each baby secure on the nursing pillow. But Irene wouldn't nurse, and all Julia wanted to do was eat. She held Julia to her breast as she tried to calm Irene. "Shh," she said above her daughter's screeching. She cringed as Irene took a deep breath and began howling again.

"What do you want?" Ellie shouted, which caused Julia to

startle, then join Irene in her cacophony of cries. When Ellie tried to feed her again, she refused.

Ellie adjusted her dress and picked up both babies, letting the pillow fall to the floor as she laid them in the cradle. They continued to cry. She brought her fingertips to her throbbing temples. She had no idea what they wanted. They were fed, changed, and bathed. "Why are you still crying?" she shrieked.

"Ellie?" Chris walked into the room, his tired voice filled with concern.

"I can't do this." Ellie turned her face toward him. "I've tried everything . . . They won't stop crying . . ."

Chris didn't say anything. She heard him walk to the cradle. Irene, who had a higher pitched cry than Julia, quieted. "What did you do?" When he paused, she yelled, "Answer me!"

"I fixed her diaper pin."

Ellie put her hand on her cheek. "It was sticking her?"

"*Ya*. But she's fine now. And Julia seems to be settling down too."

He was right. Now that Irene was quiet, Julia had stopped crying. Ellie walked to the bed and sat down, numb. She didn't even think to check the diaper pins. She'd changed Irene over an hour ago. Her daughter had been in pain that long, and Ellie didn't even know.

But Chris did. In mere seconds he was able to fix the problem. *Because he can see.*

"Ellie—"

"I'll fix your supper." She rose from the bed and walked out of the room, unable to face him. Her chest heaved with guilt. She'd hurt their daughter. Her heart ached as if it had been stabbed with a thousand pins.

She busied herself with warming up Chris's meal, but her mind was focused elsewhere. What other things would she overlook with her daughters because of her disability? How many times would she inadvertently hurt them or put them in danger?

She heard Chris's feet dragging on the floor as he entered the kitchen. He sat down on a chair, hard, not saying anything. Ellie swallowed as she placed a dish of baked chicken and black-eyed peas in front of him.

"I'm not hungry." He shoved his plate away.

Of course he was angry with her. She stood behind his chair, wringing her hands together.

"The *maed* are asleep," he said wearily. "Ellie, please sit down. We need to talk."

CHAPTER 7

E llie sat down next to her husband, noting the tired edge in his voice. "I'm sorry," she whispered, hanging her head.

"Sorry? For what?"

"For hurting Irene."

"Ellie," he murmured, reaching for her hand. "Is that why you're upset? Irene is fine. The pin barely poked her. I think she was more uncomfortable than anything else." He squeezed her hand. "It's not a big deal."

"But what if it had stuck her? What if she'd been bleeding? What if—"

"Then you and I would have handled it. We're both learning how to be parents. Next time you'll double-check the pins, that's all."

"I'll triple-check them."

He let out a tired chuckle. "That's *mei maedel*."

His calmness reassured her. And he was right—they were both learning. Relieved not only by his logic but knowing that the babies were all right, she squeezed his hand back. "You sound exhausted."

"I am."

She searched for his plate on the table. When she touched

the edge, she carefully moved it toward him. "Maybe you'll feel better after you eat."

"I'm too tired to eat."

"I'm sorry work has been so hard for you lately."

"It's not the work that's hard. It's the hours. But I'm grateful for it. So many are out of work right now. We're blessed that I have this job. Even though it threw me a curveball today."

"Did something bad happen?" she asked.

"*Nee*. Actually, I have some good news. Sort of." She felt his fingers entwine with hers. "I got a raise," he said.

She grinned, not expecting such a blessing. "That's wonderful."

"I also got a new position." He covered her hand with his other one. "In eastern Pennsylvania. Four hours away."

Ellie clutched his hand at his words. "What?"

"But it's only temporary," he said, the tone of his voice not showing any traces of its earlier weariness. "For three weeks they want me to help with a subdivision project. I don't have all the details about the job, but they're going to pay for room and board while I'm there."

"Three weeks?" she squeaked out.

His voice sped up as he talked. "It sounds like a long time, but you know how fast it will *geh*. It seems like yesterday that the *bopplis* were born."

"Then you already took the job?"

"*Ya*. I did."

Ellie yanked her hand from his. Three weeks might as well be three years.

"I didn't have time to talk to you about it or I would have. I didn't have much of a choice either. If I'd said no, they might have let me *geh* from the company. There are so many people who need work, Ellie. *Amisch* and *Englisch*. I—we—can't afford to lose this job."

Her brain knew he was right, but her panic overruled any logic. "You can't leave."

"Ellie, honey—"

"You can't *geh*." Her throat ached, as though a rock were lodged in it. "I can't do this without you."

"*Ya*, you can."

She shook her head as tears spilled down her cheeks. "I can't do this alone."

"You won't be. *Mei mamm* and *schwester* can help you with the twins during the day."

Ellie thought about Sarah Lynne. She couldn't count on her, now that she was expecting and was having a hard time with morning sickness. But she couldn't tell Chris about that.

"And I thought"—Chris cleared his throat—"well, if she would agree to it . . ."

She sucked in a breath. "You want *Mamm* to come back at night."

"More than that. I'm hoping she'll come and stay while I'm gone."

Ellie cringed and sat back in the chair. She knew Chris was right. She couldn't be here at home alone, and to ask anyone else to stay with her and the twins would be an extraordinary request. But her mother . . .

"We have to ask her tonight. I'm leaving tomorrow."

She clutched his hand, fresh panic washing over her. "So soon?"

"*Ya*." He took her face in his hands, rubbing his thumbs across her cheeks. "Ellie, I know this is hard on you. But it's hard on me too. I don't want to be gone from you or the girls."

"I know." She ran her fingers through his thick hair, setting aside her own fear for a moment. He was sacrificing a lot for the benefit of his family. She had to be strong for him and for their daughters. He didn't need to worry about them while he was gone. "We'll talk to *Mamm*," she said. Somehow she'd deal with the hurt and resentment.

He kissed her, then touched his forehead to hers. "Let's get the twins, then."

As she and Chris readied the girls for their first ride in the buggy, Ellie tried to steady her nerves. Maybe time had soothed her mother's hurt feelings. She doubted it, since time had had no effect on Ellie's emotions. But she had to set that aside and convince her mother that she not only wanted her to come and stay but that she needed her. She prayed that somehow her mother would understand.

Edna finished drying the last of the supper dishes and returned them to the cabinet. Ephraim was already in the living room, reading the paper, as was his habit in the evening. She looked out the kitchen window at the orange-and pink-streaked sky. This window always allowed her a perfect view of gorgeous sunsets. It was her idea to put the window here when Ephraim built the house. But since Ellie's accident she didn't glean much pleasure from seeing the color-soaked skies at the end of the day. How could she, when her daughter would never see another sunset?

She clenched the damp kitchen towel. Ellie and the babies were never far from her thoughts. Neither was the hurt from the fact that they had sent her away. She'd thought they would have at least visited, but she hadn't seen Ellie since the night Christopher asked her leave. Ellie wasn't able to attend church yet, not until the babies were a little older. Last Sunday she'd had to field questions about the babies and Ellie, which only drove the pain further home. Of course she never let on that she hadn't seen them.

Never mind that Ephraim had offered to go with her to see the babies. He'd only seen them once since they were born, and he'd mentioned several times wanting to visit. But Edna refused. She hadn't shared the reason she'd come home that night, just telling her husband that Ellie and Christopher were able to take care of the babies by themselves. She couldn't even admit to her husband how deeply her daughter had hurt her.

She was about to join Ephraim in the living room when she noticed a buggy pulling into the driveway. As it neared she realized who it was. She brought her hand to her chest. Ellie and Christopher.

She attempted to steady her heartbeat by breathing slowly and promised herself she would watch her tongue. Even though she had stayed away, she had longed to see the babies, and now that they were here, she didn't want to say anything that would make Ellie leave. She wanted to be sure the twins were healthy. She had prayed for them constantly while she was away from them.

A sudden panic came over her. What if something was amiss and that's why Ellie and Christopher were here? She flew out of the kitchen and through the back door, meeting them just as Christopher brought the buggy to a halt.

"What's wrong?" she blurted. "What happened to the *bopplis*?"

Ellie's brow furrowed over her beautiful, unseeing eyes. "*Nix, Mamm.* They're fine."

"Oh, thank God." She saw them nestled in Ellie's arms. Immediately she took Julia from her. "I've missed you," she cooed to the baby. She glanced at Irene. They seemed to have grown while she was gone.

Christopher came over to the other side of the buggy and took Irene from Ellie, then helped her out of the buggy. But Edna hardly noticed their movements as she checked over Julia to make sure she was okay. When she glanced up, she saw Christopher giving her a hard look, but she didn't care. She had to make sure herself that they were all right.

"*Mamm,*" Ellie said, unfolding her white cane, "we need to talk."

Edna held Julia tightly. Something was wrong. She just knew it.

"I thought you said the babies were fine."

Ellie heard the worry in her mother's voice, and the tension inside her tightened. Would her mother ever trust her with the babies? She hadn't even invited them into the house, instead jumping to the conclusion that something terrible had happened while she was gone. "*Mamm,* can we go inside?"

"Of course you can," her father said. She heard the screen door shut behind him, and seconds later felt his comforting hand on her shoulder. "I'm glad to see you, Ellie."

Her father's calmness soothed her. "I'm glad to see you too, *Daed.* I've missed you."

"Well, I told *yer mamm* we needed to visit earlier in the week but she—"

"Ephraim, we need to get the *bopplis* inside," *Mamm* said quickly. "We don't want them to catch cold."

"It's June, Edna. They're not going to catch cold."

The door slammed closed.

Daed let out a sigh. "Ellie, I don't know what's wrong with *yer mudder*. She's been acting *seltsam* since she came home last week."

"We know why," Chris said.

"*Gut*, because I need an explanation," *Daed* said. He paused. "Why do you have your cane out, Ellie? Nothing has changed here."

"I wasn't sure. *Mamm* moved a few things around at our house." She felt like she was tattling on her mother, but it was crucial that she was able to navigate any environment.

"Hmm. That's not like her either."

"Ephraim," Chris said. "We really need to talk to Edna—to both of you. Could we *geh* inside?"

"*Ya*. Sorry." Ellie felt her father take her hand and put it above the outside of his elbow, guiding her into the house the way her rehabilitation teacher had taught him. She smiled, and they all went inside and into the living room.

Ellie folded her cane and went to the chair near the door. She heard her mother speaking in hushed tones to Julia.

"Do you want to hold Irene too?" Chris asked *Mamm*.

"*Ya*." Ellie listened as Chris gave the baby to her mother, then joined her father on the couch. Her mother kept whispering to the babies over and over how much she missed them. How much she loved them. How she had prayed nothing had happened to them while she was gone. Her voice was nearly inaudible, and Chris and her father couldn't hear her.

But Ellie did. She gripped her cane.

"So what brings you here so late in the evening?" *Daed* asked.

Chris didn't say anything right away, and Ellie knew he was searching for the right words. She was tempted to speak, but waited until he was ready. Finally, he explained the job situation to her mother and father.

"You're abandoning your wife and babies?" *Mamm* said.

"That's not what he said, Edna. He has to work."

"He'll only be gone three weeks," Ellie added, trying to force a smile. She could barely do it in the face of her mother accusing Chris of neglecting his family.

"That's nearly a month." Ellie heard her mother shift in the rocking chair. "These babies are soaking wet, Ellie. Didn't you change them before you came here?"

"*Ya*—"

"It's a *gut* thing I have some diapers here at the *haus*." The back of the chair hit the wall as she rose. "I'll take care of them."

Ellie started to get up. "I can do it."

But her mother didn't reply as she walked out of the room. Ellie shrank back in her chair. The next three weeks were going to be torture.

"Ellie," Chris said gently, "*geh* with *yer mamm*."

"What's the use? She's got everything handled," Ellie said, unable to keep the bitterness from her voice.

"Ellie." This time her father spoke. "*Geh*."

Cringing, Ellie stood and walked to the hallway. "*Mamm?*" she called, not sure where her mother had taken the twins. She had to follow her mother's voice as she walked down the hall to find her in her and her father's bedroom.

"Now it's Rachel's turn. Oh, how I've missed you," her mother said.

Ellie stood in the doorway. "*Mamm?* Are you all right? You just called one of the girls Rachel."

"I did no such thing. You are the two sweetest little girls," her mother continued.

"*Mamm*, I know what I heard."

A pause. "Ellie, *geh* back into the living room with your *daed* and Christopher. I'll take care of the twins."

Ellie flattened her lips. She was being treated like a child and her mother was acting oddly. "I'm not moving. Not until we get a few things straight between us."

"Like what?"

"You left without saying good-bye."

"Your husband threw me out."

She touched her temple. "He didn't throw you out. He said you didn't have to stay with us anymore. There's a big difference."

"Humph."

Ellie took a few steps into the room, feeling for the small chair she knew was next to her parents' dresser. She sat down. "*Mamm*, please. I'm sorry we hurt your feelings. We didn't mean to. But we needed time with the babies. I wish you could understand that."

"I do. And I've done what you wished. I stayed away."

"You didn't have to. Not for a whole week."

Irene, who was turning out to be the more vocal of the two girls, started to fuss. "You and Christopher seem to be just fine without me," *Mamm* said above the baby's noise.

Ellie stood up and then sat on the bed, searching for Irene and Julia. They were lying in the middle of the bed, side by side. She felt their ears, found Irene, and picked her up. The crying stopped. "I thought you'd be happy to know that we can take care of our *kinner, Mamm.*"

"I . . . am."

"You don't sound like it." When her mother didn't respond, Ellie could see the conversation was going nowhere. There was nothing to do except ask her the question she was dreading all evening. "*Mamm,* Chris and I didn't come over here just to tell you about the job. We . . ."—she took a deep breath—"I need your help."

"Of course you do. Somebody has to be there for *mei gross-dochders.* It's not the babies' fault their father is leaving them."

"*Mamm,* stop it. You're not being fair to Chris."

But her mother continued to talk as if Ellie hadn't said anything. "I just need to pack a few things and I'll come with you."

"Right now?"

"There's *nee* sense in me driving the buggy over in the morning. I'm assuming Christopher is taking a taxi?"

"His boss is driving several of the Amish there himself."

"Then I can use your buggy when I need to." Ellie heard the snaps of her mother's suitcase open. The old hard-shell case had belonged to her grandmother.

"*Geh* get *yer daed.* I won't be able to carry my suitcase and the babies at the same time."

Ellie stood, ready to do what her mother ordered. Then she stopped, shocked at how easily she was about to let her mother take over. She couldn't live like this for three weeks. She would have to take a stand for herself now. She tucked Irene in the corner of one arm and picked up Julia with the other.

"What are you doing?" her mother asked.

"I'm taking Julia and Irene to the living room. We'll wait for you there. Please bring my cane when you leave."

"But, Ellie, what if—"

"I fall? I drop one of the babies? *Mamm*, I know this house as well as I know *mei* own. I won't fall. *Nix* will happen to *mei kinner*. I am their *mudder* and I will make sure of it." She thought about the diaper pin poking Irene earlier. Chris had been right. It was a mistake. And she would make them as she and Chris raised the girls. But she had to be given the chance to learn to be a parent.

"I wish you trusted me, *Mamm*," Ellie continued, trying to keep the pain out of her voice. "I'm blind, not helpless. Or useless."

"You've never talked to me like this before," *Mamm* muttered.

"I never had to." Ellie turned and left, her heart thumping in her chest. She probably ruined any chance of her mother staying with them while Chris was gone. Yet she didn't regret speaking her mind.

"Where's *yer mamm*?" her father asked as she entered the living room.

"Packing." At least Ellie hoped she still was. "Chris, would you mind taking Julia?"

He came to her and took the baby. As he did, he leaned closer to her. "What did you say to her?" he said in a low voice.

"Something I should have said a long time ago."

"So is she coming?"

Ellie swallowed. "I don't know."

"Let me *geh* talk to her," her father said. "Chris told me why you came. I'll tell her to get a move on."

They waited for several minutes, but neither her mother

nor father appeared. The babies started fussing, ready for their nightly feeding. She and Chris needed to get them home. "I'll check to see what's going on," she said.

"*Danki*, Ellie."

She frowned. Her husband was so tired, the babies were hungry, and her mother clearly was rethinking staying with them. What a mess.

As she made her way down the hall, she heard the murmur of her parents' voices. Her father's serious tone made her stop just outside their bedroom. Although she knew she shouldn't eavesdrop, she couldn't force herself to leave.

CHAPTER 8

Edna sat at the edge of the bed, stinging from Ellie's words. Is that what Ellie thought? That her mother considered her helpless? *Useless?* How could she believe that? All Edna wanted to do was help. To love her grandchildren and keep them safe. Yet her daughter had to twist it into something that wasn't true. She had to make it about *her.*

Edna crossed her arms, steaming with anger. If Ellie was so sure of herself, then why did she need her mother, whom she clearly didn't respect anymore?

"Edna? They're waiting on you."

She glanced up at Ephraim, who was now standing near the bed, but she didn't move. She stared straight ahead. It would take more than her husband's words to make her get up. It would take an apology from Ellie.

He frowned. "I know that face." He sat down next to her. "Don't be stubborn, Edna."

"Me? Stubborn?"

Her husband rolled his eyes. "I can see you're thinking about not helping them. And shame on you for those thoughts."

She cut her eyes at him. "You can't read *mei* mind."

"I've been married to you for forty years. I know exactly

what you're thinking. I also know that you're hurt for some reason." He angled his body toward her. "Why don't you tell me what happened."

"You tell me," she said, getting up, "since you can read *mei* mind and all that."

He blew out a breath, a noise she recognized as his long-suffering sigh. Her lower lip trembled. It seemed like she was a burden to everyone.

"I can guess. But I'd rather hear it from you. Both you and Ellie have been out of sorts for a long time, ever since she was expecting."

"And of course that's *mei* fault."

"I never said that. Ellie is as stubborn as you." He came up behind her. "And as sensitive."

She whirled around and glared at him. "What do you mean by that?"

"You both feel very deeply, which is a *gut* thing." He smiled, the wrinkles around his eyes crinkling. "It's one reason I love both of you. But it can also cause you to have hurt feelings over little things."

"This is *not* a little thing. Do you know what she said to me? She thinks I don't trust her."

"You don't."

Her brow shot up. "How can you say that?"

"Because it's true. You don't trust anyone easily. Remember how long it took you to believe I loved you?"

Her lip trembled. "*Ya*," she whispered.

He grabbed her hand. "*Nee* one knows more than I do the pain you've been through. Not just when Ellie lost her sight, but when you were young. But you have to put all that hurt behind you. Ellie and Christopher need you right now. Not just to help, but to support and respect their decisions. The *bopplis* need you, too, but the *kinner* are theirs, Edna, not yours." He gazed into her eyes. "Can you let *geh* and help them the way they need to be helped?"

She forced down the lump in her throat. She didn't want to admit it, but he was right, as he almost always was. But she didn't answer him right away.

"Edna . . ."

She nodded. "All right. I'll try." Then she paused at a shuffling sound near the bedroom door. "Did you hear something?"

"Like what?"

Edna stilled, much like Ellie did whenever she was listening carefully. She thought she heard someone outside their door. She walked to the doorway and peeked into the hall. But no one was there. "Must have been *mei* imagination," she said more to herself than to her husband.

"I'm glad you're willing to try. Now hurry and get packed. And *nee*, it's not because I want to see you leave."

"I never said—"

"You were thinking it." He winked at her and left.

Edna looked at the suitcase on the bed. She walked to the side table, picked up her Bible, and placed it on top of one of her light-blue dresses. If she was going to trust, to let go, she'd need God's help. She'd never been able to do it on her own.

She finished packing, closed the suitcase, and clicked the clasps shut. Straightening, she went to the living room. In the middle stood Ellie holding Irene, Christopher holding Julia, with Ephraim between them. Her daughter and son-in-law looked as tense as she felt. Then she met her husband's gaze. He gave her an encouraging smile.

"I'm ready," she said, managing a smile of her own. "Ephraim, carry *mei* suitcase while I take the *bop*—"

He cleared his throat.

"Um, never mind. I can carry the suitcase." She turned toward the door.

"Edna, wait." Christopher came up beside her. "If you'll hold Julia, I'll take the suitcase." He put the baby in her arms, picked up the case, and walked out of the house.

She glanced at Ellie. At least her daughter had stopped scowling. That was progress.

That night, after the twins were asleep in the cradle and Ellie's mother was settled in the spare bedroom, Chris and Ellie were finally able to climb into bed. But Ellie was preoccupied with what she'd heard during her parents' conversation. What was her father talking about, her mother being hurt when she was young? Ellie had never heard either of them speak about that before.

Chris leaned over and kissed her cheek. "Everything okay?"

"Sure," Ellie said, forcing a cheery note in her voice. "Why wouldn't it be? *Mamm*'s here now, so you don't have to worry about us while you're gone."

"I'll always worry about *mei maed*," he said, resting his chin on her shoulder.

"God will watch over us."

"I know. That doesn't mean I won't think about you all every single minute I'm gone." He traced her chin with his finger. "Are you sure everything is all right? When you came back from checking on your *mamm* at her *haus* you seemed . . . not upset exactly . . ."

She tilted her face toward his. "You are tired and imagining things." She couldn't burden him with this. Not now, not when he was leaving the next morning.

"Must be." He turned on his side, and she heard the click of the battery-operated lamp being turned off. Then he gently rolled her over and pressed her back against his chest. "Our last night for a while," he whispered in her ear. "I want to spend it with you in *mei* arms."

Despite her concern about her mother, Ellie smiled. She covered his hand with hers. Soon the sound of his heavy breathing in her ear let her know he was asleep.

Although she felt loved and secure in her husband's embrace, sleep eluded her. She was unable to get her mother out of her mind. She'd always thought *Mamm* was overprotective, even before Ellie was blind. She was less so with her older brother, Wally, but even when Ellie had her sight, *Mamm* had always peppered her with questions when she wanted to go to a friend's house, or when she started dating John, the young man who had left her after the car crash. But Ellie had thought that was simply her mother being guarded of her daughter, and now as a mother herself, she could understand that better.

Then the car accident and Ellie's losing her sight had thrown her mother over the edge, and it had taken a long time for her to let Ellie live her own life. Ellie thought about other major events in her life—her courtship with Chris, their marriage, and the birth of the twins. Each time her mother had reacted strongly. Ellie had assumed it was her personality.

But what if it was something else? Something so painful that no one, including her relatives, ever spoke of it? Whatever it was, she would have to tread carefully to find out.

CHAPTER 9

"Is something going on with your *mamm*?" Chris asked.

Ellie paused as she folded a pair of his broadfall pants. Had he suspected something? She quickly packed them in his duffel bag. "What do you mean?"

"She didn't argue about the babies being in our room, she didn't insist on feeding them this morning, and she's actually been . . . pleasant."

"Chris, *mei* mother can be nice, you know."

"I'm joking. Sort of." He took the duffel from her and zipped it up. "Whatever your father said to her last night sure made a difference."

Ellie pressed her lips together. She had also noticed the change in her mother. She was making an effort to be helpful instead of controlling. But she couldn't connect how her father's words had made an impact on her mother. She was surprised they hadn't opened some old wound, making her mother more difficult than ever.

"Whatever caused the change," Chris continued, "I'm thankful. It makes leaving you and the babies much easier knowing that you and Edna are getting along."

Ellie nodded, but she didn't see anything easy about Chris

going away. She also wouldn't go so far as to say she and her mother were getting along. Cordial was a better description. She sighed. It would be a long three weeks.

The impact of Chris being gone for so long hit her full force. "I'm going to miss you so much," she whispered, nearly strangling on the words.

He dropped the duffel bag on the floor and took her in his arms. "Me too."

"I wish you didn't have to *geh*."

He held her more tightly. "Me either. But the time will *geh* by fast. I gave your *mamm* a number to call if there's an emergency. I left it there on the dresser for you too." When she opened her mouth to speak, he put his finger over her lips. "Not that I think there will be an emergency. But I want to be prepared."

She nodded, and he removed his finger. "I understand." She took his hand. "Will it be okay to call you every night, after the *bopplis* and *Mamm* have gone to bed? I can't bear the idea of not talking for almost a month. I know *Mamm* wouldn't approve, but writing letters would take too long."

"*Ya*. It will be our secret."

The windows were open, letting in the warm summer air. A honk sounded in the distance. "That's my ride," Chris said softly. Then he kissed her, deeply, longingly, until the horn honked again. "I have to *geh*."

"Be safe. I'll pray for you every day."

"Same here—for you and the babies. And *yer mamm*, of course."

Ellie chuckled thickly. "Of course."

Chris left, and she didn't follow. Instead, she sat on the edge of their bed and bowed her head, praying for his safety while he was gone. Although he would be only four hours away, that didn't offer much comfort. After she finished, she went to the living room. *"Mamm?"*

"I'm here. Irene is on a blanket on the floor. I'm holding Julia."

She appreciated her mother telling her where the babies were in the room. She wasn't surprised that her mother was holding one of them. Even though *Mamm* seemed more at peace, she still held them any chance she had.

"It's a *schee* day outside," her mother said. "Would you like to work in the garden?"

Ellie thought for a moment. She hadn't had much time to spend there, and surely there were plenty of weeds that needed to be pulled. Then she realized this was her mother's way of offering an olive branch. She nodded, and then as an afterthought said, "Would you like to join me? We can take the babies with us, put them on a blanket in the shade under the oak tree."

Her mother didn't say anything right away. Then she replied, "That sounds nice."

A short time later the babies were napping under the canopy of the oak tree, a place where Ellie and Chris would sometimes have picnics on Sunday afternoons after church. The girls were lying on a quilt Sarah Lynne had made for them. She had described it as a center-diamond quilt, with a large pale-pink diamond in the middle, surrounded by peach-colored fabric. Ellie and her mother were a couple of yards away, tending the garden, which had indeed become fairly weedy since the birth of the babies.

"I guess I should have weeded for you while I was here last time," *Mamm* said.

"It's okay," Ellie said, checking the size of the tomato flowers on the plants. Some were pretty big, and in a month or so would be producing pea-size orbs that would eventually grow into large, beefsteak tomatoes. "Everything has been hectic since the *bopplis* were born."

They continued to work in the garden in silence except for the twittering of birds. Ellie cocked her head to listen for the babies, but all she heard was the sound of the birds—robins, finches, with an occasional blackbird squawk interrupting their delicate melodies.

But Ellie's mind wasn't on their sweet music. All she could think about was what her father had said last night. *Nee one knows more than I do the pain you've been through. Not just when Ellie lost her sight, but when you were young.*

She sat back on her heels. Her mother definitely seemed more even-keeled than she had been in a while, so this might be a good time to bring up the subject. "*Mamm*," she said tentatively, "can I talk to you about something?"

"*Ya*."

Though *Mamm*'s answer was short, it wasn't curt. She took a deep breath. "I, uh . . . I overheard you and *Daed* talking last night." She waited for her mother to say something. After a long pause, Ellie asked, "Did you hear me?"

"I heard you." Her mother's voice was tight and strained.

Ellie grimaced. She should have known it was a mistake to mention this. "I'm sorry—"

"You shouldn't eavesdrop." She heard the rustle of the grass as her mother got up. "I brought you up better than that."

"I know, but I couldn't help it."

"Someone forced you to listen to my private conversation?"

Ellie also got to her feet. She brushed the dirt off her hands. "I was checking to see if you had decided to go home with us. When I got to your room, I heard you and *Daed*."

"And of course you couldn't walk away." *Mamm*'s tone grew more tense, as if it were a tightly strung fishing line about to snap. "What did you hear?"

"I shouldn't have said anything—"

"What did you hear, Ellie?" Her *mamm*'s footsteps came toward her.

She hesitated, not wanting to continue. She and her *mamm* had been getting along all morning, and she had to mess that up by bringing up an obviously hurtful subject. But she had flipped open the can of worms, so she should see it through. "*Daed* said you were hurt when you were *yung*. I don't remember you saying anything about that when we were growing up. What happened?"

"What happened is none of your business."

Mamm's voice slashed at her, making Ellie take a step back.

"That was a private conversation," *Mamm* continued. "One that you had no right to listen to. Do not bring it up again."

"But, *Mamm*, maybe if you talked about it, you would feel better—"

"Julia's fussing," *Mamm* said.

"I don't hear anything."

Her mother didn't respond, and Ellie knew the conversation was over. But her curiosity was more piqued than before. She had several relatives in Paradise, but her mother said very little about her own childhood. Ellie had never thought much about it before, not until now. Whatever *Mamm* was hiding, it had to be more painful than Ellie could imagine.

"Ellie!" Her mother called from a few feet away.

The panic Ellie heard in her mother's voice caused her to quicken her steps and forget about her mother's secret. "What, *Mamm?*"

"There's something wrong with Julia."

"What? What is it?"

"She feels hot."

The alarm that had risen in Ellie when she first heard her mother say something was wrong with Julia subsided. "*Mamm*, she's probably warm from being outside. It's pretty hot today."

"She has a fever," *Mamm* said, her voice filled with absolute certainty.

"Are you holding her?"

"*Ya.*"

Ellie knelt by the edge of the blanket and felt for Irene. Her fingers found teeny toes, which were cool to the touch. She moved forward and scooped up her daughter. Irene didn't feel warm at all.

"We should get them in the house," Ellie said, knowing that would probably reassure her mother. When *Mamm* didn't answer, Ellie realized she had left without her.

Ellie scooped up Irene and went back to the house, finding the smooth, stone path Chris had laid when they first moved in the house. He had embedded the rocks in such a way that the edges were flush with the ground, preventing her from tripping. They led directly to the back porch steps.

"*Mamm!*" she called when she walked inside the house. Her yell startled Irene, who started to cry. "I'm sorry, little one," she whispered in her baby's ear, then cooed to her daughter until she calmed down. She cuddled Irene and listened for her mother or Julia. Finally, she heard Julia's piercing wails from the spare bedroom. When she walked into the bedroom, she heard her mother speaking in a low, almost childlike voice.

"It's okay, Rachel."

Ellie raised a brow. Rachel again? From the pain in her mother's voice it sounded like she was trying to hold back tears. Ellie wrinkled her brow. She couldn't remember the last time she heard her mother cry.

"Julia's sick," *Mamm* said in a desperate voice. "We need to get her to the hospital right away."

Ellie walked to the bed, leaned over, and placed Irene in the middle of it. "Let me see Julia, *Mamm*. Maybe she needs to nurse in order to cool off."

But *Mamm* refused to let Julia go. "I won't let anything happen to you," her mother whispered to the baby. "You're not going to die."

A shiver passed through Ellie as she heard the chilling words.

CHAPTER 10

Edna kissed Julia's forehead, feeling her hot skin beneath her lips. This couldn't be happening again. Not to her granddaughter. *Not to her Rachel.*

Ellie's voice faded as Edna's mind wandered to the past, a place she'd dared not think about for the past six decades. She thought she'd put it all behind her, had buried that agony so deep that it only came to the surface in her nightmares . . . and after Ellie's babies were born. She couldn't fail them. Not like she'd failed Rachel.

"Mamm!" Ellie's voice broke through the veil of memories. Julia's and Irene's cries chimed in. She looked up, her daughter's distraught face coming into focus. "Ellie?"

"Please give me Julia. I need to see if she's all right."

Dazed, Edna stood from the rocker and let Ellie sit. When she placed Julia in Ellie's arms, her mind had completely turned to the present. "I'll get the buggy ready."

"Nee," Ellie said. She used her forearm to check Julia's forehead. "She does feel warmer than Irene, though. Let me nurse her and see how she does."

How could Ellie be so calm at a time like this? "Ellie, listen to me. She has a fever—a very high one. If it doesn't come down she could . . ."

Ellie nestled Julia, and soon the baby started nursing. "She's okay, *Mamm*. She's nursing. If she was sick she wouldn't want to eat." But as soon as the words were out of Ellie's mouth, Julia pulled away and started crying. A sick, strangled cry.

"Ellie, please." Edna could feel the sobs rising in her throat, the helplessness in her heart. "I can't lose another *boppli*."

Her daughter's head snapped up, her blue eyes focusing off center. "What are you talking about?"

She knelt in front of Ellie. "She needs to *geh* to the hospital. She needs to see a doctor."

Julia latched onto Ellie again and started nursing. "*Mamm*," Ellie said softly. "She's okay. I promise. Look, she's eating again."

Edna saw Julia eagerly taking Ellie's milk. She stared, certain that at any moment the baby's mouth would drop away and her body would go limp. After several moments, neither happened.

"Feel her forehead now." Ellie grasped for Edna's hand. Edna let her guide the back of her hand to Julia's forehead, which was considerably cooler than before. "See? She's okay. She just got a little too warm outside."

Edna breathed out a long sigh of relief. Irene started to cry on the bed behind her.

"Would you mind giving her a bottle?" Ellie asked.

Standing, Edna nodded. Then remembering her daughter couldn't see, she said, "*Ya*. I'll get it." She left the room and went to the kitchen, only realizing how much her hands were shaking when she opened the cabinet door to get a bottle.

She leaned against the counter, trying to get her bearings.

Julia was okay, she kept telling herself. She wasn't Rachel. She closed her eyes and prayed a prayer of thankfulness, only to stop when the bitterness of the past rose like bile in her throat.

She was glad Julia was all right. But why couldn't Rachel have been? Why had God taken a tiny, innocent baby away? Even after all these years, she couldn't let go of the hurt, the regret . . . and the shame.

But she had to follow her mother's example, the way she had in the years since then. Edna straightened her shoulders and made Irene's bottle. She walked into the bedroom, picked up her fussy granddaughter, and sat down on the edge of the bed, her back to Ellie. Although her daughter couldn't see her, Edna didn't want to face her right now and the barrage of questions that were sure to come.

To her surprise, Ellie didn't say anything. They fed the babies in silence, punctuated by a few strong burps, one so loud from Julia that it was clear her granddaughter was just fine. She didn't turn around when Ellie put Julia in the cradle. "Here, *Mamm*," Ellie said as she rounded the bed and stood in front of her. "Take the rocking chair."

"Irene's nearly done with her bottle."

"That's all right," Ellie said softly. "Take your time with her. I'll *geh* finish weeding in the *garten*."

"You sure?"

She nodded. "*Ya*. I'm sure."

After Ellie left, tears welled in Edna's eyes. Her daughter was a remarkable woman in so many ways. She stood, and then through clouded eyes sat down with Irene, rocking her until the baby fell asleep. But instead of putting her in the cradle with her sister, she looked at the infant, taking in her olive-colored skin and dark eyelashes, so much like her father's. She cuddled her granddaughter close, forcing away the past and basking in the love she felt for these two precious babies.

A week passed, and neither Ellie nor *Mamm* brought up the incident with Julia. Several times Ellie had been tempted to ask her mother about Rachel, wondering who the mysterious girl was. But she kept her thoughts to herself, respecting her mother's privacy. There was a reason she'd never talked about the past, and Ellie didn't want to force her to.

But that didn't mean her curiosity wasn't plaguing her. During the second week Chris was gone, Ellie told her mother, "I'd like to *geh* see *Daed*."

"All right," her mother said, placing a plate of what smelled like perfectly crisped bacon on the table. "We can *geh* after breakfast."

"I thought I would *geh* by myself—if you don't mind watching the twins for a little while." Ellie fiddled with the edge of her napkin.

"Oh?" *Mamm* asked, sounding a bit suspicious.

"I miss him. I mean, I know you miss him too, but that's not the only reason I want to see him." The words sounded lame to her ears.

"You two have always had a close relationship." *Mamm* sat down across from her and pushed the plate of bacon toward her. "And I don't blame you for wanting to get out of the house for a little bit. It's a beautiful *daag*."

She sighed. "So you don't mind watching the twins?"

"Of course not. That's why I'm here. And don't worry; they'll be fine."

Ellie smiled. "I'm not worried." She sniffed the air. "That bacon smells *gut*."

The plate slid even closer. "Help yourself," her mother said. But despite her mother's calm demeanor, there was an underlying current of tension since the episode with Julia. Maybe her father would have some answers.

After the breakfast dishes were done, Ellie said good-bye to her twins, which was harder than she thought. She'd never been away from them, and even though she was only going down the street, it still felt like a part of her was missing when she went outside. As she unfolded her cane, she could only imagine how hard it was on Chris, being so far away. She'd talked to him briefly on the phone last night, but still hadn't mentioned what happened with *Mamm*. He didn't sound as tired as he had been the past few weeks, but he was ready to come home. Ellie said a quick prayer for him and headed for her parents' house.

It was about a half hour's walk there, and as usual she was glad they lived on a road with very little traffic. She kept to the edge of the road, staying alert as she swept her cane in front of her in a wide arc. She had walked to her parents' house many times since she and Chris were married, and even though the path was familiar, she never let down her guard. Finally, she arrived at their driveway, the comforting sound of the cows lowing reaching her ears.

She walked down the long driveway toward the house and knocked on the door. When no one answered, she headed for the barn. *"Daed?"*

"Hold on," her father's voice sounded from inside the building. "I'll be right out."

Ellie wiped the perspiration from her face. Despite it being only midmorning, the day already promised to be another hot one.

"Hi, Ellie," her father said, his boots crunching on the gravel driveway. He paused. "Did you walk here by yourself?"

"*Ya.*"

"And *yer mudder* let you?"

Ellie nodded.

"And they say there's no such thing as miracles." He put his hand on her shoulder. "How are the *bopplis?*"

"Fine."

"*Gut, gut.*" He paused, dropping his hand. "And *yer mudder?* How are you two getting along?"

"Really well." Ellie rubbed her cane in between her forefinger and thumb. "Surprisingly well."

"So you just came by to say hi to *yer* old *daed?*"

"You're not old."

"That's not what *mei* knees have been telling me. Come on, we'll go inside and have some tea. I'll have to make it first. Haven't had tea since *yer mamm* left. Haven't had a decent meal either."

She took his arm. "You could have come over."

"Nah. I think it's *gut* for you and *yer mamm* to have this time together."

"You also like the peace and quiet."

He chuckled. "That too."

A short time later they were in the kitchen. Ellie heard the rumbling of the water in the kettle as it started to boil. "When was the last time you made tea?" she asked when the teakettle began to whistle.

"Can't remember. Possibly when you were a *boppli* your-self." Earlier he had brought some ice cubes from the cooler in the basement and put them in glasses. When he finished making the tea, it was more tepid than iced, but Ellie didn't mind. She heard her father sit down across from her.

"Now . . . tell me why you're really here," he said.

She tugged on one of her *kapp* strings. She could never put anything past him, and there was no reason for her not to be straightforward. "Who's Rachel?"

He sucked in a breath. "Where did you hear about her?"

Ellie explained about overhearing his and her mother's con-versation, then about *Mamm*'s strange behavior with Julia. "She called her Rachel. I had heard her do that before, but she insisted I was mistaken. I don't know what to think."

The drumming sound of her father's fingers against the wood table filled the silence of the room. "This isn't my story to tell, Ellie. Have you asked *yer mamm* these questions?"

"Once. She didn't want to talk about it."

"She never did." His chair legs scraped against the floor. Her father's boot heels echoed as he walked toward the sink. She imagined him standing there, looking out the window. Her mother used to do that, Ellie remembered. She liked to see the sun set. How many times had she stood there and thought of Rachel?

"Ellie . . ." From the direction of his voice she could tell he had turned to face her. "If I told you about Rachel, I would be betraying your *mudder*. I won't do that."

She let go of the *kapp* string, disappointed but not surprised. "I understand. I would feel the same way about Chris."

"But I do think Edna needs to let this *geh*. And she'll never do it if she continues to keep it all bottled up inside her."

"I've tried talking to her about it."

"So have I." Her father moved closer. "I think there's only one thing we can do."

"What?"

"Show her that no matter what, we love her." He put Ellie's cane in her hand. "Let's *geh*."

CHAPTER 11

Edna sat on Ellie and Christopher's front porch, enjoying the late-morning air. Despite the heat, there was a lovely breeze that made the rising temperature bearable. She had brought the cradle out with her and placed both babies inside. She used her foot to rock the cradle back and forth. They weren't asleep, but they weren't fussing either. She kept glancing at them, keeping them close to her, making sure neither was too warm or uncomfortable in any way.

She looked out at the yard in front of her. As she had over the past few days, she thought of her behavior with Julia. She'd foolishly overreacted. Fortunately Ellie hadn't brought it up, but that still didn't temper her embarrassment that she thought her *granddochder* was deathly ill when she wasn't.

A buggy turned into the driveway, and she immediately recognized it. She smiled. Although she was enjoying her time with the babies and Ellie, she missed Ephraim. He parked the buggy near the barn, and after several moments, he and Ellie appeared.

"I see you're enjoying the morning, Edna," he said, escorting Ellie up the steps.

"*Ya.* It's been a fine *daag*. What are you doing here?"

He bent over and picked up both babies in one swoop. Edna started. "Ephraim, what—"

"I think I deserve some quality time with these *bopplis.*" He flashed her a grin and opened the screen door.

Edna shot up from the chair. "You don't know the first thing about taking care of twins."

"I took care of *mei* own two *kinner,*" he said.

"Excuse me?" She put her hands on her hips, ignoring Ellie's laughter in the background. "*Who* took care of our *kinner?*"

"It was a dual effort. Well, we gotta *geh.* Time for Irene and Julia to hear all about my favorite fishing hole."

The door shut behind him before she could say anything else. She turned to Ellie, who was still smiling. "Are you going to let him take the girls like that?"

"He's their *grossvatter.*" She carefully moved to the porch swing and sat down, still holding her cane. "Plus, it will give us a few minutes alone."

"What do we need that for?"

Ellie's expression grew serious. "So you can tell me about Rachel."

Ellie paused, waiting for her mother to respond. Instead, all she heard was the sound of horse's hooves on the road as a cart went by. She could tell the difference between a cart and a buggy by the sound the wheels made. When the cart and horse passed and her mother still didn't say anything, Ellie sat back in the swing. "I want to know what happened to her."

"It's not your business. Rachel is . . . personal."

"I know. *Daed* told me."

Her mother gasped. "What did he say? I can't believe Ephraim would do that to me."

"Wait," Ellie said. "He didn't tell me anything, other than he wants you to be free."

"I am." *Mamm* sat down. "Rachel is in the past."

"Not anymore." Ellie leaned forward. "I don't think she ever was. Please, *Mamm*. Tell me what happened."

She heard a sob catch in her mother's throat.

"She was . . ." *Mamm* sniffed. "She was *mei* sister. And I was supposed to take care of her. It was *mei* job to keep her safe." She choked on the next words. "She died because of me."

Ellie got up from the swing and sat at her mother's feet. She reached out until she found *Mamm*'s hand. "How old was she?"

"Just a baby. Not even six months old. *Yer* grandmother had to take *yer aenti* Roberta to the emergency room—she'd fallen out of a tree and hit her head. *Vatter* was at work, and *Mutter* asked me to watch Rachel. But as soon as Roberta and *Mutter* left in the taxi, Rachel started to cry. She wouldn't stop."

"Oh, *Mamm*." Ellie stroked her mother's hand. *Mamm* squeezed her fingers, stilling Ellie's movements.

"She was very hot too. I didn't know it at the time, but she had a high fever. I tried to cool her off with a cold cloth. I gave her a bath. But she kept crying. She wouldn't stop . . ." *Mamm*'s voice cracked. "I had to put her in the cradle. I closed the door because I couldn't take the crying anymore." *Mamm*'s voice sounded soft. Young. As if she was reliving the nightmare at that moment. "Finally, she stopped crying. Then I went to *mei* room and played with *mei* dolls. I . . . forgot about her."

Ellie's heart filled with pain. "What happened?"

"*Mamm* and Roberta were gone for a long time. Hours. It was almost dark when I remembered I was supposed to be watching Rachel. I ran into the room. I looked in the cradle, and she wasn't moving. I touched her. She was cold. So very cold."

Tears streamed down Ellie's face. "How old were you?"

"Seven." She pulled out of Ellie's grasp. "Old enough to take care of a *boppli*."

"It wasn't *yer* fault she died."

"I forgot about her, Ellie. I should have taken her next door to the neighbors. They would have known what to do. But I forgot all about her. If I hadn't put her in the cradle . . . if I hadn't shut the door . . ."

Ellie rose and put her arms around her mother. "I'm so sorry."

Mamm stiffened. "*Mutter* never blamed me. Neither did *Vatter*. I remember them saying she died from the fever, but other than that we never spoke of it again, right up until the day they died. It was as if Rachel never existed."

"But she did, *Mamm*. And she still does. In *yer* heart. You can't keep blaming yourself. You have to know it wasn't your fault."

"It was God's will. That's what *mei onkel* said. But that was little comfort."

Ellie sat back down. "We don't always understand God's will. Remember, that's what you told me after the accident."

"*Ya*," she whispered. "I remember."

"And Rachel is in heaven. She has her angel wings. You need to let her *geh*." She laid her head in her mother's lap. "You can't keep worrying about the twins. Or about me. All this fretting is keeping you from enjoying your grandchildren."

"I realize that, Ellie." She stroked Ellie's back. "And I thought

I had come to terms with it. When Wally and you were born, I wasn't afraid. Not like I am now."

"Because you kept us safe."

"*Ya*," she whispered. "I kept you safe."

Ellie lifted her head. "*Mamm*, don't you see? It's God who's in control. Even when we think we are, God's will is always done. We have to do our part, but we also have to accept when God's decisions aren't ours."

Mamm touched Ellie's cheek. "Like with your blindness."

"Like with your Rachel."

"Ellie, I . . . I'm not sure how I can forgive myself for what happened to her."

"Let's take the first step." She reached out and touched her mother's cheek. "Let's pray."

Chapter 12

Ellie paced the front porch, her stomach in knots. *Mamm*, sitting in a chair, her knitting needles clacking away, cleared her throat.

"You're going to wear down the porch boards," she said. "Be patient. He'll be here soon."

Ellie checked her Braille watch. "He's half an hour late. What if their van got into an accident?" An ache formed in her chest, close to panic as her own car accident flashed in front of her. Almost instantly she felt her mother standing beside her.

"What did you tell me about worrying?" *Mamm* said.

"That it doesn't change anything." Ellie sat down in the swing. Why couldn't she take her own advice? Chris's three weeks had turned to four, and he was finally due home. Unfortunately, he was late. She had talked to him almost every day, but the phone was a poor substitute for him being here.

Mamm sat back down in the chair, picked up her needles, and started knitting again. She was making two dark-blue sweaters for the girls. The sound of her foot rocking the cradle back and forth against the porch boards was in perfect rhythm with her flying needles. Since their talk on the front porch that day, Ellie and her mother had grown closer. *Mamm* had been less tense, although she still went a little overboard when it came to taking care of the girls. But now she wasn't any more doting than Chris's mother, who had been by several times to see the twins. Sarah Lynne, who was still struggling with morning sickness, was only able to visit twice, but according to Barbara everything was going well with the pregnancy.

The clicking of the needles abruptly stopped. "I believe I owe you an apology, *dochder*."

Ellie turned her head toward her mother. "For what?"

"For not helping you the way you needed me to."

"*Mamm*, everything has been fine."

"I'm talking about before. I should have trusted you with the twins."

Surprised, Ellie said, "*Danki, Mamm*. I appreciate that."

"I see how *gut* you are with the babies. How organized everything is here." Mamm sighed. "Christopher was right to ask me to leave. I was in the way."

"Is that what he said to you?"

"Not in so many words. But he did the right thing." She started knitting again. "You know I didn't think much of him when we first met."

"You did make that pretty clear."

"Now, Ellie, you couldn't blame me, could you? He had left the Amish. How was I supposed to trust him?"

"By trusting me."

Her mother paused. "You're right. I promise I'll do a better job of that from now on."

The sound of a car turning into the driveway drove Ellie out of the swing. "Is he here?"

"Looks like it," *Mamm* said. She didn't move or stop knitting.

Ellie carefully but quickly went down the steps. She heard the sound of a car door slam. She stopped in the middle of the yard. "Chris?"

"I'm here." He drew her close.

She hugged him tightly, whispering in his ear, "I'm so glad you're home."

"*Mei* too." He pulled away from her. "Hi, Edna," he called.

"Christopher."

He chuckled and said in a low voice, "Same old Edna."

Ellie lifted her head. "*Nee*. She's not the same. She's better."

"What do you mean?"

"I'll tell you all about it. But there are two little girls waiting for you. You won't believe how big they've grown."

"I can't wait to see them. Let me get my duffel bag." When he took her hand, she leaned against him and whispered, "Later I'll give you a proper welcome home."

He laughed, and she smiled. They walked up the front porch steps together, and she stayed back as Chris picked up his daughters, telling them how beautiful they were and how much their *daed* had missed them.

Mamm came up beside her. "It's time for me to *geh* home."

Ellie turned to her. "You can stay, *Mamm*. Chris won't mind."

"*Nee*, Ellie. You all need time together. As a *familye*."

"I'll miss you."

"I'm only down the street, *dochder*. Don't worry. You'll see me soon enough."

Before her mother could walk away, Ellie hugged her, her own heart filling with love as her mother hugged her back. They had both changed since the babies were born. A month ago she wasn't sure if she and her mother would ever get along again. Now she knew they would always be close . . . and she thanked the Lord for that.

Surprised by Love

CHAPTER 1

E mily Schwartz looked up at the early morning August sky. The sun hadn't broken through the darkness yet, and the balmy temperature made it a wonderful time for stargazing. Thousands dotted the inky black sky. She knew there were millions—no, billions—more scattered across the endless expanse. She adjusted her telescope, took off her glasses, and peered into the eyepiece. Not that she could see much. The telescope was a small, inexpensive instrument, better suited to a child than a true student of the stars. Still, it was all she had, and her parents didn't give her a hard time about using it. One day she hoped she could afford a good one.

She continued gazing at the stars, moving her telescope around to get the best views. She turned on her head lamp, scribbled down a few notes in her small spiral notebook, then tucked her pencil behind her ear and looked in the eyepiece again. When the sun's morning rays streaked the horizon with soft lilac and peach hues, she folded up her telescope, took it inside, and went up to her bedroom.

"Stargazing again?" her mother asked when Emily entered the kitchen to help with breakfast. She was making pecan waffles—a family favorite. Emily reached for her apron so she could make another favorite—bacon.

Tying the apron around her waist, she nodded. "I didn't want to waste a clear morning."

"Humph." *Mamm* flipped over the iron griddle and put it back on the gas burner. "I wish you would apply yourself as diligently to finding a husband."

Emily suppressed a sigh. Her mother was relentless when it came to Emily's romantic life. Make that her nonexistent romantic life. "God will supply a husband for me." *If it's his will.* Emily wasn't completely sure that it wasn't.

"I wish he would hurry up then," *Mamm* muttered.

Emily laid strips of thick bacon on the pan her mother had set out earlier. "You can't rush the Lord, *Mamm*."

"Of course not." She gave Emily a sharp look. "But I can light a little fire under you."

Emily frowned. Her mother was up to something, she was sure of it. As the youngest of six, Emily was the last one still living at home. Her three brothers and two sisters were married and had started families of their own years ago, which made her parents' move from Shipshewana to Middlefield difficult. Most of her siblings and all of their children still lived in Shipshewana. But the opportunity to open their own natural food store in a community that wasn't overpopulated with them was too great to resist. And in the four years since their arrival, no one could deny the shop was a success.

Unlike her parents, Emily had been happy to move. She wanted a fresh start, and she'd gotten one here. She was content with her job at the store, the community, and of course her astronomy hobby. Being unattached gave her extra time to devote to it. She considered her stargazing time a perk of the single life. If only her mother could see things the same way. But Louwanda Schwartz had her own particular, and outspoken, view on life.

By the time the waffles were brown and the bacon crisp, *Daed* walked into the kitchen. They all sat and, after prayer, dug in to their food. Emily nibbled on a hot slice of bacon while saying an additional silent prayer that her mother would drop Project Find Emily a Husband. Emily's father wasn't interested in that kind of talk. Besides, she was only twenty. Just because her siblings had all married by her age didn't mean she had to.

Fortunately, her mother and father were discussing their visit to Shipshewana coming up in a couple weeks. When they finished eating, *Daed* pushed away from the table and stood.

"I'm planning to spend some time in the greenhouse. Unless you need me at the store."

Mamm shook her head. "We shouldn't be too busy this morning."

"*Gut.* I'll order some more of those organic candles this afternoon. We ran out faster than I thought we would."

"You should probably double the order."

Daed nodded, then left. Emily ate the last bite of her waffle and started clearing the table. "I'll get the kitchen."

"*Danki.* I've got some paperwork in the office that needs *mei* attention." She removed her apron and hung it on the hook in the adjacent mudroom, then left for the office, which was in the back of the store, across the driveway from the house. Her mother took care of the books while her father managed the ordering and grew specialty herbs, vegetables, and plants in their garden and greenhouse. They sold nearly as well as the candles.

It didn't take long to finish the dishes. Emily hung her apron next to *Mamm*'s, then walked over to the store. The front door was already unlocked, and she turned the Closed sign to Open. Time for another workday to begin.

She straightened the baking goods shelves, which were the most popular and usually the messiest. She'd pulled forward a small bag of gluten-free flour when Reuben Coblentz walked through the door. In addition to natural foods, they also sold fresh organic produce from local farms. The Coblentzes were one of their best sources. The food they brought in was always delicious.

"Hi, Emily," Reuben said, flashing a smile that some girls in the community thought was handsome. And she supposed it was. At least to the girls who were interested in that sort of thing. "Got a delivery in the back." He angled his thumb toward the back of the store. He wasn't wearing his usual straw hat. "*Yer daed* ordered a lot of rhubarb for some reason."

"I'm sure he'll put it to *gut* use." She pushed up her glasses and walked toward him. "I'll meet you around back—" Her toe caught the edge of the rug in front of the door and she tripped into Reuben's arms.

Not again. On instinct Reuben reached out and kept Emily from landing on the ground. This wasn't the first time she'd tripped on the rug. More like the third, at least when he was around. They should get rid of it before Emily did some real damage to herself.

He looked down at her. She was a petite girl, several inches shorter than he was. She also wore glasses with the thickest lenses he'd ever seen. Maybe that was the reason she kept tripping. "You okay?"

"*Ya*." She straightened, pushed her glasses back up, and smoothed her *kapp*. "*Danki*. I'll meet you around back."

He noticed the slight rosy hue of her cheeks and smiled to himself as he walked around the building to the horse and wagon he'd brought. In addition to rhubarb, there were tomatoes, corn, and other vegetables, plus a few plants his sister Sarah had started to grow in a new greenhouse last year. Their father and Reuben's brother-in-law, Judah, who was married to Reuben's other sister, Esther, had partnered and expanded the farm, which increased business. Schwartz Natural Herbs and Foods wasn't the only place Reuben delivered to, but it was one of his favorite stops. Emily never failed to do something that made him smile, or even outright laugh. She was unique, for sure.

He climbed up into the wagon and handed her the lightest box of rhubarb. He always packed a couple of them extra light for her, since the time she insisted on carrying a heavy case of tomatoes, only to drop them on her foot, splattering the vegetables on the ground. They were able to salvage some, but he wasn't so sure about her dress, which was stained with tomato juice and pulp when she stepped on one of the tomatoes and fell on the ground. Come to think of it, he hadn't seen her in that light-green dress since.

"Everything looks so *gut*. I can smell the green beans from here."

"Really?" He put several crates on the open end of the wagon, then jumped down. He stacked two crates of apples on top of each other and lifted them. "You can smell green beans?"

"Of course. Can't you? And the apples smell amazing."

Emily smiled, revealing two slightly crooked front teeth, then turned and went inside.

She must have a supernatural sniffer or something. He breathed in but all he could smell was dirt. Shaking his head, he followed her through the back door after he propped it open with a nearby rock. "Where do you want these?"

"Against that wall." There was a small storage area to the right, and he set the crates on the ground. She placed the rhubarb next to the apples.

He looked at her again. Despite the goggle-like glasses, she was kind of cute in her own peculiar way. But he thought a lot of girls were cute. And pretty. He wasn't blind, and he'd been on more than his fair share of dates, something those cute girls didn't appreciate. But he wasn't ready for commitment. It had taken him long enough to figure out he wanted to join the Amish church, which he'd done a few months ago. He wasn't about to take the plunge and get married, not anytime soon. And not until he'd considered it thoroughly.

Pushing the thoughts away, he said, "I'll get the rest."

She rubbed her nose, which displaced her glasses again. "I can help."

"It's *mei* job, remember? What would *mei daed* say if he found out I was slacking off work?"

Emily giggled and two dimples appeared near the corners of her mouth. "You say that every time. I know you never slack at work."

"That wasn't always the case."

She tilted her head at him. "And that was the past." She smiled again and walked out the door, giving him no choice but to follow her. Fortunately he'd packed three light boxes today.

After they brought everything in, Emily said, "We've got some fresh apple cider on the counter. Would you like a cup?"

"Sounds great."

They went to the front of the store. A couple of English customers had arrived, and he nodded to them. They smiled and went back to perusing shelves filled with organic food, herbs, supplements, and vitamins. The Schwartzes' store was popular with Amish and English alike and was gaining a reputation for its quality items and fair pricing.

Emily went to the end of the counter and picked up a paper cup from a small stack near a jug of cider. A small handwritten sign said, "One sample per customer, please." She poured cider into the cup, then handed it to Reuben. The bell above the door rang, and Deborah Yoder walked in. Reuben gave her a polite nod, which she returned with a glare as she walked past. He flinched and glanced at Emily to see if she noticed. If she did, she didn't let on as she poured herself a half cup of the cider.

He fought the urge to look at Deborah again. They'd gone out twice a few months ago, but there was nothing between them. Apparently Deborah felt differently, and he heard through the always lively grapevine that she was upset with him. Maybe he should have explained that he wasn't interested instead of ignoring her. But that meant more entanglement than he wanted. She'd get over it. Yet from the sharp look, she still wasn't too happy with him.

The bell sounded again, and Emily's mother, Louwanda, came in. He flinched again, this time for a different reason. Louwanda was a nice woman, but a little more forceful than most of the women he knew. In contrast, her husband, Andy, was a quiet, mellow man.

"Hello, Reuben," Louwanda said, a bright smile on her face.

She glanced at the cup in his hand. "Andy's cider is delicious, isn't it?"

"*Ya*. It always is."

"The *mann* has a God-given gift for gardening and food, that's for sure." She held a letter-size envelope in her hand and turned to Emily. "I'm happy to say that plans are coming together quite nicely for our family reunion."

"That's *gut*." Emily straightened a stack of flyers on the counter, and Reuben noticed she wasn't looking at her mother. He also noticed she didn't seem excited by the news.

He finished the last of the cider and was about to hand the cup back to Emily when Louwanda said, "Guess who's also going to be there?" Before Emily could answer, she said, "Wayne Jantzi."

"What?" Emily's face turned gray.

"I just got the confirmation today." She held up the letter, her smile stretching from one plump cheek to the other. "Well, actually yesterday. Our neighbor brought it over this morning. Apparently there is a new mailman and he misdelivered a bunch—"

"Wayne will be there?"

Reuben looked at Emily. There was no mistaking her complexion now—she was nearly the color of his mother's freshly washed white sheets. He'd seen Emily flustered plenty of times. Not just here at the store, but also at church, a couple singings they'd both attended, and once when they were at a barn raising. Emily had been serving the food, and she accidentally flipped a huge spoonful of macaroni salad on the front of Judah's shirt. Reuben still wasn't sure how she accomplished that.

But he'd never seen her this pale. She almost seemed to be in shock.

"*Ya*." Louwanda's grin grew even wider, which Reuben hadn't thought possible. Unlike Emily, she didn't wear glasses, and her gray eyes shone with delight. "In fact, he was very interested to know you were coming this year."

"He . . . was?"

Reuben thought Emily would wilt right there. Without thinking, he moved to stand a little closer, in case he had to break her fall again.

"Oh, I guess I'll just tell you." She lowered her voice. "Wayne's mother and I have been corresponding. We have so much in common, especially two children who are unmarried and available."

Emily leaned against the counter. "You told his *mamm* I was available?"

A little of the delight faded from Louwanda's face. "Goodness, Emily. Is that all you have to say? I thought you'd be excited about this opportunity."

"Excited?"

Reuben knew he should leave. This was none of his business. But his feet stayed put. He didn't like how vulnerable Emily seemed right now. And he could sympathize with her. Now that he'd joined the church, his own mother kept dropping some not-so-subtle hints about his future and how it should include a wife and *kinner*. He hadn't realized Emily's mother was pressuring her too. And whoever this Wayne guy was, it was clear Emily had no idea he was interested in her.

"Do I have to spell this out for you?" Louwanda shot Reuben a furtive glance. "In front of Reuben and all our customers?" she whispered through pressed lips.

Normally Reuben would have chuckled at her dramatics. Louwanda couldn't be more different from Emily. But right now he didn't see anything funny about the situation.

When Emily didn't respond, Louwanda shrugged. "Since you don't mind people knowing *yer* personal business, I guess it won't bother you if I say that Wayne is already planning your first date."

Emily gasped. "Th-that's not possible."

"It is possible." Louwanda grinned and held up the letter. "I have it in writing. You should make a new dress. It's not like you can't afford one. You're very miserly with *yer* money, Emily. Maybe something in a pretty lavender shade. That will bring out *yer* eyes." She looked her daughter up and down and sighed. "Too bad we can't do anything about your glasses."

"There's *nix* wrong with her glasses," Reuben blurted, then pressed his lips together. *Stay out of this.*

"Of course there isn't," Louwanda said, lifting her chin. "I just wish everyone could see her pretty blue eyes more clearly."

"*Mamm.*" Emily took a step forward, knocking over the can of pencils she'd just straightened. She tried to put them back, but her hands were shaking. She gave up. "Wayne and I can't *geh* on a date," she said.

"Nonsense. You can't say *nee* without giving him a chance. He comes from a nice family, and from what I remember he was quite *schee*—"

"I can't *geh* out with anyone!"

Reuben glanced behind him at one of the English customers nearby. She looked at the three of them for a moment. Since Emily was speaking in *Dietsch*, he was pretty sure the woman didn't understand what she was saying, but anyone could tell by the rising, strained tone of her voice that something was wrong. Reuben smiled and nodded at the customer, trying to reassure her that everything was all right. She gave him a tight smile in return, then moved to the next aisle.

"I don't know why *yer* behaving like this." Louwanda moved closer to Emily. "We'll talk about this later," she said through pressed lips. "*Nee* need to make a scene in the store."

"There's *nix* to talk about," Emily said, her voice raising even higher.

"Emily—"

"Because I'm not available."

Reuben swung his gaze to her. That was surprising news. "*Yer* not?"

"*Yer* not?" Louwanda repeated.

"Nope." She crossed her arms over her chest and lifted her chin, looking like a trembling, yet defiant, sparrow. "You'll just have to tell Frau Jantzi that you were mistaken."

Louwanda's eyes narrowed. "Why haven't I heard about this before?"

"I don't have to tell you everything."

"How could you keep something so important from me?" Her expression pinched with hurt.

"I'll be going now," Reuben said as he started to inch away.

"Who is it?" Louwanda's voice now matched Emily's. So much for not making a scene. One of the customers slipped quietly out of the store. Andy wouldn't be happy about that.

Emily backed away from her mother. "I don't have to tell you."

"Because *yer* lying," Louwanda said.

Reuben paused. Now her mother was crossing a line.

"I'm not lying!"

"Then tell me who *yer* seeing!"

Reuben hurried his steps toward the door. The last thing he wanted was to get in the middle of these two women, even though he thought Louwanda was being unfair. And ridiculous. What was the big deal, anyway? So what if Emily wasn't dating anyone? That was her choice and her business. And none of this involved him. Thank God.

He was reaching for the door handle when Emily said, "Fine. I'm seeing Reuben Coblentz."

What have I done?

Emily's stomach hit the ground. She scanned the store for Reuben, panicking, then blew out a breath when she didn't see him. Thank God. The last thing she needed was for him to hear her say he was the man she was dating. Which of course wasn't true. She liked Reuben well enough. He was kind, he was easygoing, and he seemed to have a good head on his shoulders.

But why had she said his name? Sheer panic. That was the reason. She couldn't believe her mother was meddling so much that she would try to set her up with someone back in Indiana. Wait, yes, she could. But why of all people did it have to be Wayne Jantzi? He couldn't be a part of this. He wouldn't. She knew that much. Her mother said she had proof in the letter, which didn't make sense. But her mother wouldn't have said it if it wasn't true.

She wrung her fingers together. She didn't want to lie to her mother, but desperate times made her brain malfunction. She wasn't sure when he'd left since she'd forgotten all about him the moment her mother had mentioned Wayne.

"Reuben?" Her mother smiled, then laughed. "Really?"

"Why are you laughing?" She said a silent prayer of thanks that he wasn't here to witness this. She still wasn't sure why she'd said his name. Or why her mother was skeptical. *Mamm* didn't think she was *gut* enough for Reuben?

"I'm not laughing." She chuckled again. "It's just, I'm surprised you would use him for an excuse."

Great. Her mother didn't believe her. Then again, she was lying. And since she rarely lied, at least on purpose, she had no idea how to proceed.

"I'll let Wayne's mother know you'll be available for whatever plans he has in mind." She touched Emily's shoulder. "Trust me, Emily. You don't have to be afraid of dating Wayne."

"I'm not afraid—"

"Besides, the two of you are perfect for each other."

Nee, we're not. She fretted again. She'd figure out later how to deal with this, but she had to stop her mother from telling Wayne's mother she wanted to see him. Because he was the last person she ever wanted to see. "Reuben and I are . . . we're going out tonight."

"You are?" *Mamm* turned, surprise lighting up her face.

"Um, *ya*. I'm meeting him later."

Mamm looked at her for a long moment. "*Yer* serious, aren't you?"

She gulped. "*Ya*."

Clasping her hands together, *Mamm* said, "How wonderful! And here I was doubting you. I'm sorry, *lieb*. Tell Reuben he's invited for supper tonight."

"But . . . he can't—"

"Why not?"

Emily swallowed again, her mother's expectant gaze making her wilt. Oh, she was in trouble now. "Because . . . because . . ."

Reuben suddenly appeared at her side. "Because we already have plans for supper."

CHAPTER 2

Emily froze as Reuben moved closer to her. Oh *nee*. He'd been here the entire time. How much had he heard?

"But I appreciate the invitation," he said, moving even closer until the top of her shoulder touched his bicep.

Her palms broke out in a sweat. "Reuben"—she smiled up at him with what she hoped was a sweet, flirty smile, but she was sure it wasn't anything close—"I thought you already left."

"*Nee*. Not yet." He smiled at her, but she saw the strain at the corners. "I've been here the whole time."

She gulped. He definitely wasn't happy with her, and she didn't blame him. She was sinking deeper into the mire of her own making.

He turned to *Mamm*. "We can't join you for supper tonight because Emily and I are going on a buggy ride." He looked down at her again. "Right, Emily?"

Confused, she frowned. What was he talking about?

"Remember?" He nudged her a little with his elbow. "We have a lot to discuss tonight."

"You do?" *Mamm*'s smile grew wide. She may have had her doubts before, but Emily could see she now believed the two were an item.

Reuben nodded. "I'll be by to pick you up at six sharp."

"O-okay."

He gave them both a nod, then left the store. Just as he disappeared several more customers came in.

"We'll talk about this later." *Mamm* walked away to help one of their regular customers. "Bertha," *Mamm* said, her face shining as bright as twenty head lamps, "what can I help you with this week?"

Emily leaned against the counter, her shoulders slumping. At least she had a bit of a reprieve from the prying. But that didn't mean she had any idea how she was going to fix this mess.

"Emily."

She turned to see Deborah Yoder behind her. She was a couple years older than Emily, and they weren't exactly friends. More like acquaintances. Emily gathered her wits and smiled.

"Hi, Deborah. What can I do for you today?"

"Stay away from Reuben."

Emily's mouth dropped open. "What?"

Deborah leaned closer, lowering her voice. "He'll only hurt you. Trust me on this." She gave Emily a knowing nod, then left the store.

Emily paused. Deborah didn't have to bother with the warning, since there was nothing between her and Reuben. No, her heart was safe. That hadn't been the case in the past.

The rest of the day was busier than usual, for which Emily was grateful. She and her mother didn't have time to talk about anything, and by the time they closed the store it was already five thirty.

"Hurry and freshen up for your ride with Reuben," *Mamm* said, practically pushing her out the door toward the house.

"Ride with Reuben?" *Daed* asked as he walked toward them and lifted a bushy brow. He hit a button on the register and pulled out the cash drawer. He'd worked with them in the store that afternoon and spent the last hour explaining to some new customers where he sourced his honey and produce.

"Our Emily is going on a buggy ride with Reuben Coblentz." *Mamm* clasped her hands together, a gesture Emily was starting to find irritating. "Isn't that wonderful, Andy?"

"Only if she thinks so." He looked at Emily. "Do you?"

She nodded, unsure of how else to respond. Without a doubt Reuben was going to be upset with her and would let her know in no uncertain terms. For a brief moment she thought about feigning illness, but that wouldn't be fair. Reuben deserved an explanation, although she wasn't sure she could give him one. Not to mention she had to figure out what to say to her parents. Lying to her mother was bad enough, but now her father knew too.

"All right then," *Daed* said. "You two have fun. But not too much fun." He winked.

Normally she would be cheered up by her father's good humor, but right now she felt like curdled milk inside. She went upstairs and looked at her dresses. The one she had on was fine, but her mother would expect her to change into something different. As she combed through the few she had, she realized her mom was right. She did need to make a new one or two. She was decent with a needle but hadn't felt like sewing much lately. She'd rather read, or even better, spend the nights and early mornings looking at the stars.

She selected a dark-green dress, hoping Reuben wouldn't notice the small dark stain on the top of one shoulder. How did it get there? Shrugging, she changed, looked at her reflection in the mirror, straightened her *kapp*, and pushed up her glasses. She remembered Reuben defending her glasses to her mother. *Mamm* wasn't being cruel. She'd always told Emily she had beautiful eyes, then reminded her not to be prideful about them. And Emily wasn't. She wasn't even all that bothered about her thick lenses, with the exception of being teased when she was in school. Which made her think about Wayne . . .

"Stop." She grimaced at the mirror, then left her bedroom and went downstairs. Reuben would be here any minute, and she wouldn't keep him waiting.

Unfortunately, her mother had parked herself on the couch in the living room. "I'll *geh* outside and wait for Reuben," Emily said, going to open the door.

"You'll do *nee* such thing. He can come to the door and ask for you himself."

"*Mamm*, it's not that serious."

"*Nee?* I thought it was. Serious enough that you don't want to *geh* out with Wayne. But if you and Reuben aren't an item, I'll write to Wayne's mother right now and tell her plans are on." When she opened the top drawer of the end table near her chair, where Emily knew she kept her stationery, Emily hurried over to shut it.

"We're serious." She folded her hands and smiled at her mother so wide her mouth hurt.

"For goodness' sake." *Mamm* shook out her hand. "You almost smashed my finger in that drawer."

"Sorry."

Mamm sighed. "You've always had a bit of an endearing clumsiness about you. I hope Reuben appreciates that."

She thought about falling into his arms this morning when

she tripped on the rug—again. She doubted Reuben appreciated that part of her, or any part, at this point. Her stomach tightened and she glanced at the clock. Almost six and she still didn't know what to say to him.

At six sharp a knock sounded on the door.

"How nice," *Mamm* said. "I appreciate promptness."

Emily flashed her a desperate look and hurried to open the door. "Hi," she said, her voice sounding like a bullfrog had taken over. She cleared her throat. "Come in."

He did, not looking at Emily but at her mother. "Hi, Louwanda."

"Andy should be here any minute. Why don't you sit awhile? I can make some *kaffee*—"

"*Mamm*—"

"*Danki*, but I really would like to take Emily on that buggy ride." He looked at her. "I've been waiting to talk to her privately all day."

"I see." *Mamm* flashed Emily a knowing look. "Well then, don't let me hold you up."

Emily motioned for Reuben to walk out the door, but he gestured for her to go first. She hung her head as she walked outside and down the porch steps. She stood at the bottom and squeezed her eyes shut.

"What are you doing?"

She opened one eye and looked at him. "Waiting for you to yell at me."

"I'm not going to yell at you." He moved past her. "Let's *geh*."

"*Geh* where?" she asked, running to catch up with him.

"On a buggy ride." He turned and sighed. "That's why I'm here, right?"

"Right." She followed him and climbed inside the buggy. He pulled out of the driveway and headed down the road. Emily fisted her hands in her lap. She should say something, but no words would come out of her mouth.

After several minutes of silence, Reuben slowed the buggy to a more leisurely pace. "Mind explaining what's going on?"

She turned to face him. "I'm sorry, Reuben. *Mamm* wants me to go out with Wayne Jantzi and I can't go out with him. But she's determined to see me married off and won't listen. I'm fine not being married. More than fine. I have my life and hobbies, and marriage and a family would interfere with all of that—"

"What does that have to do with me?"

"I panicked."

He glanced at her. "That's it?"

She nodded. "I don't do well under pressure."

"So I see." He made a right and turned down a road with lots of white-sided Amish homes. "You know, you could have made up someone."

"That would be lying."

"Isn't that what you're doing now?"

"*Ya*, but making someone up would be really lying."

He gave her a side eye. "You realize *yer* not making sense."

She sighed. "I know." She looked down at her lap. "I'll explain everything to her when I get back."

"If you do, will she still want you to *geh* out with Wayne?"

Emily nodded.

"And you don't want to *geh* out with him."

She shook her head, hard. She also prayed he wouldn't ask her why. She wasn't prepared to give that explanation.

Reuben rubbed his chin. "What if we did start dating?"

Reuben wanted to swallow his tongue. What had possessed him to say such a thing? He gripped the reins as he looked at Emily. Even behind her thick lenses he could see how wide her eyes were. She couldn't believe what he was saying either.

But he couldn't take it back. In fact, he wouldn't. If there was one thing he disliked, it was coercion. And while her mother might have good intentions, she was being overbearing and pressuring Emily. Emily didn't deserve that. No one did. And what harm would it do to help her out a bit?

"You . . . you want to date me?" Emily said in a small voice.

"*Nee*. Of course not. I mean, not really date." He turned onto a short gravel road. He knew who owned the property, and there was a field at the end of the drive. The guy wouldn't mind if they stopped for a minute. Reuben didn't need his attention divided.

He halted the buggy near a patch of grass, where his horse could graze while he and Emily talked. He angled his body so he could face her. "Would it help if we went out a couple times before your reunion? That way *yer mamm* would leave you alone about dating Wayne."

She bit her bottom lip and stared at him. "It would, but you don't have to do that. I need to stand up to her."

"*Ya*, you do, eventually. But if you tell her the truth, she'll probably set you up with Wayne anyway."

"That's true."

He sat back in the buggy. "Parents. Why won't they just let us live our lives?"

"I don't know." She sighed and seemed to relax. A horsefly

landed on her lap and she brushed it away. "I don't understand why she thinks me and Wayne are a *gut* match."

"Maybe she's desperate." At Emily's hurt look he quickly added, "She wants to marry you off, right?"

"Desperately."

"I understand. I've been getting more pressure from my *mamm* too. Esther's married, and Sarah has been dating her boyfriend for a while. They've all but planned the wedding. You'd think that would be enough, but now *Mamm*'s turning her attention on me." He brightened. "You know, this plan would probably be a nice break for both of us. *Mamm* will stop dropping her not-so-subtle hints if she thinks I'm seeing someone. And *yer mamm* will let *geh* of the idea of you dating what's-his-face."

"Wayne." Her face pinched.

Reuben nodded. Despite knowing it wasn't any of his business and he shouldn't dig deeper into Emily's privacy, he said, "Must be quite a guy if *yer* that bothered by him."

"Actually, he is quite a guy." She sighed and looked at him. "At least now. He wasn't always. Let's just say he and a few others weren't all that nice to me when we were kids."

"Ah." He knew children could be cruel, but he hadn't really experienced it when he was younger. He'd been well liked, and since he was good at sports, he was always chosen first or second for teams. He made decent grades and now made a decent living working the family business. He glanced at Emily. "He must have hurt you."

She nodded, looking down at her lap. Then her head sprang up. "So how will we do this dating thing?"

"Easy. We *geh* out."

"Together?"

"*Ya*, together." He laughed. "That's what dating is about. Being together."

"But we're not really dating."

"Right."

"Then why do we have to be together?"

Reuben rubbed his forehead with his fingers. He knew Emily wasn't dumb. She was excellent with customers and knew everything about the goods her family sold. They talked often when he made deliveries, although the conversations were rather short. But right now she was being as thick as an oak log. "Because if we're not together, we would be lying."

"Wouldn't we be lying anyway?"

"*Ya*, but . . ." He frowned. Now he was confused. This all seemed so clear a minute before. "Are you saying we shouldn't?"

She paused. "I don't want to drag you into *mei* problems. At least any more than I already have. I'm really sorry about this."

"Don't be. Like I said, this will be beneficial for both of us. We don't even have to be specific that we're dating. We can just *geh* out and do things. Give the illusion of being a couple without being a couple."

"Are you sure?"

"Positive." Then a wave of self-doubt came over him. "Unless you don't want anyone to think we're dating."

"*Nee*, I don't mind that. I mean, it's all right with me." But she didn't look at him when she spoke.

He frowned. This was new. He'd never had any girl cause him to doubt himself before. He shoved it aside. This was Emily after all. A little plain, a little odd, and just a friend. It wasn't like they were really dating after all.

"We should probably get back," Emily said after several seconds of awkward silence.

"It's still early, though."

"I know. But the longer we stay out, the more questions *Mamm* will have."

Compassion filled him. "She's been pressuring you that much?"

Emily stared out into the field in front of them. "I think she's worried I'll never get married."

He laughed. "You're what, only nineteen?"

"Twenty. All my siblings were married by my age."

He lifted a brow. "Wow. That's young."

She nodded. "I think it's more than *mei* age, though." She looked at him, tilted her head. "Do you think I'm *seltsam?*"

The question caught him off guard. He took her in for a moment, her pale features, thick-lensed glasses, and small chin. She kept to herself a lot, which he guessed could be weird, especially for a girl. But she'd never struck him as being unhappy or discontented. And if she was happy with herself, wasn't that what mattered?

"*Nee*," he said, shaking his head. "*Yer* not *seltsam.*"

"I'm pretty sure *Mamm* thinks I am. She doesn't understand why I don't like to *geh* to singings, or that I'd rather have *mei* head in an astronomy book than a cookbook." She gave him a sideways glance. "I can cook, by the way."

He wasn't sure why she told him that, but the astronomy part got his attention. "You like the stars?"

"I love them." She angled herself toward him again. "My telescope isn't very strong and I can't see very far, but I've learned a lot from books. It's amazing what God has created—billions of stars and planets and nebulas and quarks and—"

"Quarks?"

"They're particles of matter. Scientists haven't directly observed them, but theoretically they exist."

He was right. Emily wasn't dumb. She was outright smart. "And you like studying about these things?"

"*Ya*." She glanced at her lap again. "I thought about going to college once and becoming an astronomer."

"What changed *yer* mind?"

"I couldn't leave *mei* faith. I realized I could enjoy astronomy as a hobby and teach myself what I wanted to know. I've never regretted *mei* decision."

"Must be nice to be that sure of *yerself*." When she gave him an odd look, he added, "I'm serious. It took me a while to figure out whether I wanted to join the church or not. I didn't even have anything else pulling at me. I'm happy working with *mei daed* and brother-in-law. I believe in our faith and follow the Ordnung."

"Then what held you back?"

"The permanence of it, I guess." Now it was his turn to stare at the field. "It's a commitment, one I don't take lightly. I wanted to be one hundred percent sure."

"I understand that." She smoothed her dress. "It's the same with marriage. Just because *mei* siblings knew early on who they wanted to marry doesn't mean I have to. When or if I get married, I want to be absolutely sure."

"Exactly." He grinned, glad they had something in common. That would make this thing they were doing, whatever it was, easier.

They ended up talking so long, they were surprised when the sun dipped past the horizon. "Sorry," Reuben said, gathering the reins. "You said you wanted to *geh* home an hour ago."

"It's fine." Emily sighed. "I'll handle *Mamm*."

"Like you did this afternoon?"

"I told you I don't do well under pressure."

He laughed and elbowed her playfully. "I'm kidding." He pulled on the reins to turn the buggy back the way they'd come. "Actually, Emily, I think this is going to work out well for both of us."

By the time Emily arrived home, she was fully relaxed, something she hadn't been since her mother first brought up Wayne. She'd enjoyed her time with Reuben and was relieved he wasn't upset with her. She was also glad she could help him out the way he was helping her. She'd had no idea he was dealing with marriage pressure from his parents too. What she did know was that he liked to date. A lot. Emily thought he was unusual in that respect, since most of her peers tended to date in secret and usually only when they were at least a little serious with each other. But that was his business, not hers.

By the time he pulled up in front of her house, it was dark. "Sorry," he said again. "Do you want me to *geh* inside and run interference?"

She shook her head. "I'll be fine." He really was a nice *mann*. He could have left her out to dry after she lied to her mother, but instead he was helping her. And helping himself. But that didn't diminish the fact that he was doing her a huge favor.

"So what time should I be over for supper tomorrow?"

She lifted a brow. "Supper?"

"*Ya*. I'm sure *yer mamm* will ask again, so we might as well get it over with."

If they were really dating she might have been a little hurt by his cavalier words, but she knew what he meant. "How about six o'clock?"

"Sounds *gut*. Want me to bring anything?"

"Just *yerself*." She smiled and turned to get out of the buggy, then faced him again. "*Danki*, Reuben. I really appreciate this."

She could see his brilliant smile despite the darkness. "See you tomorrow."

Emily watched him drive off, then took in a deep breath. The gas lamp was still on in the living room, even though her parents liked to retire early. She steeled herself and walked into the house.

"*Yer* back so soon?" *Mamm* said. She was perched on the edge of her chair, while Emily's father was napping in the chair opposite her, a seed catalog lying across his lap. "I thought you two would be out for a while."

"We both have work in the morning."

Mamm huffed. "That's *nee* excuse." Then she smiled. "When are you seeing him again?"

"He's coming for supper tomorrow."

Her mother's squeal woke up *Daed*. "What?" he said, the seed catalog hitting the floor as he bolted upright.

"Reuben's coming over for supper tomorrow!" *Mamm* clasped her hands together, her eyes shining.

"Oh." *Daed* yawned. "That's nice. I'm going to bed."

"Andy, how can you sleep at a time like this?"

He glanced at the clock. Then back at his wife. "That's what I do at bedtime." He looked at Emily. "*Gute nacht*."

"Night, *Daed*." Emily couldn't help but smile. She counted herself lucky that her father was so uninterested in her social life.

She couldn't bear it if both her parents were chomping at the bit for her to get married.

"Oh!" *Mamm*'s eyes widened. "What does Reuben like to eat? What's his favorite dessert?"

"Um . . ."

"Surely you know such a common thing about the man *yer* going out with."

"We, uh, haven't talked about food."

"Really?" She lifted a doubtful brow. "But all men like to talk about food."

"Reuben doesn't." At least she hoped he didn't. This drove a point home—they needed to exchange some basic information before supper tomorrow. "*Mamm*, we haven't been dating that long." Two hours to be exact, but she didn't need to know that.

"No bother. I'll make some baked chicken and dumplings," she said. "That's something everyone likes."

"*Danki.*"

"And rhubarb pie. The rhubarb he brought over today looked *appenditlich.*"

Emily stood. "That sounds perfect." She feigned a yawn, taking the opportunity to end the conversation before *Mamm* drilled her any further and she couldn't answer her questions. "I'm heading upstairs to bed."

"*Nee* stargazing tonight?"

She wanted to. It would be another cloudless night and she would see tons of stars. But since she was pretending to be tired, she needed to play it through. "Not tonight."

"All right. Have a *gut* night."

"*Gute nacht, Mamm.*" She started up the stairs.

"Emily?"

"*Ya.*" She paused on the third step.

"Are you happy?"

She saw the hope and sincerity in her mother's eyes, which reminded her that no matter how annoying her mother could be about the marriage topic, she did honestly mean well. "I am. Truly."

Mamm's smile beamed. "I'm so glad. That's all I want for you."

Emily returned her smile, then went upstairs. She changed into her nightgown and kerchief, said her prayers, and slid between cool sheets and a worn, soft quilt. She thought about her mother's question.

She really was happy. She and Reuben got along, which would make dating for appearances easy. She actually looked forward to supper tomorrow night. She enjoyed her job and her hobby and was content in the community. And her mother was pleased, which added to her happiness. Even when she and Reuben eventually "broke up," she would get some kind of respite from the pressure of getting married.

But what made her happiest was that she would never have to see Wayne Jantzi again.

Chapter 3

Reuben found himself looking forward to supper at Emily's. When he told his mother he was going out again, she gave him a stern look. She'd been giving him such looks for years. As usual he ignored it, told his father good-bye, and headed out to get the buggy.

He pulled into Emily's driveway and continued down to the barn. The store was across the driveway from their house and there were several hitching posts there. He wondered if he should park there instead when Andy came out of the barn.

"Evening, Reuben." He wiped his palms across his pants, which no matter the season seemed to have grass and dirt stains on them. He was a man of the land, that was for sure.

Reuben understood that, since he too felt a kinship with the land as a farmer. "*Gut* to see you, Andy."

"You can bring *yer* horse into the barn. I've got to *geh* inside and clean up. Louwanda's picky about that." The older man smiled. "Nice to have you over. Just come through the back door when *yer* done."

Reuben nodded and settled his horse in the barn. He was about to *geh* inside when he heard a shriek coming from the front yard. He ran around the house and saw Emily up in a tall oak tree. She was dangling from a thick branch.

"Emily!"

"Help!"

He ran toward the tree. She wasn't too high up, but high enough that if she let go, she could be injured. He positioned himself under her, his foot landing on a hard object. Assuming it was a rock, he kicked it to the side and held out his arms. "I've got you, Emily."

"You want me to let *geh*?"

When he looked up at her, he noticed she wasn't wearing her glasses. "*Ya*, I want you to let *geh*. I'll catch you."

"What if you don't?" She tightened her grip.

"You want to hang there all day?"

She looked up at the branch, then squinted down at him. "You promise you'll catch me?"

"Emily, I promise."

Closing her eyes, she let go of the branch. When she landed in his arms, the force of her weight caused him to stagger back. She wasn't heavy, but he hadn't been fully prepared for impact. He tripped and fell backward, landing on his backside with Emily on top of him.

"Ooof!"

Reuben tried to catch the breath that had been knocked out of him, but found it difficult with her face so close to his. Without her thick glasses, he could see what her mother was talking about. She had blue eyes that were the clearest he'd ever seen, and long black eyelashes. The bottom ones reached almost to the top of her cheek. Her dark eyebrows were perfectly shaped, her complexion flawless. When she suddenly wrapped her arms around his neck, he couldn't breathe at all.

"*Danki*, Reuben." Her eyes were wide and misty. "I could have broken *mei* neck."

His hands tightened at her waist. "*Yer* . . . welcome." He gazed into her eyes, feeling a tingle in his chest like nothing he'd felt before.

Then she rolled off him and began searching the ground with her hands. "*Mei* glasses. They fell off when I lost my balance on the branch."

He stood and went to help her. She was crouched down and squinting. "Can you see them?"

He looked around and saw the sun glinting off an object a few feet away. As he neared, his stomach dropped. "I think so." He bent down and picked up a pair of broken, thick-lensed glasses. This must have been what he kicked out of the way. The frame was bent and one of the nosepieces was gone. He turned to her.

"I'm sorry."

"For what?" She walked toward him, her nose scrunched as she stumbled along.

Cute. But there was nothing cute about this situation. He held up the glasses. "I accidentally stepped on them when I was under the tree."

She squinted harder as she took the glasses from him. "Oh *nee*," she said, moving them closer to her nose. Then she sighed. "It's *mei* fault. They've been slipping down a lot, and I should have taken them to get readjusted a long time ago. I kept putting it off." She looked up at him. "Don't worry about it."

"I'll pay for them."

"It's okay, really." She smiled. "This will teach me to be more careful with them."

"At least let me take them to get repaired."

"I would need to go with you. They usually take a few measurements when I get new frames."

Even better. He could pay for the new frames, because despite what she said, it was his fault they were broken. Another upside was that they could spend a little more time together. To keep up the ruse. That was the only reason. Now that he was committed to this, he was determined to see it through. "I'll get a taxi and pick you up tomorrow. Unless you need to make an appointment."

"I can walk in for a repair." She looked at the broken glasses in her hand. "Are you sure?"

"Positive."

"All right. I have an extra pair inside that I use for emergencies." She turned toward the house.

He followed. "What were you doing in the tree?"

"Trying to get him down." She turned and pointed to one of the branches. A small cat, a little larger than a kitten, sat there calmly washing his paw.

"He seems fine," Reuben said. "He'll come down on his own."

"I felt so bad for him. He's a stray, and he's come around here a few times. When I saw him up in the tree meowing . . . I couldn't leave him stuck up there."

Suddenly the cat raced down the tree. As if knowing Emily was his would-be rescuer, he rubbed against her leg. She knelt and squinted at him. "Don't you do that again."

"Uh, *yer* talking to his tail."

"Oh. Right." She stood. "I'm sure he heard me." She walked toward the house and slowly made her way up the porch steps.

Reuben chuckled as he followed her. He had no idea she was so visually impaired. The thick glasses were a clue, but she really couldn't see anything. When they entered the living room, she said, "I'll be right back." She touched the back of the couch, then grabbed the banister, fumbling a bit as she went up the stairs.

Delicious smells came from the kitchen. Emily came downstairs a few moments later, and Reuben was stunned. This pair of glasses was in almost worse shape than the ones that were broken. The middle piece was taped together, and only half a frame surrounded one of the lenses. He had no idea how it was holding the lens in place. "Can you wear those?"

"Temporarily. They're not *mei* prescription anymore, so things are a little blurry. But at least I can see enough to get around." She frowned. "I look stupid, don't I?"

"*Nee.*" He reached out and touched the thick piece of tape covering the nosepiece. "You look fine."

"You don't have to tell a fib."

"I'm not." She did look fine. Once he was used to the glasses, he could see past the lenses to those beautiful eyes. He remembered how he had gazed into them, and his heart started racing.

"I'm sure *Mamm* has supper ready." She headed for the kitchen.

He paused, willing his heartbeat to slow. He'd never felt like this around any of the girls he dated. And he wasn't even dating Emily, but his pulse thrummed. What was going on here?

Emily had been embarrassed plenty of times in her life. Being a klutz and wearing thick glasses tended to cause more than her fair share of humiliation. But her face had never been so hot as when she was lying on top of Reuben. She never should have climbed up that tree. But thankfully he had been there to break her fall, or she might be sitting in the emergency room right now.

But it wasn't just thankfulness she was feeling. Something else had gone through her when she was so close to him. She'd had no idea he had a small freckle underneath his left eye, or that his irises were a mix of brown, green, and gold. His arms were strong, and being that close, she could see the dark stubble on his chin. For some reason, she wanted to touch it. And because of that she sprang up as if her dress had been on fire.

The odd feeling inside still hummed in the background when he'd touched the tape on her extra glasses. Adding to her humiliation, this was the only other pair she had. Her mother wanted her to get rid of them, but Emily was petrified of something happening to her good ones and not having another pair to wear. She was already getting a headache from the blurriness, but this was much better than having to feel and trip her way around the house.

They entered the kitchen as her mother was pulling the rhubarb pie from the oven. She turned, and when she saw them she grinned. But her smile disappeared as her gaze landed on Emily. She set down the pie, took off her oven mitts, and walked over to her. "Why are you wearing those?" she said in a loud whisper. Her mother had no idea what it meant to be subtle.

"I accidentally broke her other pair."

They both looked at Reuben. Emily didn't blame him at all for breaking her glasses. She'd been putting off getting them adjusted. But she appreciated his reaction—taking her to the eyeglass shop and now taking the blame. He really was a good guy.

The flutter in her heart started again. She placed her palm over it, then realized what she was doing and threw her hands behind her.

"How in the world did that happen?" *Mamm* asked as *Daed* walked into the kitchen. As always before supper, he was showered and dressed in clean clothes.

Emily gave her mother the shortened version of the story while her father and Reuben sat at the table and started talking about growing vegetables.

Mamm shook her head when Emily finished the story. "That could only happen to you, Emily."

Emily shrugged. Her mother was right. She wasn't a walking disaster, but she was close.

She helped bring supper to the table. After prayer, they started to eat. Reuben and her father continued to talk, both having farming and gardening in common. Reuben was telling *Daed* about the success of his sister Sarah's greenhouse.

"The plants are growing really well," he said, then put a bite of chicken and dumplings in his mouth. After he finished eating, he added, "Next month's harvest should be excellent."

"I'm thinking about building another one," *Daed* said.

"Let me know if you need some help."

Emily was surprised by the offer. After their relationship ended, she expected to have minimal contact with Reuben. Things would go back to the way they were before. She knew her father wouldn't start working on the greenhouse until late fall, months after she and Reuben "broke up." She had to hand it to him, he was taking this fake relationship very seriously.

She glanced at her mother, who practically had stars in her eyes. If Emily didn't know better, she would have thought her mother was smitten with him. Then again, who wouldn't be?

After supper, Emily offered to wash the dishes. "Why don't

you and Reuben sit outside? I'll bring dessert," *Mamm* said. "I heard it was supposed to be another clear night."

"From who?" Emily asked.

"Um, you must have mentioned it." She moved behind Reuben and Emily and started shooing them out the back door. "I'll bring *yer* pie and *kaffee* out in a minute."

Emily looked at Reuben when they were on the patio. "Sorry," she said.

"For what?" He looked down at her and smiled.

"*Mei mamm*'s a little too eager to leave us alone."

"I know a few girls who would love for their mothers to do that."

"Really?"

Reuben's smile turned into a confused frown. "Obviously *yer mamm* trusts us."

"Why wouldn't she?"

He sat on one of the patio chairs. "I don't have the most trustworthy reputation when it comes to *maed*."

She sat in the chair next to him. "Because you date so much?"

Reuben nodded and leaned back. "Can't blame people for drawing conclusions."

"Well, they shouldn't. That's not fair to you or the *maed* you *geh* out with."

"Sometimes the rumors are started by those *maed*. Can't blame them for that either." He looked down at the concrete patio floor. "Some of them are pretty mad at me."

"Still, starting rumors isn't the right thing to do." She knew that all too well.

"Neither is leading girls on."

She stared at him for a moment. It was still too early for

twilight, and contrary to her mother's statement, it wasn't supposed to be a clear night. Already the clouds were gathering into one solid cover. There would be no stargazing tonight. In the fading sunlight, she could see the troubled look on Reuben's face. Regret. A feeling she, too, knew very well.

The back door opened and her mother appeared, carrying a tray. Reuben popped up to take it from her, which led to another beaming smile. "How kind of you," *Mamm* said, handing it to him. He set it on the patio table between their chairs.

"If you need anything else let me know. I'll be right inside." *Mamm* hurried back into the house.

Emily got up to serve the pie and coffee to Reuben, but he waved her off and handed her a steaming mug.

"The pie looks delicious," he said, handing her a piece. "Is this from today's delivery?"

She nodded and sat back down. A cow lowed in the distance. "*Mamm* makes excellent pie. I've tried to duplicate her crust, but I can't get it right."

He sat and pushed his fork into the large piece of pie. Juice ran from the fruit between flaky layers of crust. He took a bite and swallowed. "*Yer* right. Best pie I've ever had."

They ate in silence, but it was a nice silence. Emily gazed up at the sky, wishing they could see the stars tonight. She would love to show Reuben the different constellations, the location of the North Star, and maybe, if they were lucky, a shooting star. She'd only seen one and would love to share that moment with Reuben.

Wait. She put her hand over her heart again.

"You okay?" Reuben put his fork down.

She nodded quickly and shoved the rest of her pie in her mouth.

"*Gut*," she said through a mouthful, then grimaced. "Sorry. That was rude."

He chuckled. "You've got some pie on the corner of *yer* mouth."

Of course she did. She wiped it away. "Did I get it?"

"*Ya*." He picked up his mug and took a sip. "What time do you want to go to town tomorrow?"

She thought for a moment. "Early afternoon would be best." She paused. "You really don't have to *geh*."

"So you've said."

"I don't want you to *geh* to any trouble, or to take you away from work."

He took another drink of his coffee, then set the mug on the table. "I don't mind a little escape from work every now and then, especially in the summer." He glanced up at the sky. "Too bad it's cloudy. I was hoping you could show me your telescope." He locked his gaze on her. "We'll do that next time."

Next time. A shiver coursed through her. Oh *nee*. She was in trouble. She wasn't experienced at all in the dating department, but she knew what she was feeling for Reuben right now. Attraction. Surprising attraction. She leaned over. "You don't have to be so nice. I'm sure *Mamm* isn't spying on us."

He looked surprised. "I wasn't being nice because I have to. I really do want to see *yer* telescope. I've never looked through one."

"Oh." Now she felt stupid. Confused, stupid, and unfortunately, still attracted. "I'm sure you have to get back home," she said, bolting from her chair.

"Not really—"

But as he spoke she stepped backward, bumped into the

chair, and started to fall. Before she hit the ground he caught her—again.

But instead of letting go the way he normally did, he held on to her. "We seem to be finding ourselves like this a lot lately."

Her eyes widened as he pulled her upright, and kept his arm around her waist. "Because I'm so clumsy," she said, her voice sounding breathy.

"I don't mind clumsy." Reuben gazed at her intently.

The back door opened and they broke apart. This time it was *Daed*, not *Mamm*, who came outside, holding a large roll of paper. He moved the coffee cups and pie plates to the side. "I thought you and *yer* sister might want to look at this," he said, unrolling the paper and putting it on the patio table. "It's *mei* plans for *mei* new greenhouse."

Reuben quickly moved to the table and started looking at the plans. "Nice," he said. "This is pretty big."

"I'll probably scale it back. This is just a rough sketch."

Emily took a step back and smoothed her dress, not that either man was paying attention to her. Which was good, because right now she could barely get her wits about her. Even though she knew Reuben was being nice and keeping her from falling—again—she couldn't help but wonder if he felt the same sharp jolt she had when she was in his arms. Her face heating, she slipped back into the house, leaving Reuben and her father to talk about the greenhouse.

"Where's Reuben?" *Mamm* asked. She was seated at the kitchen table, writing a letter. She wrote weekly to Emily's two sisters and three sisters-in-law back in Shipshewana.

"Outside with *Daed*. They're discussing greenhouse plans."

"For goodness' sake." She put down the pencil and stood. "*Yer vatter* can be so thick at times."

"It's okay. Reuben was ready to *geh* home anyway." At least she thought he was. He'd have to be, especially since he'd kept her from landing on her behind more than once today. Her cheeks heated.

Mamm sat back down, mollified. "Well, you'll see him tomorrow anyway. If you need the day off, you can have it."

"Just the afternoon." She pushed on her glasses, even though they weren't slipping, then remembered the big hunk of tape in the middle of them. Not to mention the half of a frame, plus another bit of tape on the side. She groaned inwardly. How could she possibly think Reuben would be attracted to her when she looked like this? When she was even more of a klutz around him than normal?

She had to remember they were pretending. A stab of guilt passed through her. She looked at her mother, who was writing again. She didn't like lying to her or her father. But it was better than the alternative—Wayne Jantzi.

She also had to remember that Reuben didn't take commitments lightly. After his confession about waiting to join the church, it made sense to her that he would be fully invested in playing the role of dutiful boyfriend. Reuben wasn't a man to do things halfway. Any feelings she thought were between them were due to him playing his role to the hilt—and nothing else.

CHAPTER 4

It took all of Reuben's concentration to focus on what Andy was saying. He liked the man, but he could drone on about his garden, herbs, and now, the greenhouse. Normally he'd be interested in those things, but his mind was somewhere else. Reuben nodded and glanced over his shoulder. Emily had gone inside. He hid a frown. He'd wanted to say good-bye to her at least. But she'd been so eager for him to leave that he didn't dare go back inside.

That bothered him. He was a decent-looking guy and a decent-acting guy. Nothing really special. But he was available, and that was the most likely reason why he had so much female attention. But not from Emily. When he'd held her in his arms after her second near-fall of the day, he hadn't wanted to let her go.

Which puzzled and unnerved him—two more things he wasn't used to feeling.

Andy rolled up the plans. "Feel free to keep them as long as you want."

Reuben glanced at the house again, positive Emily wasn't going to come out. She could at least say good-bye the way most people would. But when it came to Emily Schwartz, Reuben was realizing she wasn't like most people.

He headed home, the plans next to him on the seat in the buggy, still thinking about Emily. He smiled as he thought about her taped-up glasses. His smile widened as he remembered her beautiful blue eyes. Then he thought about the cat in the tree. Of course she would take a risk to rescue it. That was the kind of woman Emily was.

Despite all her great qualities, it didn't mean he wanted to take their relationship any further. They were fulfilling a purpose for each other, and it was a temporary one. When Emily returned from her family reunion, they would stage their breakup and go back to the way things were.

Satisfied he had set his thoughts back on the right track, he put his horse up in the barn, then went inside. His mother was in the living room, working on a crossword puzzle. "Hi," she said, taking off her reading glasses as he walked into the room. "Did you have a nice time tonight?"

"I did." He set the rolled paper on the coffee table. "That's for *Daed* and Sarah. Andy said they could look at his plans for a second greenhouse if they wanted to."

"How nice of him."

Reuben nodded as he started up the stairs.

"He'd make a *gut* father-in-law for you," *Mamm* said.

Reuben almost tripped. "Father-in-law?"

"*Ya.*" She put her reading glasses back on. "Or are you planning to break her heart like you've broken the others?"

He went back down the stairs. "I haven't broken anyone's heart."

"*Nee?* What about Lora Yutzy? Her mother said she was upset for weeks when you didn't ask her out a second time."

"Her mother shouldn't be gossiping," he muttered.

"And maybe you haven't literally broken hearts, but you have left hurt feelings in your wake." She looked down at the puzzle book in her lap.

"I . . ." He couldn't respond because it was true. He'd never really thought about how the girls felt. He'd moved on and he expected them to as well. It was only one date for most of them, although he did go out with Julia Miller twice. Or was it three times? He scowled. How pathetic that he couldn't remember, and they deserved better. They were nice. Friendly. They were all pretty in their own way. But since he felt nothing but friendship for them, there was no reason to keep dating. He was being practical, that's all.

Yet his mother's words started to dig at his conscience. "You're making me out to be a jerk."

She peered up at him over her glasses. "If the shoe fits."

He sat down across from her. "You really think I'm a jerk?"

Mamm removed her glasses again. "*Nee*, Reuben. I don't think that, because I know you. *Yer* a kind, thoughtful, generous *mann*. But that's not the impression you're leaving on these *maed*. And if you think *yer* going to end up dropping Emily like a rock, it might be better if you end things now."

Well, that put a kink in his and Emily's plan. Sometimes his mother surprised him, and he was definitely stunned now. "I'm not going to drop her," he said. At least not yet. And for once it would be mutual. Emily wouldn't be hurt. Neither one of them would be.

She lifted a brow. "It's that serious between you two?"

"Uh, it's gotten a little more serious recently." Very recently.

Mamm smiled and leaned forward, the censure in her eyes

replaced with a spark of excitement. "I'm so happy to hear that. I wasn't sure if you'd ever settle down enough to get married."

"Married? But—"

"And I really like her. Emily is such a nice girl. A little different, but there's nothing wrong with that. She should come over for supper soon."

"Okay." He didn't know what else to say. He couldn't tell his mother the truth. Not only would it ruin Emily's ruse, but *Mamm* would be doubly disappointed in him. As it was, it bothered him that she felt the need to chastise him about his dating habits.

"We'll have two weddings in the near future. How exciting." She set aside the puzzle book.

"Two?" he said weakly.

"*Yers* and Emily's . . ."

Reuben paled. "And who else?" The words sounded like he was speaking with a throat full of peanut butter.

"Sarah's."

"Oh. Right."

She grinned. "She hasn't said anything, but I have a feeling she and Peter will be announcing their engagement soon."

Talk about an unusual couple. His sister Sarah was a beautiful girl, probably the prettiest in the district, and he wasn't being biased. Even his brother-in-law, Judah, had been smitten with her at one time. Then he regained his senses and fell in love with Esther. Sarah, who had the pick of eligible men, had started seeing Peter, a short, stocky guy who definitely wasn't her type. But it was clear to anyone how much they cared for each other.

Reuben's temples thumped. He wasn't used to thinking this hard about relationships, especially when it came to his sisters—or himself. And he had to make something perfectly clear to his mother.

"I'm not going to rush into anything," he said, standing. "You don't have to start planning a wedding for me anytime soon." He started for the staircase again.

"I know. You never do anything without thoroughly thinking about it before committing."

That gave him a moment's pause, then he went upstairs. But instead of getting ready for bed, he walked to his bedroom window and looked outside. The sky had cleared up a little, and there were patches of stars twinkling between layers of clouds.

He leaned his head against the glass. His plan with Emily had seemed so simple, but now felt complicated. And wrong. But what could he do? If he came clean, Emily's mother would send her straight to Wayne, and from the strong reaction she'd had to the man, Reuben knew he couldn't let that happen. Whatever had gone on between them, it was clear she wanted nothing to do with him.

The word *jerk* hung over him like one of the thick clouds in tonight's sky. He'd never thought himself as a jerk. Practical, yes. Realistic? Of course. But a jerk? Had he really hurt the girls' feelings that much, or was his mother being overdramatic, as she tended to be sometimes?

He moved away from the window, undressed, and readied for bed. Before he pulled back his bedclothes, he kneeled on the floor, the urge to ask for forgiveness for his behavior overwhelming him. When he was finished, he got into bed. But it was still a long time before he fell asleep.

True to his word, Reuben picked up Emily in a taxi the following afternoon. They went to her eye doctor and visited the optician, who said the glasses couldn't be fixed.

"You'll have to get a new pair of frames," she said, setting the glasses on the table.

"I'll take the same ones I had before."

"Let me see if we still have them." She went to a display of frames, found the one she was looking for, and picked it up. Meanwhile Reuben was walking around the boutique, looking at all the different frames.

The optician took the frames over to Emily. "Have you given any thought to getting thinner lenses?"

Emily shook her head. "I'm fine with my same ones."

Reuben walked over as the optician said, "Thinner lenses would be more comfortable for you. The frames won't be as heavy."

"They're more expensive, though."

The optician sat at her computer and started typing. After a minute she wrote a number down on a small notepad, tore off the sheet, and handed it to her. "Here's the price."

Emily's eyes widened as she saw the number. She couldn't see spending this amount of money on thinner lenses. Especially when she was saving for something special.

"You also won't have such a coke-bottle effect," the optician added.

"That's okay." Emily handed the paper back to her. "I'll just have *mei* regular lenses."

"All right. Let me get the order started for you." As she typed, Reuben pulled Emily aside.

"Why don't you get the thinner lenses?" he asked.

"Because it seems frivolous to spend so much money when I can have a cheaper pair."

"But they would be more comfortable."

She looked up at him. Why would he care about her comfort? Yet he seemed sincere. "I can't," she said in a low voice.

"Why not?"

"Because," she said, turning her back to the optician, "I'm saving money for a new telescope."

"Oh."

"I need to take some measurements," the optician said.

Emily sat across from her, and after the measurements the order was complete. It would take two weeks for the new glasses to arrive, since her prescription was so strong. "Can I do a little repair on your current glasses?" the optician said.

Emily had forgotten about the unfortunate extra pair of glasses. She nodded and handed them to her, then sat back down, since she couldn't see anything.

"Look at this," Reuben said, handing her a flyer.

She brought it close to her face so she could read it. "A show at the planetarium?" she said, squinting as she looked at him.

"Would you like to *geh*?"

She continued to look at Reuben, unable to see his face clearly. Everything was a blur around her. "But it's at five o'clock."

"*Ya.*"

"The taxi will be here to pick us up soon."

"I can arrange for another ride."

His persistence surprised her. "You don't have any plans tonight?"

He shook his head. "I'm kind of interested in seeing this myself."

That surprised her too. She had no idea he was interested in astronomy. Her stomach fluttered as the optician came back. She put on the repaired glasses and looked in the mirror, suddenly self-conscious.

"Is something wrong?" the optician asked.

Emily scrutinized herself in the small mirror. Her glasses looked old and worn, but at least the tape was gone. "No, they're fine." And they were. It wasn't like she had much of a choice anyway. She was more confused by the fact that it even bothered her.

She turned to the optician. "Thank you for fixing them."

"You're most welcome. You can check out up front."

After they finished and walked outside, Reuben said, "Well? Do you want to *geh*?"

"*Ya*," she said, her excitement at seeing a planetarium show overtaking her sudden shyness. "I do."

"Great." They took a few steps away from the store before Reuben abruptly stopped. "Hold on," he said, lifting one hand. Then he hurried back inside the optometrist's office.

Emily figured he was borrowing their phone to arrange another ride. She leaned against the building and watched several cars go by. After about fifteen minutes she started pacing in front of the store. It shouldn't have taken him that long to schedule a taxi. Just as she was about to go inside and see what was keeping him, he came out of the store.

"Sorry. That took longer than I thought."

"Is Terry picking us up later tonight?"

His brow furrowed. "Huh?" Then he blinked and nodded. "Um, *ya*. She said she'd come back and pick us up from the show around six thirty."

"That's nice of her. I hope she didn't mind the extra trouble."

"She said she didn't." Another car whizzed past them.

"The show doesn't start for a couple hours," Emily said. "What do you want to do in the meantime?"

"We can grab a bite to eat. There's a restaurant nearby I like. Bixby's Café."

"I've never been there."

"They have great chili." He paused. "If you like chili, that is."

"I do."

As they walked toward Bixby's, which was a couple blocks away, they fell into easy conversation. She found out his favorite foods, favorite color, and other basic information. She would be well prepared if her mother asked her any more of these simple questions about him. In turn, she told him how much she liked French fries, hot dogs, and apple pie.

"How American of you," he said with a wink.

She grinned. "I'm pretty simple."

He halted, his expression growing serious. "I wouldn't say that about you." He tilted his head. "I wouldn't say that at all."

Before she could question him he started walking again. What did he mean by that? She was a simple woman, especially when it came to food. She hurried to catch up with him, and they didn't say anything when he opened the door to Bixby's for her.

The café was small but busy. There was an empty booth in the back of the restaurant, and she followed him to it. When they sat, a waitress with short purple and black hair immediately appeared. "Hi, Reuben," she said, setting down two glasses of water. "Haven't seen you here lately."

"Been busy with the farm."

"And with someone else, I see." She gave Emily a knowing smile and handed her a menu from underneath her arm. "Today's lunch special is a chicken bacon wrap with fries. I assume you'll have a bowl of chili?" she asked Reuben.

"*Ya.*"

Emily looked at him. He was subdued, something she'd never experienced. She glanced at the waitress again. She seemed nice, if a bit colorful. But Emily got the sense that Reuben was now uncomfortable, and she wasn't sure why. "I'll have a bowl of chili too," she said, trying to break the tension. "I hear it's really *gut.*"

"It's one of our best sellers. Anything to drink?" She scribbled their order on a pad.

"Milk for me," Emily said.

"I'll take an iced tea."

The waitress picked up the menus. "I'll be back in a jiff."

After she left, Reuben said, "Sorry about that."

"About what?" Emily took a sip of water.

"What Carly said. About me being busy with someone else."

Wait, were Reuben's cheeks turning red? "I didn't think anything about it."

He let out a long breath. "That's *gut.*" But when he leaned back in the booth, he was still frowning. Then he looked at her. "Do you think I'm a jerk?"

Emily's eyebrows flew up. "What? Who called you a jerk?"

"Believe it or not, *mei mamm.* Well, she didn't call me a jerk, but she might as well have." He rubbed the back of his neck. "I think she might be right."

"She's definitely not right." Emily crossed her arms. "Why would she say something like that?"

"Um, well . . ." He rubbed his neck again. "She wanted to be sure I didn't break your heart."

"Why would you do that?"

"Because we're dating? Because apparently that's what I do to the *maed* I date."

"Oh." She ran her finger along the edge of the red table. She didn't have experience dating, or even understanding how to date. But she did know all about a broken heart. Which made her think of Wayne. And thinking of Wayne threatened to spoil what was turning into a lovely day, so she shoved him out of her thoughts.

"Then it's a *gut* thing we're not dating," she said, smiling. "*Nee* need to worry about *mei* heart."

"Right."

Carly appeared with their drinks and chili. They bowed their heads in silent prayer, then started to eat. After a few spoonfuls she said, "*Yer* right. This is *gut*."

"Not as *gut* as *mei mamm*'s, but close." He took a sip of his tea. "Glad you like it."

While they ate they made more small talk, but in the back of her mind Emily couldn't stop thinking about what Reuben had said. And this time instead of Wayne popping up in her mind, Deborah Yoder did. *Stay away from Reuben.* Emily hadn't even known the two of them went out. She didn't pay much attention to everyone else's social life, and she had only gone to a couple of singings over the past few years, something her mother wasn't happy about. "How are you going to find a husband if you don't even look?" she'd said. And Emily had given her mother her standard answer. God would provide. She knew that in her heart.

Yet despite Deborah's warning—and Reuben's mother's own concerns—Emily didn't see Reuben as a jerk. A jerk wouldn't have saved her from the embarrassment of lying to her parents. He would have let her twist in the wind if that were the case.

"Emily?"

She blinked, his voice bringing her out of her thoughts. Her gaze landed on the freckle above his cheekbone, then moved to his multicolored eyes. Handsome eyes, like the rest of him. But good-looking didn't mean well-mannered or kind, and Reuben was all of those. The flutter she'd felt in the optician's office reappeared.

"Uh, *ya?*"

"You went quiet all of the sudden. Anything wrong?"

She shook her head and scraped the last bit of chili out of the bowl. Without answering him she put it in her mouth, then took a drink of milk. "Done," she said, pushing the bowl away.

He tilted his head, something she noticed he was doing lately when he looked at her. Then he glanced at her empty bowl. "Do you want seconds?"

"*Nee*, but I do want dessert."

"Two apple pies, coming up."

By the time they were finished with their meal, they had thirty minutes to get to the planetarium. As they walked outside, Emily said, "We should find a phone and get a taxi to take us to the show."

"Already done. The taxi will be here in a few minutes."

Emily was impressed that he'd thought of everything. "You're definitely not a jerk," she said softly.

"Others would disagree." He looked down at the ground and kicked a small stone on the sidewalk.

"Reuben." She took a step forward, forgetting she had no idea how to properly act around a man, that they were supposed to be dating even though she was clueless about relationships. All she was focused on was him. "Look at me."

He lifted his head, and she could see the disappointment in his eyes. He was being hard on himself for no reason.

"You're not a jerk." She locked her eyes on his. "You're the nicest man I've ever known."

CHAPTER 5

When they arrived at the planetarium, Emily thought she had made a mistake. After she tried to reassure him, the taxi had pulled up. He hadn't said a word, or even looked at her, on the ride over. When they got out of the car, he paid the driver and went to the ticket counter, still quiet. She rushed her steps to catch up with him. Had she said something wrong? Had she been too close to him when she spoke? She must have done something.

Reuben pulled out his wallet. "Two tickets," he said.

"I can pay for mine."

"I've got it."

"But you paid for lunch."

He finally turned to her. Instead of the irritation she was sure he was feeling, he gave her a smile that hit clear to her toes. Then he leaned forward and said in a low voice, "This is what I do when I'm on a date."

She watched him purchase the tickets, a bit stunned by his words and even more stunned by her reaction to them. A date? But they weren't on a date. Even if they were pretending to be on a date, it wasn't a real date. By the time she'd traveled that confusing train of thought, he was gesturing for her to go with him into the planetarium.

When they entered the dim auditorium, a different type of excitement filled her. She'd been here a few times but it never failed to inspire her. They found their seats just as the room darkened and the planetarium lit up with the show. She saw images of stars, planets, nebulas, all to a classical soundtrack that thrilled her. But she knew even something as awe-inspiring as this only barely scratched the surface of the amazing universe God had created.

At one point she shifted in her chair and put her hand on the armrest. It touched Reuben's arm, also lying there. When she started to pull away, he slipped his hand into hers and held on to it.

Her breath caught and she glanced at him. He kept his eyes on the show, his profile illuminated by bright and twinkling stars on the ceiling above them. His hand was large, callused from farmwork, and warm. Her pulse felt rapid. Somehow a trip to the optometrist had turned into a date—one that felt very real to her.

She leaned back against the chair and tried to focus on the show. But how could she do that when Reuben was holding her hand? Surely he'd let it go any time now. But he held on until the lights in the planetarium turned back on.

They walked out of the building and waited on the sidewalk for their ride home. Reuben was staring at the sky, which was still full of evening summer light, obscuring even the brightest stars. His hands were in his pockets now, and he was acting as if nothing had happened in the planetarium.

Emily frowned. She didn't imagine him holding her hand for a good part of the show. But why would he do that, then act like he hadn't?

"The North Star is right about there, isn't it?" He pointed at the sky.

She moved to stand next to him. He was off by a few inches. She was about to tell him, but on instinct she reached up and moved his arm to the correct position. "There. That's the North Star. Too bad you can't see it."

He looked down at her. They weren't alone, as people were still filing out of the building. The show hadn't been full, but it was closing and everyone was leaving. He dropped his arm and looked at her with enough intensity that she felt a shiver down her spine. "What happened between you and Wayne?" Then he shook his head. "Never mind. It's not *mei* business." Then he looked over her shoulder. "Taxi's here."

She followed him to the small sedan that would take them home. He sat in the front next to the driver while she sat in back. She was glad for it, since Reuben made small talk with the driver and she was left to process what had happened at the planetarium. It was all so confusing. She'd never held hands with a boy—or a man, for that matter. And Reuben wasn't just any man. He was a friend, who was pretending to be her boyfriend for a short period of time. He was helping her out, and that's what friends did. She hadn't even minded him asking her about Wayne, and she would have told him about it if the taxi hadn't arrived.

But she wasn't so naïve that she didn't know the feelings she was developing for him were anything but friendly. Which was definitely unexpected—and definitely a problem.

The rest of the week Reuben focused on his job and tried not to think about Emily. But that was hard today, especially after the time they'd spent together in town. When the taxi dropped her off at her house, she had barely looked at him before hurrying inside. Then again, he should have expected that. He had held her hand without her permission after all.

He slammed his hoe into the ground. He was cultivating a row of beans, something he could do in his sleep. Unfortunately, that gave him plenty of time to kick himself for holding her hand. He still wasn't sure why he'd done it, only that when she had lightly brushed against him, it was like his hand had a will of its own. But that wasn't exactly true. He knew exactly what he was doing. He just couldn't stop himself—because he didn't want to.

She had a soft, delicate hand, and it fit nicely in his. He'd really enjoyed himself during the planetarium show. Emily's enthusiasm for astronomy was infectious, and he'd learned a lot. There was only one thing he didn't understand—his unexpected feelings for Emily.

Then again, how could he not feel something for her after her gentle reassurance that he wasn't a jerk? The sincerity and warmth he'd seen in her eyes, even behind those thick lenses, had jarred him. And touched him. And confused him more than anything else had in his life.

"Need a drink?"

He stopped his hoe and looked at Judah, who was holding out a jug of water. Reuben took it, flipped off the lid, and took a big swig. It was Friday, and by now Judah had usually gone back to the home he and Esther shared a mile down the road. "Didn't realize you were still here," he said, capping the jug and handing it back.

"I'll be leaving in a minute." He took the jug from Reuben. "After we have a little talk."

"What about?" Reuben leaned on his hoe.

"Is something going on with you?" Judah tilted his head.

Reuben blanched. "What makes you think so?"

"Well, you almost put a nail in your hand the other day when we were repairing the cow's fence. And you forgot to make a delivery to that English produce stand out on Route 608. That's not typical of you."

He gripped his hoe. "Everything's fine. Just have a lot on *mei* mind."

"Like?"

Reuben knew his brother-in-law was concerned, but that didn't mean he had a reason to pry into Reuben's business. "Just . . . stuff."

"A *maedel*, possibly?"

Reuben slammed the hoe into the ground again, barely missing his toe. "*Nee*," he said. "I don't know why you'd say that."

"Because usually it's a girl that makes a man's mind slip. I know it was when I fell for your sister."

"Well," Reuben said, tackling the ground again and making sure his foot was well out of the way, "I'm not you."

Judah didn't say anything for a moment. Then he said, "Esther wants you to come over for supper tomorrow night."

Reuben didn't respond. He'd planned to stop by the store and maybe wrangle a supper invitation from Emily tomorrow. "I'm busy. We can do it another time."

"She'll be disappointed. It's been a while since you've seen each other, other than at church." Then he added, "You can bring yer *maedel* if you want."

Reuben was about to deny it again, but he changed his mind. Hadn't he promised to commit fully to their ruse? And just because he was confused about his feelings didn't mean he could go back on his word to Emily.

"All right," he said. "We'll be there."

Judah grinned. "I knew it. Who is it? Esther will be dying to know."

"Emily Schwartz."

"Really?" He rubbed his chin. "That's a surprise."

"Why? Because she's got thick glasses? And she's klutzy? And she has a fascination with stars and planets?"

Judah took a step back. "What do stars and planets have to do with anything?"

He blew out a breath. "Never mind. Do you want me and Emily to come over or not?"

"We do, we do." He shook his head. "You don't have to be so touchy about it. We eat around six thirty."

"Fine. See you then."

After Judah left, Reuben stopped hoeing. He wiped the sweat off his forehead and frowned. He had been overly defensive about Emily to Judah—because he had thought those things about her in the past. He really was a shallow jerk, despite what she thought.

He knocked off a little early, showered and changed, then hitched up the buggy and went to Emily's. She was locking up the store when he pulled up. "Hi," she said, giving him a shy smile.

His heart skipped a beat as he climbed out of the buggy. "Hi." He smiled in return. He couldn't help it, seeing those dimples in her cheeks.

"What brings you by?" she asked.

We're supposed to be dating. He paused. He was getting too caught up in the ruse. That had to be the reason he was having these feelings, and why he hadn't been able to let go of her hand in the planetarium. And the feelings weren't real because the relationship wasn't real.

"Reuben?" She pushed up her glasses.

"My sister Esther invited us over for supper tomorrow. At six thirty."

"Oh. How nice. Should I bring anything?"

He shook his head. "Knowing her she'll have more than enough. She's a great cook. Sarah, on the other hand, not so much. So I'll pick you up at five thirty?"

"It takes an hour to get to Esther's?"

It didn't, but he had planned to drive the buggy extra slow. He needed to get to know Emily better—for the purposes of their fake relationship only. What better way than to spend an hour in the buggy together? But he couldn't tell her all that.

"Um—"

"Emily, would you mind bringing in a couple tomatoes from the greenhouse?"

They both turned as Louwanda came out of the house. Great. He wasn't in the frame of mind to deal with her right now.

"Oh hello, Reuben." Louwanda gave Emily a knowing smile. "I didn't realize we were having company. Are you staying for supper?"

Reuben didn't miss Emily's scowl in return. "*Nee*," she said quickly. "He just dropped by to, uh, tell me something."

"But we have plenty of beef stew."

Reuben found himself hoping Emily would extend the invitation. When the awkward silence continued, he realized she wasn't going to. "I have to get home," he said, backing away a few steps. "I just came to invite Emily to *mei* sister's tomorrow evening."

Louwanda's expression brightened enough to rival the morning sunlight. "That sounds nice. Very nice."

Good grief, he had to get out of here. "I'll see you tomorrow, Emily."

"*Ya*, tomorrow."

Reuben climbed into his buggy and pulled out of the Schwartzes' driveway. On his way home he frowned. Why didn't Emily want him to stay for supper? It was a prime opportunity to cement their false relationship in her mother's mind. Now he wondered if she really wanted to go with him to Esther's, or if she was just being polite.

He shouldn't have held her hand at the planetarium. That had been a mistake. He wasn't used to making mistakes when it came to dating, and dating Emily—even pretend dating Emily—was new territory for him.

But he couldn't deny that a small part of him wished it were real.

Emily stirred the beef stew around in her bowl. She should have invited Reuben to stay for supper. She'd wanted him to stay. Which was why she didn't ask him to.

"Emily?" *Mamm* looked at her. "Is there something wrong with the stew?"

She shook her head and took a small bite. Her mother made delicious beef stew, but Emily couldn't enjoy it. She felt like she was drowning in guilt and confusion. She didn't like lying to her mother, and she didn't like the attraction she felt for Reuben.

Well, she liked it, but it also made everything worse. How was she going to get out of this? It wasn't as if he was interested in her beyond their agreement. She hadn't seen him all week until today, and her mother had been dropping subtle questions, and some not so subtle, about his whereabouts.

Now she knew for sure the reason he held her hand was to keep up appearances. That was all. They hadn't known anyone at the planetarium, and it had been so dark inside, no one would have seen them. But she knew enough about Reuben now, and when he committed, he committed completely.

No, Reuben wouldn't break her heart. She was allowing that to happen all on her own.

She choked down her stew and cleaned the kitchen after supper, telling her mother to go relax in the living room. After she finished cleaning, she went outside. But instead of looking at the sky in anticipation of nightfall, she sat down on one of the patio chairs and wrung her hands. She couldn't *geh* on like this. Even if it meant her mother would go back to setting her up with Wayne.

Tomorrow, she would make everything right.

Something didn't sit well with Reuben when he went to pick up Emily. Actually, nothing was right about this. It had been nagging at him ever since they decided to pretend to date. Even though they had started off with good intentions, the deception was wrong. Tonight they would have to pretend to be dating even though they weren't—and even though he wanted to. It was growing more complicated by the day, and he was getting more and more uncomfortable with the lying.

In his mind there was only one way to fix this—take the chance and ask Emily to date for real. He came up with the answer in the middle of the night when he gave up trying to sleep. Then he went back and forth about the wisdom of the decision. What if she said no? He'd never been worried about being rejected before.

The door opened as soon as he hit the front porch. Emily stepped outside and closed the door behind her. He noticed she was barefoot. "Hi," she said, looking at her feet.

A knot of dread formed in his stomach. "Ready to *geh*?" he said, knowing full well she wasn't.

She shook her head. "Reuben, we need to talk."

CHAPTER 6

Emily's throat felt like it was stuffed with cotton. Why did Reuben have to look so handsome right now? His short-sleeve blue shirt brought out the color in his eyes, and he wasn't wearing his hat. His brown hair was neatly combed, and so thick she wanted to run her fingers through it. But she never would, and it was time to face reality.

"I'm sorry for dragging you into *mei* mess," she said, clasping her fingers together.

"You didn't drag me into it. I offered to help, remember?"

She nodded. How could she forget the day he'd suddenly become so important to her? And now she realized it wasn't because he'd saved her from endless matchmaking and the humiliation of a lie. He was important because of who he was. A kind, smart, caring man who didn't deserve to deal with Emily's deception.

She squeezed her eyes shut. She had to stay focused. She opened her eyes and said, "I'm not going with you to Esther's. I'm going to tell *mei* parents the truth."

His mouth dropped open. "Why?"

"Because it's the right thing to do—for all of us." She felt tears forming in her eyes. "I'm so ashamed," she whispered. "I never should have started all this."

"Emily—"

She looked up at him. "*Danki* for everything you've done. And I promise I'll tell *mei* parents this was all *mei* doing. They won't blame you for anything."

"What about Wayne? You know *yer mamm* is going to *geh* back to her matchmaking ways."

"And I'll have to handle that." She let out a bitter chuckle. "I guess that's *mei* fault for not being firm with her. And I have to face Wayne sooner or later. I can't avoid him for the rest of *mei* life, especially when I go back to see *mei* family at the reunion in Shipshe." She looked at Reuben again, her heart aching. "You don't have to pretend anymore." She turned around and went into the house.

I'm not pretending.

Reuben stood on the porch, dumbfounded. He'd been prepared—at least sort of prepared—to tell Emily his real feelings. And then she dumped him. Not technically of course, but the hurt was genuine. He had half a mind to go inside the house and convince her not to say anything to her parents. That he would fix everything by dating her for real.

But obviously she didn't want that. She was ready to face her mother's meddling and go to the reunion and see Wayne. Wait, was that what happened? Had she changed her mind about Wayne? She never told him what happened between them. Had they been dating and Louwanda didn't know it?

Jealousy twisted inside him, along with anger. Fine. If that's how she wanted it, that's how it would be. It wasn't like he couldn't find someone else to date. It wasn't like there weren't other women out there in Middlefield.

But none of them were like her.

"Hi, Reuben."

He turned to see Andy walking toward him. The man was never in a hurry, always calm with a ready smile. Reuben gave him a short nod, then collected himself and met him at the bottom of the porch steps. He didn't need to let on that he'd just been rejected by the man's daughter before he'd even had a chance to tell her the truth.

"Louwanda said you and Emily were going to Esther's for supper tonight."

"We were." Reuben shrugged, trying to seem casual, when inside he felt anything but. "Seems she changed her mind."

"Oh? I'm surprised."

"You're not the only one," Reuben muttered.

"Well, whatever's going on I hope you two work it out. I tend to stay out of *mei kinners'* business, unlike Louwanda, even though she means well. But I have to agree with her when she says you two make a *gut* pair." He clapped Reuben on the shoulder. "See you soon."

Reuben made his way to the buggy as he heard the front door of the Schwartzes' house shut. Even Andy thought he and Emily were a good idea. Emily was the only one who didn't.

He clenched his teeth as he drove home. The mix of pain and hurt squeezed his heart. So this was what it felt like. Had the girls he'd disappointed gone through the same thing? If so, this was the least of what he deserved.

"You what?"

Emily bit the inside of her lip as her mother's eyes grew stormy. She pressed her palms flat on the kitchen table and looked at her father, who was drumming his fingers on his leg, a sure sign he was upset. And there was nothing she could do but take her lumps.

"I lied about Reuben and me. We're not dating."

"But you went out on a buggy ride." *Mamm's* voice raised. "He came over for supper. He invited you to his sister's house, for goodness' sake!"

"I know." Emily curled her fingers into her palms. "And I'm sorry. He was helping me." She told her parents about Reuben being in the store and overhearing her and her mother's conversation about Wayne. "When we went on the buggy ride, we decided to keep up the ruse."

"The lie, you mean," *Mamm* huffed.

"*Ya*. The lie."

"Why would he agree to do that?" *Daed* asked, his voice quiet.

"Because he's also been getting pressure from his mother to marry."

"So this is all *mei* fault?" *Mamm* shook her head. "Don't blame me for your deception."

"I'm not—"

"Because all I want is for you to be happy."

"Is it?" *Daed* turned to her. "Or do you want the bragging rights of all *yer kinner* being married?"

"Bragging rights?" *Mamm* put her hand to her chest. "I don't know what *yer* talking about."

Daed pushed away from the table. "I'm going for a walk. You know what you need to do, Louwanda." He left the kitchen and went outside.

"Andrew Schwartz, get back here . . ." *Mamm* turned to Emily, glaring.

This was unexpected. She hadn't thought her parents would get into a fight over this. In fact, her parents rarely fought, especially since she and her siblings were grown now.

"I'm sorry," she said, her voice squeaking. "I didn't mean to upset you and *Daed*."

"But you did." *Mamm* kept her eyes on Emily until Emily thought she would wilt. Then without warning *Mamm*'s shoulders slumped.

"Oh, Emily. I'm so sorry." She put her head in her hands. "*Yer daed* is right. This is *mei* fault."

"*Nee, Mamm*. I'm the one who lied."

"But I'm the one who pushed you to it." She lifted her head and looked at Emily, her eyes shiny with tears. "I really do want *yer* happiness, but I'm afraid all I've done is make you miserable."

She thought about the time she'd spent with Reuben. She had been anything but miserable. She touched her *mamm*'s hand. "It's okay."

"*Nee*, it's not. I've been meddling and I shouldn't have. *Yer daed* warned me, but I wouldn't listen." She clasped Emily's hand. "I'm listening now. What's going on between you and Wayne Jantzi?"

Emily breathed out a long sigh. "*Nix, Mamm*."

"Then why don't you want to see him? You've gone to great lengths to avoid him."

"Because I'm embarrassed." She pulled away from her mother.

"I used to like him, when we were in school. And after we were in school. I always hoped we would be married someday, even though he's rarely said more than a few words to me. And then . . ." She turned away.

"What?" *Mamm* asked gently.

"I decided to take matters into *mei* own hands. I asked him on a date when we were both seventeen. In hindsight I should have waited until he was alone and not eating lunch at Pamela's Pantry with his brother and their friends."

Mamm cringed. "He said *nee*?"

"Not only that, he laughed at me. Said he wouldn't date me if I was the last woman in Shipshe." She sighed. "They all laughed at that one."

"I don't see why. That's not even a clever response."

Emily chuckled. Now that she was talking about it— something she had never done, with anyone—the whole thing seemed immature. But she'd nursed that hurt all these years. Wayne had been the only boy for her growing up. He was popular, handsome, and he had seemed nice, until that day. In many ways, he was like Reuben.

But Reuben was nothing like him. Her heart pinched.

"If I had known all that, I never would have mentioned it to his mother in the first place."

"That's the one thing I didn't understand," Emily said. "I know Wayne wasn't interested in me, so why did he change his mind?"

"Uh . . ." *Mamm*'s face turned red. "As far as I know, he hasn't."

"What?"

"I was hoping I'd never have to tell you this." She wiped her hand across the side of her *kapp*, but didn't look at Emily. "I might have fudged a bit about Wayne."

"Fudged?"

"I mean lied. I thought if you went back to Shipshe, I could find a way to get you two together. Wayne's mother had a family recipe for banana pudding that I wanted to make for the reunion, so I wrote her and asked for the recipe. I casually mentioned that you were still single, and wondered what Wayne was up to. When Susanna sent me the recipe, she casually mentioned that Wayne was single too."

"Does Wayne know about this?" Emily asked, her stomach twisting in a fresh knot of embarrassment.

"*Nee, nee.* As soon as you said you and Reuben were dating, I wrote her back and told her you had found someone."

Emily leaned back in the chair. "Thank you, Lord."

"Can you forgive me?" *Mamm*'s eyes were filled with pleading. "I know I did a terrible thing."

"So did I." Emily leaned forward. "Can you forgive me too?"

"Of course." *Mamm* took Emily's hand and squeezed it. "This calls for some raspberry pie, don't you think?"

"Any time is *gut* for raspberry pie."

As she was finishing up her last bite, complete with fresh whipped cream, *Mamm* asked, "So there really isn't anything between you and Reuben?"

"*Mamm!*" She sighed. "I thought you were through meddling."

"I am, I am. It's just that *yer daed* and I both thought you made a *gut* couple."

"Even *Daed*?"

"*Yer daed* isn't as oblivious as he pretends to be." She pressed her fork on the last tiny bit of crust on her plate, then put down the fork. "Never mind. Don't answer that question. I won't pry or meddle anymore."

"Promise?"

"Promise. You're trusting God with *yer* future. It's time I did too. Now, it's almost dark. I'll get these dishes. Why don't you go and do that stargazing you love so much?"

Emily bounced up from the chair and went to give her mother a kiss on the cheek. "I love you," she said.

"Love you too."

A short while later Emily was on the back patio, her telescope pointed at the stars. But she couldn't concentrate on the night sky. Her mother's question kept nagging at her. If things had been different, could she and Reuben date for real? It was pointless to think about it. She'd learned her lesson from pining for Wayne Jantzi. She wasn't about to spend another minute wishing for Reuben Coblentz.

But that didn't mean she was over him either.

CHAPTER 7

Emily looked at all the tables set out for the family reunion. The day was nice for it. She'd arrived with her parents two days earlier by taxi. They'd closed the store until they returned to Middlefield Tuesday.

She hadn't spoken to Reuben since that day on her front porch. She'd seen him at church, but they avoided each other. She hoped that with a little time the ache in her heart would disappear, but if anything, it had grown stronger when she'd seen him. Yet she refused to behave the way she had with Wayne. She wouldn't wish for something that could never be.

Spending some time away from Middlefield would help. It had been nice to see her siblings again, and she realized how much she missed them, and how ridiculous she'd been to let her past keep her from coming home.

She spent the next hour visiting with family—her brothers and sisters, aunts and uncles, and too many cousins to count. She was about to join some of her younger cousins in a game of volleyball when she felt a tap on her shoulder. She turned around, and her jaw dropped.

"Wayne," she said. "What are you doing here?"

He shifted on his feet. He was still handsome, with dark-black hair, nearly black eyes, broad shoulders, and a dimple in his cheek. She expected to feel the familiar pounding of her pulse she always felt when she was around him. Instead, she felt . . . nothing.

"I, uh . . ." He grimaced.

Now he was acting odd, not the confident young man she remembered. "Is something wrong?"

"Could we talk?" He glanced around Emily's grandparents' large yard where all her relatives were either eating or playing games. "Somewhere a little more private?"

She gestured to the large tree in the back corner of the yard. A tire swing hung from one of the huge branches. When they were standing under the tree, he turned to her. "I'm sorry," he blurted. "I was a big jerk to you before you left Shipshe. I never should have acted that way toward you back then."

His confession surprised her, and made her smile. "It's okay." And it was. She was over him, over the girlhood pain he and his friends had caused.

"*Nee*, it's not. When I heard you were coming back for the Schwartz reunion, I knew I needed to see you. I had to make things right."

"*Danki*," she said. "I appreciate it."

"So *yer* not mad?"

Emily chuckled. "Not at all."

Relief crossed his face. "You've always been a nice *maedel*," he said. Then he looked at her. "Do you want to get a cup of *kaffee* sometime while *yer* here?"

"*Nee*," someone said from behind her. "She doesn't."

She turned at the sound of Reuben's voice. For the second time her mouth dropped open.

"Sorry I'm late. The driver who brought me got hung up in

traffic. Next time we'll come together. No more of this separate ride business."

Wayne looked at him, his gaze narrowing. "And you are?"

"A friend," Emily said.

"Her boyfriend," Reuben said at the same time.

Wayne's gaze darted between them. "Never mind about the *kaffee*, Emily." He gave her a lopsided grin. "I'm glad things are okay between us."

"Me too."

After Wayne left, Reuben moved to stand in front of her. "What was that all about?"

"That was Wayne."

"I got that." He took a step toward her. "What did he mean by things being *gut* between you?"

If she didn't know better, she would have thought Reuben was jealous. But that wasn't possible. "He apologized."

"For what?"

She gave him a shortened version of the conversation, along with an even shorter version of her former crush. "Now that I've answered *yer* questions, it's *yer* turn to answer mine. Why are you here?"

For the first time she could remember, she saw Reuben Coblentz look uncertain. "Because . . . because . . ."

"Emily!" her cousin Fannie called. "Are you playing volleyball or not?"

"In a minute." She turned to Reuben. "My parents are sitting at the far end of that table over there." She pointed across the yard. "I'm sure they'd like to see you. Help yourself to the food. We have plenty." Emily started to walk across the yard toward the volleyball net.

"Emily . . . wait."

She stilled at the warmth in his voice, the gentle urgency of his fingers on her shoulder.

"What?" she said softly as she looked up at him. When her eyes met his, her pulse sped up like it never had before.

"Let's make it real." He took a step toward her.

"Make what real?"

"You. Me." He smiled. "Us."

"But we don't have to. *Mamm* said she's going to stop interfering, and there's *nix* between me and Wayne." Which was true. But none of that explained the hitch in her breath as Reuben took another step closer.

Then he took her hand. "Come with me."

She was too stunned to say no as he led her behind the tree, well out of the view of any watchful eyes. When he let go of her hand, his fingers lingered on hers before he drew away. "It's time for me to come clean, Emily. When we started this, I was just trying to help you—and myself, of course. I've always been selfish that way."

"*Yer* not selfish—"

He held up his hand. "*Ya*, I am. And despite what you said, I'm a jerk. At least I have been to the *maed* I've dated. But that ends. Now."

Her heart did a backflip. "You like me?"

Reuben nodded. "*Ya*, Emily. I definitely like you. I came all the way to Shipshewana to tell you that. And to ask you if you'd like to *geh* out with me when you get back to Middlefield." He paused, his expression growing serious. "I'm finished with breaking hearts. *Yers* is the only one I want."

His words reached into her soul. "Really?" she asked, her

trembling voice nearly swept away by the warm afternoon breeze.

He chuckled. "Are you just going to stand there and ask me questions?"

"What—"

His lips met hers in a gentle, quick kiss. "You were saying?"

She pressed her lips together, savoring the moment. Then she smiled, completely at peace. She knew she could trust this man with her heart and her future. Reuben Coblentz never committed to anything unless he was absolutely sure. *God will provide*. And it looked like he had, in the most unexpected way.

"*Nix*," she said. "I wasn't going to say anything. Except *ya*. I will *geh* out with you when we return home."

"Exactly what I was hoping for." Reuben grinned. "We better get back before we're missed."

She gave his hand a squeeze. "I wouldn't mind if we were."

A week later a car pulled in the driveway of her parents' home. Reuben had stayed in Shipshewana overnight with her older brother and his family before returning to Middlefield, much to her mother's delight. "I knew there was something real between you two," *Mamm* had said. "I'm rarely wrong about these things."

"*Yer* always wrong about those things," her father said.

"Well, this time I'm right, and that's what counts."

Now the taxi was here to take her to pick up her new glasses. Reuben opened the passenger door, stepped outside, and called to her. "Ready to *geh*?"

She nodded and got in the car. A short while later they were inside the optometrist's office. "Hi, Ms. Schwartz," the optician said. "The glasses just arrived yesterday. I'll go in the back and get them."

When she returned and handed Emily the glasses, Emily frowned. "I don't think these are right," she said.

"They are," the optician said with a confident nod. "Try them on."

She slid on the light frames and looked around. Everything was crystal clear. "Wow," she said, amazed.

"How do they feel?"

"Great!" They were so light on the bridge of her nose that it would take a little while to get used to them. "Why do they feel so different?"

"We used the thinner lenses."

Confused, Emily said, "But I only paid for the regular ones."

The optician leaned forward. "*Yer* young *mann* made up the difference."

She looked at Reuben, who was whistling on the other side of the room trying to pretend he wasn't listening. She went to him and batted him lightly on the arm. "Why did you do this?"

He looked down at her, his eyes turning a little smoky. "Those glasses definitely suit you."

"I can't take them," she said, slipping them off.

He took them out of her hand and put them back on her face. "*Ya*, you can. Now you'll be more comfortable and you'll still get *yer* telescope." He leaned forward. "And if you say another word about it, I'll kiss you right here in front of everyone."

He hadn't kissed her since they left Shipshewana, and she was almost tempted to call his bluff, if there hadn't been so many people around. She gave him a playful grimace and went back to the optician. "I'll take them."

After they left the store, Reuben took her to the planetarium. "Another surprise?" she said, pleased.

He leaned and whispered in her ear. "Where else can I hold *yer* hand in the dark while we get to watch a fantastic light show?"

And as soon as they were seated and the lights dimmed, Reuben made good on his words.

A Gift for Anne Marie

CHAPTER 1

A nne Marie Smucker pulled back the light-blue curtains and peered outside into the darkness. On her rural street, the only available light was the tall streetlamp a few houses down. She tapped her fingers against the window frame and squinted. *Where is he?* Her best friend Nathaniel was never late for game night.

She let the curtains fall and breathed in the scent of wintergreen and cinnamon. The spirit of the holiday was in the air. Her mother had started decorating for the season—placing pine boughs, cinnamon sticks tied with winter-white ribbon, and dried orange slices in a small arrangement on an end table near the front window in the living room. Like all her decorating, she kept it simple, yet lovely.

A few minutes later she went into the kitchen. Her mother stood by the stove, peeling off the foil from a pie plate. "What's that?" Anne Marie asked.

"A new pumpkin pie recipe I tried yesterday. I'm hoping it

will be *gut* enough for this year's Christmas cookbook." Her mother looked at her. "Would you like to try some?"

Anne Marie frowned. "Pumpkin? *Nee.*"

"I thought you liked pumpkin."

"That must be your other *dochder.*"

"I only have one *dochder,* and she's handful enough."

Anne Marie chuckled as she moved closer to her mother and peeked at the pie. Flawless, as usual, with a golden, high-edged crust. It looked appetizing—to someone who liked pumpkin.

Mamm picked up a knife and sliced a small wedge. She put the piece on a nearby saucer. "Nathaniel's not here yet?"

"Nee." She frowned.

She heard a light tapping sound on the window of the back door. She turned and saw her friend Ruth Troyer waving a mitten-covered hand.

Anne Marie opened the door and let Ruth inside. "This is a surprise."

Ruth smiled, the tip of her nose red from the cold air. "I hope you don't mind me dropping by for a minute." She looked at Anne Marie's mother. *"Frau* Smucker."

"Hallo, Ruth. Would you like a piece of pie?" *Mamm* asked.

"Nee. I just need to speak with Anne Marie for a minute." Ruth came closer to her and leaned in, her honey-colored eyes wide with curiosity. "Is Nathaniel here?"

Anne Marie shook her head. "He's a little late tonight."

Ruth let out a breath. *"Gut."* She lowered her voice. "Is there somewhere we can talk?"

"We can *geh* into the living room."

Once they entered the room, Ruth walked to the coffee table where Anne Marie had laid out the Scrabble board and tiles. "I see you're ready for your game night." She looked at Anne Marie. "I wish you'd come to the singing with me and Hannah tonight. You used to like them."

"I did when I was younger. I don't really see a reason to *geh* anymore."

Ruth frowned. "Because you're busy with Nathaniel?"

It seemed like the temperature in the room dropped twenty degrees. Anne Marie blinked. "Is something wrong, Ruth?"

Her friend paused. "Not really. It's just . . ." Ruth clasped her hands together, her mittens making a soft clapping sound as they met. "I need your help."

"Of course."

"But I need to know something first."

Anne Marie nodded. "What's that?"

"Are you and Nathaniel together?"

That was the last thing she expected Ruth to say. "What? Of course not."

Ruth blew out a breath. "*Gut.* Then you can help me get Nathaniel's attention."

"Attention? Why?"

Ruth cocked her head and rolled her eyes. "I have to explain it to you?"

Anne Marie paused. Then her eyes widened. "You like Nathaniel?"

She rolled her eyes. "You're just as oblivious as he is."

"What?"

Ruth put her hands on the back of the chair near the coffee table. "I don't know what to do to get him to notice me. I've dropped so many hints on him the past couple of weeks, I'm surprised he doesn't have a headache. I even asked him to tonight's singing. But then he reminded me about Sunday game night, which *of course* he couldn't miss."

Was that a touch of bitterness in Ruth's tone? "I didn't know you felt that way about him," Anne Marie said.

"Now you do. So, will you help me?"

Anne Marie turned up the damper on the woodstove in the corner of the room. "I'm not sure what I can do."

"You can give us your blessing."

She whirled around, confused. "Ruth, I'm not Nathaniel's keeper. He's free to court anyone he wants to."

Ruth dug her hands into her coat pockets. "You know how shy he is, so if you'll just give him a nudge in *mei* direction. A small one. Then I'll take care of the rest." Before Anne Marie could respond, Ruth added, "I have to *geh* or Hannah will have a fit." She touched Anne Marie on the arm. *"Danki."*

"You're wel—"

But Ruth had disappeared before the words left Anne Marie's mouth.

She stood there in the living room, feeling the warmth of the woodstove and looking at the Scrabble board, trying to absorb what her friend had told her. Ruth liked Nathaniel. She hadn't seen that coming. She also hadn't thought her friend would be so forward about it. And she wouldn't consider Nathaniel shy. Reserved, sometimes. But not shy. As she walked back to the kitchen, she tried to picture Ruth and Nathaniel as a couple. But she couldn't see him with Ruth. She thought about other young women in the district. Who would she pair up with Nathaniel? For some reason, she couldn't imagine him with anyone.

"Ruth blew out of here in a hurry." *Mamm* wiped down the

counter to the left of the white cast-iron sink. "Is everything all right?"

"*Ya.* I guess."

Mamm lifted a questioning brow. "What does that mean?"

"Sorry I'm late." Nathaniel appeared in the kitchen doorway. "Jonah let me in." He'd already removed his jacket and hat, his thick, dark-brown hair popping up in hanks all over his head. He tried smoothing it down, but it was no use. He'd always had trouble taming his hair. When they were sixteen he had come over to help her spread sawdust on the floor of the barn. Before they started, he'd tripped into the huge pile. She remembered how the small chips of wood and dust had stuck in his hair, how she'd run her fingers through the thick strands to help him get it out . . .

"Something smells *gut.*" He lifted his nose as he stepped into the kitchen.

Anne Marie shook her head, clearing her mind of the memory, and the tingly sensation suddenly coursing through her.

"What are you making, Lydia?" Nathaniel asked.

"Pumpkin pie." *Mamm* cast a sharp look at Anne Marie. "Keep your comments to yourself."

Anne Marie held up her palms. "I wasn't going to say a word."

"Are there samples?" Nathaniel asked.

"Of course." Her mother cut another slice. "I'm glad *someone* appreciates my cooking."

"Now that's not fair," Anne Marie said. "You know I like everything you make. Everything that doesn't contain pumpkin, that is. Plus, your cookbooks are in such high demand, we can barely keep up production. Clearly, many people in Paradise love your recipes." She moved away from the counter. "That reminds me, I can help you bind the rest of the cookbooks and fill the Christmas orders. It's just a couple weeks away."

"I think you have enough to do with your candle orders," *Mamm* said.

"I can handle both."

"Always thinking about work." *Mamm* shook her head. "We have time." She looked at Nathaniel, then at Anne Marie. "Now *geh* play your game."

When they entered the living room, he moved one of the chairs closer to the coffee table and sat down. He leaned over and started selecting tiles. But Anne Marie's mind wasn't on Scrabble. She was still thinking about Ruth's request. How should she tell him that Ruth liked him? Just blurt it out? Hint at it? She had no idea what Ruth meant by nudging Nathaniel in her direction. She'd never played matchmaker before.

He glanced up. "You going to sit down?"

She looked at him. Saw the competitive gleam in his eye. Ruth could wait—they had a game to play. She grinned and sat down.

He wiggled his dark brows. "Ready to lose?"

"Um, *nee*. When was the last time you beat me at Scrabble?"

"A month ago."

"I let you win."

He smiled and clasped his hands behind his head. "Keep telling yourself that."

Determined to prove him wrong, they began to play . . . and she forgot all about Ruth.

Nearly two hours later, the game was almost tied. Nathaniel didn't know how she did it. But with stealthy play and a lot of thought—sometimes so much thought he had to prod her to take her turn—she'd racked up the points. She twisted the end of one of her *kapp* strings as she surveyed the board. Her thin finger traced a line across the top of one of her tiles leaning against the holder, her blond eyebrows forming a *V* above her pale-blue eyes. He tapped his foot, glancing at the clock hanging on the wall. "Anytime now."

"Don't rush me. I'm thinking."

"Think a little faster. I have to get home."

"Ready for more pie?" Nathaniel looked up to see Lydia walk into the living room carrying a tray with one piece of pie and two glasses of tea. Anne Marie took a glass. She sipped, her attention still on the board. Nathaniel accepted the pie and tea. *"Danki."* He took a huge bite, the taste of cinnamon and pumpkin exploding in his mouth. There was a good reason Lydia Smucker's holiday cookbooks sold out every year right before Christmas. He scooped a smaller portion with his fork and held it out to Anne Marie. "Sure you don't want a little taste?"

She smirked at his offering. *"Ya.* I'm sure."

"You don't know what you're missing." He waved it in front of her. "It's the best pumpkin pie I've ever had."

"That's kind of you to say, Nathaniel," Lydia said.

He moved his fork closer to Anne Marie. "I know why you won't try this."

She folded her arms. "Why?"

"Because you're afraid you might like it. Then you'll have to admit you were wrong."

"Fine." She grabbed the fork and stuck the tip of her tongue to the pie. She closed her mouth and smacked her lips. "I tasted it. I still don't like it."

"More for me, then." He finished off the bite, looking up at Lydia. He paused at her puzzled look, the fork still in his mouth. "What?"

Anne Marie's mother looked at him, then at her daughter. "*Nix*. Just . . . *nix*." She turned and left the room.

"What was that about?" Nathaniel asked after he polished off the bite.

Anne Marie shrugged, still focused on the game board. With a swift movement she grabbed the rest of the tiles on her stand and placed them on the board. *T A S T Y.* She gave him a triumphant smile.

"More like ironic." He set down the empty dish. "Congratulations. You won."

Her smile widened, the tiny scar at the corner of her mouth disappearing. He remembered the day she'd gotten it. They were both seven, and he'd pushed her a little too hard in the swing at school. She face planted on the ground and the ragged edge of a stone had sliced her lip. Thirteen years later, he still felt bad about it.

After cleaning up the game, he and Anne Marie walked to his buggy. "Same time next week?" He grabbed the horse's reins. "Although I'm picking the game this time."

"Life on the Farm?"

"Of course." He unwrapped the reins from the hitching post underneath the barn awning and took the blanket off his horse. He folded it and tossed it in the buggy.

"Before you *geh* . . ." She moved nearer, rubbing her arms through the thin long sleeves of her dress. "I have something to tell you."

"Okay." He faced her.

"Um . . ." She looked away.

Nathaniel frowned. "Is something wrong?" She had never been hesitant to talk to him before.

"*Nee.*" She faced him again, drawing in a breath. "Ruth Troyer likes you." The words flew out of her mouth like a caged bird being set free.

He leaned against the buggy, his cheeks heating against his will. Ruth was one of the prettiest girls in their district, but he had never thought about her romantically.

"Well?" Anne Marie drew her arms closer to her chest.

"Well what?"

"What are you going to do about it?"

"I don't know. Give me a minute to think."

"You should probably ask her out." Her eyes narrowed in the faint yellow light from the lamppost down the street.

He didn't respond. He'd gone out with a couple of *maed* in the past two years. Yet he wouldn't have called the dates successful. More like awkward. And forgettable.

"Don't be so gun-shy." Anne Marie rubbed his horse's nose.

"Don't be so bossy."

She glanced at him. "Sorry." She faced him. "Nathaniel, if you don't ask her out, you'll never know if you're well suited. Maybe ask her to next week's singing."

"What about our game night?"

"We can miss it for one week. Especially for a *gut* reason."

Nathaniel climbed into the buggy. "I'll think about it." He looked at her. "Why are you so eager for me and Ruth to *geh* out?"

She took a step back and looked at the ground. "Because . . ."

"Because?"

She finally met his gaze. "I just think you two would be a *gut* couple. That's all." She turned and hurried toward her house.

"*Gut nacht*," he called after her.

She gave him a half wave and ran inside, like she couldn't get away from him fast enough.

Huh. He frowned, wondering why she was acting strange all of a sudden. Things were fine all evening until she brought up Ruth. Was something else going on? Maybe, but knowing Anne Marie he'd have to pry it out of her. Or wait until she was ready to tell him.

He tapped on the horse's flank with the reins and headed home, his mind on Anne Marie, not Ruth Troyer.

CHAPTER 2

After Nathaniel drove off, Anne Marie walked into the living room, rubbing her hands together to warm her cold fingers. She'd done her duty where Ruth was concerned. Yet something didn't feel right. Ruth was one of Anne Marie's closest friends. She was kind to everyone, one of the more intelligent people she knew, and of course, extremely pretty. Yet despite all of Ruth's wonderful qualities, one question kept nagging at her.

Was she good enough for Nathaniel?

She snatched up the half-empty tea glasses off the coffee table, feeling guilty for even thinking such a thing. Who was she to judge Ruth? Still, she had to wonder. Nathaniel deserved someone special. Someone who could appreciate his quiet nature, his almost obsessive attention to small details, his ability to make sure everyone around him felt comfortable, his—

"*Yer* boyfriend gone already?" Her younger brother Christopher walked into the room.

Anne Marie grimaced. Fifteen-year-old brothers were a thorn. The tea glasses clanked together in her hand. "That joke is getting old."

"Not as old as you." Christopher laughed and left the room.

Anne Marie sighed. Christopher never missed a chance to

tease her about Nathaniel. At least her other brother, Jonah, left their friendship alone. She entered the empty kitchen. *"Mamm?"* No answer. Odd, since the pie remained uncovered on the counter and her mother never left food sitting out. Anne Marie placed the foil over the pie plate and crimped the edges. Then she started on the dishes. She had just finished washing the last tea glass when her mother scurried into the room.

"Danki for cleaning up, Anne Marie. I meant to do that. I went upstairs for a moment and got distracted." A small smile formed on her mother's face as she grabbed a rag and started wiping down the table.

Anne Marie put the glasses away. "You seem happy tonight. Any particular reason?"

"I'm excited about Christmas," *Mamm* said quickly. She looked at Anne Marie. "Aren't you?"

"I will be once all the candles are made."

Her mother patted her on the shoulder. "I'm so glad you've taken over that part of our business. I just couldn't do both anymore."

"I'm happy to do it. And remember, I can help with the cookbooks too."

Her mother shook out the rag over the sink. "I don't want you to spend all your time working. You need to *geh* out and socialize more."

"I plan to visit *Aenti* Miriam before she has her *boppli*."

Her mother lifted her brow. "Anyone else?"

"If I have time."

"We make time for the people who are important to us."

"Which is why I'm going to visit *Aenti* Miriam." At her mother's sigh, Anne Marie held up her hands. "What?"

"Never mind. *Gut nacht*, Anne Marie."

Anne Marie shrugged and completed the finishing touches in the kitchen before heading to her room. She unpinned her *kapp*, giving one last thought to what her mother said. Lately *Mamm* had been making comments about Anne Marie spending more time with her friends. Anne Marie was satisfied with her life— she loved her candle business, and she saw her friends more than her mother realized. Just because she didn't go to singings or date didn't mean she didn't have a social life, or that she wasn't happy.

Yes, things were fine the way they were.

Anne Marie turned off the battery-powered lamp on her bedside table and snuggled under several thick quilts her aunt Miriam had made over the years. She thanked God for all the blessings in her life before closing her eyes and drifting to sleep.

After what seemed like only seconds later, the door to her room flew open. Her mother rushed to the bed. "Anne Marie! Seth is here."

She sat up, bleary eyed. "What?"

"It's Miriam. She's having the *boppli*."

"But it's early yet—"

"Get dressed. We must hurry."

Anne Marie scrambled out of bed, the sense of peace she'd felt before falling asleep replaced by alarm over her aunt going into early labor. She said a short, heartfelt prayer for her *aenti* Miriam's safety, and for the health of the unborn child.

Anne Marie bit at her nails as she paced the length of Miriam and Seth's small living room. Her mother had taken their son, Seth Junior, back to their house. Anne Marie thought it a wise decision. She flinched as Miriam's screams pierced the air.

She glanced at *Onkel* Seth standing by the window. He leaned against his cane. He and her aunt were only a few years older than she was. His handsome face and strong body bore the scars of a reckless youth. Now he was a responsible *mann* and father who deeply loved his family.

"Miriam will be all right," she said, crossing the room to stand next to him. She looked outside the window at the pink-and-lavender-tinged clouds streaking across the horizon, signaling the rising sun.

Another scream. Seth's knuckles turned white. "It wasn't this bad with Junior," he whispered. "I feel so helpless."

She grabbed his hand. "Then let's pray for God's help."

They both stood in front of the window, holding hands, each of them saying their own silent prayer for Miriam. When Miriam screamed again, Seth gripped Anne Marie's hand. She winced. As his wife's cries subsided, he loosened his grip.

"Sorry." He pulled out of her grasp.

"It's okay." She put her hand behind her and flexed her sore fingers.

At the sound of a newborn's cry, they both turned around. Seth's shoulders slumped. "Thank God."

A few moments later, Nathaniel's mother, Mary, entered the living room, a huge smile on her face. A midwife for years, Mary had delivered Seth and Miriam's son. "A girl, Seth. You have a *maedel*."

"Can I . . . ?" He glanced at Anne Marie. "I mean, we, *geh* see her?"

Mary nodded, her smile widening. "*Ya*. She's beautiful, Seth. Both *mudder* and *boppli*."

Anne Marie followed Seth into the bedroom. Her aunt Miriam was propped up in bed with several pillows behind her, her hair still damp from the strain of childbirth. She smiled wearily.

Seth hobbled to the bed and sat next to her. He brushed back a lock of Miriam's hair and glanced down at the newborn. "She's amazing," he murmured. "And *schee*." He looked back at Miriam, gazing into her eyes. "Just like her *mudder*."

Anne Marie swallowed. For years her aunt had been insecure about her appearance, which was considered plain, even among a plain people. Yet Seth never hesitated to tell her how pretty she was.

Miriam and Seth looked at their new daughter. She was perfect, with fair skin and a dusting of dark hair on top of her head.

"We should let them be," Mary whispered to Anne Marie.

Anne Marie nodded and they both slipped quietly from the room.

In the living room, Mary sat down on the hickory rocker near the window, her plump hips wedged between the chair's curved arms. At the same time, Anne Marie's mother walked through the front door.

"*Gut* timing," Anne Marie said.

"Then she's had the *boppli*?"

"*Ya*," Anne Marie said. "A beautiful girl."

Mamm knelt next to two-year-old Junior and removed his tiny jacket. "Let's meet *yer* new *schwester*."

The little boy nodded, letting *Mamm* take his hand.

Golden sunlight streamed through the front window. Anne Marie pulled the shade halfway. "Looks like a pretty *daag*."

"Which is needed after such a long night." Mary took a white handkerchief out of her apron pocket and dabbed her broad forehead. "But Miriam handled it well." She sighed, smiling at Anne Marie. "The women in *yer familye* have little trouble birthing *boppli*. Which is fortunate for you. Whenever you have *kinner*, that is."

Anne Marie glanced away. Mary never hesitated to speak plainly or, in some instances, boldly.

"Miriam and the *kinn* are doing fine," *Maam* said as she walked into the room. "And of course, Seth is relieved."

"He has a wonderful little *familye*." Mary rocked in the chair, scrutinizing Anne Marie. "I've spent years helping women have *boppli*. I wonder when I'll help *mei* future daughter-in-law have one of her own?" She turned to *Mamm*. "It's in the Lord's hands, I know. But *mei* Nathaniel isn't getting any younger. Neither is your Anne Marie."

"I'm standing right here," Anne Marie said, a bit irritated.

Both women looked at Anne Marie. Mary leaned forward. "Do you have something to tell us? Maybe about your Sunday evening 'game nights'?"

"What? *Nee.*"

Mary leaned back in the chair and sighed. "Oh. Well, *nee* harm in hoping, is there?"

Anne Marie looked to her mother. She remained silent but had a sly grin on her face. Why wasn't she saying anything? This wasn't the first time Mary had hinted about Anne Marie and Nathaniel dating, and her mother knew that they weren't. She wished she could tell Mary that Nathaniel had an admirer so his mother would leave her alone. But he wouldn't appreciate it. "I think we could all use some *kaffee*," she said, scrambling out of the room before Mary could say anything else.

CHAPTER 3

Nathaniel sat at his bench and repositioned the gas lamp on his worktable, brightening the light and shining it on the watch mechanism he was repairing. As he adjusted the jewels in the pocket watch, he sensed someone looking over his shoulder.

"*Sehr gut*, Nathaniel." His father nodded, peering down at the watch. "That was not an easy repair."

Nathaniel snapped the back on the pocket watch and wound it. He brought it to his ear and listened to the steady ticking. It had been dead when the owner brought it into his father's clock shop earlier last week. "I need to polish it up a bit—"

"Not too much." His father straightened, the tip of his iron-gray beard touching the middle of his barrel chest. "We don't want it too fancy."

Nathaniel nodded. *"Ya."*

Daed clapped him on the shoulder. "You'll make a fine repairman, *mei sohn*. Like your *grossvatter* and *mei grossvatter* before him." He walked back to his desk in the small repair shop.

Nathaniel smiled, looking around at all the clocks on the walls. His favorite was the century-old cuckoo clock from the Black Forest of Germany. The mechanism had been dismantled because, as his father said, it drove him cuckoo. But it was a fine piece of craftsmanship, like so many of the clocks and watches in the shop.

He pulled out a soft cloth and lightly buffed the outside of the pocket watch. He enjoyed working in the shop, repairing the watches, even trying his hand at carving some of the wood casings containing the clocks. He'd been born into this job, and his father had mentioned how thankful he was for it, Nathaniel being his only child. The business would pass on through the family for one more generation at least.

Just before five that evening, he and his father began closing up the workshop. While he was putting all the tools away in their specific compartments in his toolboxes, his father walked up beside him. He took off his glasses and wiped the lenses with his handkerchief. "You were at the Smuckers' the other day, *ya?*"

Nathaniel nodded. "Game night with Anne Marie."

"How did their wood supply look? I know Lydia's got those two *buwe* to help out, but it won't do for them to run out of fuel during the cold months." As a deacon of the church, his father's responsibility was to make sure the widows of the district were taken care of. Lydia and her family had always been self-sufficient, but his father never took his responsibility lightly.

"They have a *gut* pile laid in, enough to last a couple of weeks. I'll help Jonah and Christopher chop more on Friday after work."

"Take that afternoon off. Don't want you chopping wood in the dark." He put his glasses back on. *"Danki, sohn."*

"Glad to do it." He checked the clock on the wall.

"Mamm probably has supper ready. You know how she gets if we're late."

"Last time I checked she was taking a nap. Spent all night delivering Miriam's *boppli.*"

Nathaniel smiled. "That's right. Anne Marie has a new little cousin, Leah. Lydia was finishing up a quilt a couple weeks ago when I was visiting. A gift for the *boppli*."

"That reminds me. Wait here." His father went to the back room. Nathaniel straightened his chair, wondering why a baby quilt would remind his father of anything. A few moments later, he returned carrying a small, old-fashioned clock. He placed it on Nathaniel's workbench.

"What's this?"

"A *familye* heirloom. *Mei* great-grandfather made it. Gave it to his *frau* for a wedding gift, and *mei grossvatter* gave it to *mei grossmutter* when they got engaged. Then she passed it down to me."

Nathaniel picked it up. It was fairly ornate for an Amish piece. The elaborate silver overlay on the corners of the slate-blue box containing the clock had tarnished over the years. "How old is it?"

"A hundred years, at least. It came from Switzerland. Has been in our family a long time."

"Needs some restoring," Nathaniel said.

"I thought you could handle the job."

Nathaniel set the clock down. "Who's it for?"

"You."

"Me?"

"*Yer* mother said it was past time I gave it to you."

Nathaniel looked at the clock again. "It's not that I don't appreciate it, but I don't need a fancy clock like this."

"Eventually you'll give it to someone special. I'd better check on *yer mamm*. Maybe heat up some leftover soup for her so she doesn't have to worry about supper." He left the workshop, a small bell tinkling as the door shut behind him.

Nathaniel looked at the clock again. Picked it up. Ran his fingers over the slate body, the tarnished embellishments. It was a fine clock, and with a little elbow grease, he could make it as beautiful as it originally had been.

He set the clock down, his hand lingering on the smooth case. It would be a great gift for someone . . . someday. But not anytime soon.

That Friday, Anne Marie sat at the kitchen table and cut candle wicking. She measured each strand at nine and a half inches, cut it with sharp scissors, then tied a small metal washer at one end to weight it. These would be used for simple white taper candles, which she would dip this afternoon in her candle workshop behind the house. She had three dozen to make today if she was to stay on track with her Christmas orders.

After she weighted the last wick, she went to the kitchen sink for a glass of water. She looked out the window as she drank. Dried, crunchy, brown leaves, the remnants of fall, swirled around the gravel driveway. Although it was December, it still hadn't snowed yet. But each day snow threatened, bringing with it dense, overcast skies and brittle wind.

Anne Marie watched her mother stroll across the yard, the strings of her white *kapp* flying out behind her as she made her way to the mailbox. *Mamm* pulled out a few pieces of mail. She thumbed through them quickly, then stopped. Pulled one out. And smiled.

Anne Marie set her glass on the counter and watched as *Mamm* pocketed the letter in her dark-blue jacket and headed for the house. At the same time, Nathaniel's buggy pulled into the driveway. He paused next to her mother, who said a few words to him before he drove toward the barn.

The kitchen door creaked open and her mother walked into the room. "Nathaniel stopped by to help the *buwe* chop firewood."

The gesture didn't surprise her. He was always thoughtful. But Anne Marie was more curious about what her mother had in her pocket. "Anything interesting in the mail?" she asked, leaning against the counter.

Mamm dropped a stack of letters on the table. "Just the usual. A couple of bills. Those never seem to stop coming." But instead of frowning, her mother seemed happy. She looked past Anne Marie for a moment before she started to leave. She made a sudden stop at the doorway and turned around. "Anne Marie, could you do me a favor?" *Mamm* reached into her pocket.

Anne Marie leaned forward, dying to know what was in the letter. "Sure."

Her mother pulled out an index card and handed it to her. "This is a new recipe I planned to try today. Would you mind preparing it for me?"

Anne Marie took the card, trying to mask her disappointment. Chicken and corn soup. "I've never made this before."

"It's a simple recipe. I have all the ingredients in the pantry and the stewing hen is in the cooler on the back porch."

"All right, but—"

"*Danki*, Anne Marie." Before she could say anything else, her mother left.

Anne Marie frowned. What did her mother have to do that was so important she couldn't test a recipe? Anne Marie had always helped her mother cook, but she wasn't as skilled in the kitchen, which was why she took over the candlemaking part of the business.

Anne Marie picked up the pile of mail, shuffled through it, and cast it aside. Why had her mother lied to her? Well, not lied, exactly, but she wasn't being completely truthful either. Something was going on . . . something her mother didn't want her to know.

CHAPTER 4

After spending a couple of hours outside with Jonah and Christopher chopping, splitting, and stacking wood, Nathaniel was dripping with sweat, despite the cold temperature. "I think we have enough wood laid to last until next Christmas."

Jonah dropped his stack on top of a neat, towering pile. "We need more. Just to be sure."

"Aw, Jonah. Nathaniel's right," Christopher said. "We got enough."

"I think Jonah's the wise one, Christopher." Nathaniel leaned his axe against the woodpile. "Nothing wrong with laying in a little extra. How about I *geh* inside and get some drinks?"

"I'll *geh* with you." Christopher started toward the house.

Jonah reached out and grabbed his brother by the arm of his jacket. "*Nee*, you're not getting out of work that easy."

Nathaniel headed toward the house, chuckling at Christopher's grumbling. He neared the kitchen, recognizing the scent of chicken and onions stewing. Lydia must be trying a new recipe.

But when he walked in, he saw Anne Marie standing over the stove. She was staring at the pot, absently stirring the contents.

"Anne Marie?" He walked toward her, then tapped her on the shoulder.

She jumped, turning toward him. The wooden spoon flipped out of her hand, hit her forearm, and landed on the floor.

"I'm sorry." Nathaniel grabbed the spoon and set it near the sink. "I didn't mean to startle you."

Anne Marie snatched a dish towel off the counter and wiped the hot food from her arm. "It's all right. I wasn't paying attention."

He watched as a welt formed on her arm. "Here," he said, taking the rag from her and running it under cold water. He pressed it against her arm.

"Really, Nathaniel, I'm okay."

"Just making sure." He pulled the rag away. The redness had calmed. Without thinking, he blew a breath lightly across the burn. He froze, still holding her hand. What made him do that?

Her eyes widened and she pulled away from him. "Uh, see? I'm fine."

She yanked open the drawer and retrieved a clean spoon. "My fault for not paying attention." She focused on stirring what was in the pot. "Did you need something?"

If she could ignore the weird moment between them, he could too. And it really wasn't that strange. He'd tried to cool off the burn, that's all. He forced a casual tone. "I came in to get some water for me and your *bruders.*"

"You know where the glasses are." She glanced at him and smiled.

Now things were back to normal. Relieved, he opened the cabinet door. "I'm surprised to see you cooking," he said, turning on the tap. "Smells *gut.*"

She shrugged. "I suppose. It's a new recipe, so it will probably taste awful."

"Let me try it." He took the spoon and scooped out a small bite of what looked like a thick soup. After he'd tasted it, he said, "Not bad. Needs a little salt."

She grabbed the saltshaker and shook it vigorously. He took it from her. "Not that much."

Anne Marie sighed. "*Mamm* should be making this, not me. But *nee*, she's too busy."

"Doing what?"

"I don't know." She went back to stirring the soup.

Nathaniel knew better than to pry, especially when Anne Marie was in one of her moods. He retrieved two more glasses and filled them with water. "Better get back to chopping."

She didn't respond. He resumed his work, but his thoughts were still on Anne Marie, wondering why she was irritated with her mother.

He had finished stacking another batch of logs when Jonah approached and said, "Nathaniel, can I talk to you for a minute?" Jonah took off his hat and wiped the sweat from his damp bangs. "I wanted you to know how much I appreciate your help with the wood."

"Anytime your *familye* needs something, just let me or *mei daed* know and we'll take care of it."

"I know." Jonah shoved his hat back on his head. "It's just . . ."

"What?"

Jonah looked into the distance. "I'm seventeen, ya know. Christopher is fifteen. We're not *kinner* anymore."

Nathaniel rubbed his cold hands together, seeing where this conversation was going. Jonah had always been serious-minded and mature for his age. "*Yer* doing a *gut* job taking care of *yer familye*, Jonah."

He looked at Nathaniel, his mouth twitching slightly. "You think so?"

"*Ya*. But it doesn't make you any less of a *mann* to accept help." Jonah nodded. "When we need it."

"Right. And I trust you'll let me know if you do."

"I will. I just didn't want you to think we were helpless."

"I've never thought that." He picked up his axe. "But *mei mamm* says many hands make quick work, so let's get this done already."

Jonah nodded, the sharp wind lifting up the ends of his dark-blond hair. "*Danki*. For understanding."

Nathaniel tipped his head in Jonah's direction. He was glad to see him taking responsibility for his mother, sister, and younger brother. But it also proved that he wouldn't need Nathaniel's help as much.

Even as he continued splitting the wood, Nathaniel's thoughts drifted back to Anne Marie. He hadn't thought about it much before, but eventually she'd find a boyfriend and a husband. She was already encouraging him to date Ruth. What would happen when they didn't need each other anymore? It was something he couldn't—and didn't—want to imagine.

An hour later Anne Marie finished making the soup. Her mother was right—it hadn't been that hard to make. The most difficult part had been the most tedious—picking the meat off the chicken bones. She took a taste and thought it was decent, but nowhere near her mother's standard.

She let the soup simmer on the stove so it would still be warm when her mother came home, whenever that would be. She'd left a few minutes ago without an explanation—and without giving Anne Marie a chance to ask her about the pocketed letter.

She looked down at the red mark on her arm. A shiver ran through her as she remembered Nathaniel's gentle breath on the welt. He was being nice, of course. But that didn't keep goose bumps from forming on her skin at the memory.

Anne Marie entered her mother's bedroom looking for some salve to put on the burn. Her bed was neatly made with her grandmother's quilt and one of Aunt Miriam's beautiful lap quilts folded across the end. The faded fabric of the old quilt contrasted with the sharper colors of Miriam's quilt. But both were beautiful.

She went to her mother's side table and opened the drawer. *Mamm* kept everything from adhesive bandages to sewing needles to ink pens in the messy drawer, the only untidy place in their house.

Anne Marie searched through the deep drawer, lifting objects and looking for the small cylinder that held the homemade salve. She spied it in the far back of the drawer. As she moved the random contents aside to reach for the jar, she touched a stack of papers held together with a rubber band. She pulled it out. Letters.

Unable to help herself, she looked at the return address. Thomas Nissley, Walnut Creek, Ohio. Her brow scrunched. As far as she knew, her family didn't know anyone in Walnut Creek.

She should put the letters back. But curiosity won over indecision and she slipped one of the envelopes out of the pack and lifted the already opened seal. She began to read, ignoring her guilt.

"Anne Marie?" Nathaniel walked into the kitchen. He'd left Jonah and Christopher to stack the rest of the firewood before sundown. Before he went home he wanted to check on Anne Marie's arm. It was a small burn, but he couldn't leave without making sure she was okay.

He faced the empty kitchen and looked at the pot of soup on the stove. His stomach rumbled. He fetched a spoon from the drawer and took another taste. Now it was perfect. Even though she always denied it, Anne Marie was just as good of a cook as her mother. "Anne Marie, do you care if I have some more of this soup?" he called out.

She didn't answer. He headed into the living room. Not finding her there, he started walking through the house, calling her name. When he was midway down the hall, he spied a light peeking through the crack at the bottom of Lydia's bedroom door. He frowned. He had seen Anne Marie's mother leave earlier in the day, so why was the light on in her room?

Nathaniel pushed open the door a little farther and saw Anne Marie sitting on the bed, reading a letter. Next to her, more letters were littered on the pastel quilt covering Lydia's bed. The lines on Anne Marie's forehead deepened. "Anne Marie?"

Her head shot up, and he saw the fury in her eyes. She stood, holding out one of the letters in her hand. "How could she do this?" she said, thrusting the letter at Nathaniel.

"Do what?"

She whirled around, her cheeks as red as holly berries. She started to pace. "I can't believe this."

"Anne Marie—"

"It's one thing to keep a secret. I mean, I've kept my fair

share of secrets." She glanced at him. "But to do this?" She held up the letter.

He walked over to her and thought about putting his hand on her shoulder, but quickly changed his mind. "Anne Marie, calm down. It can't be that bad."

"*Ach*, it's bad. *Sehr* bad." She opened the letter. "'My dearest Lydia,'" she read aloud. "'I never thought I would feel this way about a woman again. It gives my heart wings to know you feel the same way.'" She pursed her lips in a sour expression. "Gives his heart wings? What kind of romantic nonsense is that?"

Nathaniel didn't think it was too bad. But he did feel like an intruder.

Anne Marie plopped on the bed, her shoulders slumping. "She's been writing to him for months. Apparently she's in love with him." She looked up. "Oh, and he's coming for Christmas. When was she going to tell us? When he landed on our doorstep? 'Oh, by the way, this is Thomas, my secret beau that I didn't bother telling anyone about. Merry Christmas!'"

Nathaniel bit his lip to keep from chuckling. Anne Marie in a snit was entertaining. But he didn't want her anger directed at him. He cleared his throat and sat down next to her. "I'm sure your mother had her reasons for not telling you."

"They better be *gut* ones."

"What's going on here?"

Nathaniel froze at the sound of Lydia's sharp voice. He glanced at her standing in the doorway, her nostrils flaring much in the same way Anne Marie's had moments ago.

Lydia crossed her arms over her chest. "What are you two doing in my bedroom?"

CHAPTER 5

Anne Marie jumped from the bed and faced her mother. "Don't be upset with him. He was only checking on me."

Her mother uncrossed her arms, lowering them to her sides. "Nathaniel, I think you should leave."

Nathaniel rose. He glanced at Anne Marie, concern in his eyes. She looked away. He slipped out the door, not saying anything to either of them.

Lydia shut the door behind him. She looked at the letters on the bed. "I see you've been snooping."

"I wasn't snoop—"

"Don't lie." Lydia scooped up the letters.

"I was looking for salve for my burn—the one I got making your recipe, by the way." She lifted her chin. She sounded childish, but she didn't care.

Lydia folded the letters carefully and began putting them in the envelopes. "How did the soup turn out?"

"Soup? Don't you think we have something more important to talk about?"

Her mom turned to Anne Marie, her eyes starting to blaze. "I'm trying not to lose my temper. I'm very disappointed in you."

"Disappointed in me? You're the one keeping secrets."

She averted her eyes. "I was going to tell you and the *buwe* about Thomas."

"Before or after the wedding?"

Lydia froze, keeping her gaze from Anne Marie.

Dread pooled inside Anne Marie. "*Nee* . . . you're not . . ."

Her mother sat down on the bed. She moved the letters to the side and patted the empty space beside her. "Anne Marie, sit down."

"I'm fine standing."

Lydia sighed. "All right. As I said, I was waiting until the time was right. You've been busy with your candlemaking, and I've been trying to get things ready for the cookbook."

It sounded like a list of excuses to Anne Marie. "Who is Thomas?"

"He's a *mann* I knew from my childhood. He used to live in Paradise. When he was twelve, he moved to Walnut Creek. Like me, he married and had children, although now they are grown and have their own families. He's lived alone for several years."

Anne Marie refused to feel sorry for him. But she couldn't help but soften her stance a little. "How did you start talking to him again?"

"He came to Paradise six months ago, to visit his *bruder's familye*. I was delivering some soaps and candles, and when I saw him . . ." Her eyes grew wistful. "He recognized me right away."

"How *romantic*." Anne Marie nibbled on her finger, unable to keep the bitterness out of her tone. "Love at first sight."

"*Nee*, it wasn't like that. You have to understand, Anne Marie. I loved your *daed* very much. I never thought I'd fall in love with someone else. But something changed these past few months.

Thomas started writing me first. Friendly letters, reminiscing about childhood. Then the letters became more personal."

"So I read."

Her mother scowled. "You're not making this easy, *dochder*."

"You should have said something to me. To all of us."

Mamm raised her voice. "I'm not allowed to have anything of *mei* own? Any privacy?"

Anne Marie opened her mouth, then shut it. She looked at the letters. Her mother was right. But that didn't change anything.

"Thomas is visiting his *bruder* for Christmas. He'll be coming here to meet you and Jonah and Christopher." Her mother stood, squaring her shoulders as she faced Anne Marie. "You will treat him better than you've treated me today."

Anne Marie pressed her lips to keep from saying something she'd regret.

"Since you want to know everything," *Mamm* continued, "I went to see Miriam today. I needed her advice about Thomas."

"And?"

The hardness in *Mamm*'s eyes softened. "He asked me to marry him." She smiled. "And when he comes here for Christmas, I'm going to tell him *ya*."

Although the words made Anne Marie take a step back, she couldn't deny the look of love in her mother's eyes. She looked away, guilt gnawing at her. She'd been unfair to her mother. And immature.

"Say something, Anne Marie. Please."

Anne Marie finally looked up, the glistening tears in her mother's eyes melting away the betrayal. "I want you to be happy, *Mamm*." She took a deep breath, forcing out the words. "If Thomas makes you happy, then that's what counts."

Her mother hugged her. "*Danki*, Anne Marie." She stepped back, wiping her eyes. "I understand why you were upset. It's a lot to take in, especially when we start packing for the move—"

"What move?"

Her mother paused. "The move to Ohio."

Anne Marie's chest felt like a load of baled hay landed on it. "Moving? We're *moving*?"

"Thomas's home is in Walnut Cre—"

"Our home is *here*."

"And his business is there. I can produce my cookbooks anywhere. Although I probably won't anymore. I want to focus on making a *gut* home for our *familye*."

"We have a *gut* home." She spread her arms, gesturing to the space around them. "We always have."

"And we will have one in Walnut Creek."

"What about Miriam? *Grossmutter* and *Grossvatter* have already moved away. You'll leave her here alone?"

"I talked to her about that too. She'll miss us, but she understands. And Seth's family is here. She'll hardly be alone." *Mamm* took Anne Marie's hand. "I know it will be a big adjustment for everyone."

She pulled her hand from her mother's. "I won't leave. I can live with Miriam and Seth."

"You can't. You know how small their *haus* is."

"I'll sleep on the couch."

Mamm rubbed her fingers across her forehead. "Miriam and Seth would take you in if you asked, but you know it would be a hardship. And unnecessary, since you would have a home with me and Thomas."

Anne Marie blinked away the tears. Her mother and Thomas.

It sounded strange. Unnatural. But her mother spoke of her future husband as if he'd always been a part of her life. She spoke of Thomas with love.

Her heart constricted. What about her life? Her friends, her candlemaking business? She had to start everything over because her mother fell in love?

"Now that you know," *Mamm* said, sounding more cheerful than she had in a long time, "we can start packing. The wedding will be in early January. We'll move right after that."

Anne Marie fisted her hands together. She couldn't do this. She couldn't leave everything she knew. Everyone she loved.

"*Mamm?*" Jonah's voice sounded from the opposite end of the house. "Anne Marie?"

Her mother sighed. "I guess it's time to tell the *buwe*." She looked at Anne Marie, hope in her eyes. "It would help if you could be supportive and an example for your *bruders*. You're not the only one having to sacrifice."

Anger bubbled up inside her. Unable to speak, she rushed past her mother, past Jonah and Christopher in the living room.

"Hey!" Jonah said, spinning around. "Where are you going?"

"Out." She opened the front door and ran into the cold evening, the screen door slamming behind her.

Nathaniel guided his buggy down the road, tucking his chin into his coat to ward off the chill. Good thing his horse knew the way home, as he wasn't as focused on driving as he should be. Anne Marie consumed his thoughts.

She was overreacting, but he sympathized with her. He

couldn't put himself in her place, since his parents had been married for years. Just thinking about one of them being with someone else was impossible. But Lydia deserved to be happy. So did Anne Marie.

A car behind him honked its horn, pulling his attention back to the road. As the vehicle zoomed past, Nathaniel looked in his side mirror. He squinted in the pale light of dusk. Someone was walking behind him. As he slowed his buggy, he could see it was Anne Marie.

He pulled the buggy to a stop, holding the reins as he came to a halt on the shoulder of the road. Although her street wasn't busy, it was best to be cautious. As she neared, he could see her rubbing her hands over her arms.

"Anne Marie," he said, moving toward her but keeping a grip on the horse. If he let go, his horse would head straight home. Anne Marie stopped a few feet away. "What are you doing out here?" he asked. When she didn't say anything, he tilted his head toward the buggy. "Get in."

She shook her head but walked toward the buggy.

"Wait." He slipped off his jacket and handed it to her. "You're freezing. Put this on."

"Then you'll freeze."

"I'll be all right."

She looked at the coat for a moment, then took it. The edge of the sleeves reached past her fingertips. Then she climbed into the buggy. When they were on their way, he said, "Want to talk about it?"

"*Nee.*" Her voice sounded thick.

His heart lurched. Anne Marie was several things: a bit excitable, a little melodramatic, and occasionally annoying. She was also tough. During their long friendship, he'd only seen her cry once, and that was when they were talking after her father's funeral. Whatever happened between her and Lydia after he left was serious.

Without thinking twice, he reached for her hand. She gripped it. Her fingers were cold, but they soon warmed in his palm. Neither of them spoke as he drove to his house. When he pulled into his driveway, he stopped in front of the clock shop. "Are you ready to talk now? We can *geh* into the workshop. *Nee* one will bother us there."

She nodded. Looked at him with tears in her eyes.

And his heart melted.

CHAPTER 6

"Here. This will warm you a little more."

Anne Marie took the mug of coffee from Nathaniel. "I never knew you had a coffeepot in here."

"It's in the back. We use a camping stove to percolate it. *Daed* can't *geh* more than a couple of hours without his *kaffee*."

She took a sip of the hot, strong brew as she sat on Nathaniel's workbench. He pulled a chair over and sat across from her, holding his own mug. "Now are you ready to tell me what's going on?"

Anne Marie paused. She didn't want to say the words out loud. But Nathaniel would find out soon enough, as would the rest of the district. She wanted him to hear it from her. "We're moving."

He frowned. "Who's moving?"

"My *mamm, mei bruders* . . . me." She explained everything to Nathaniel.

He became very still, as he usually did when he was deep in thought. But his expression remained unreadable. Finally he leaned forward. "I know you're upset, Anne Marie, but this isn't the end of the world."

The warmth she'd felt from the coffee and his coat dissipated.

"That's easy for you to say." Her eyes narrowed. "Your world hasn't been turned upside down."

"Look, I don't like the idea of you moving either." He stared at his coffee. "I really don't like it," he mumbled.

"What?"

He looked at her again, a muscle twitching in his left cheek. "At least you're not moving too far."

"Nathaniel, it's Ohio. That's a day's ride on a bus."

"*Ya*. Just a day's ride. It could be worse. You could be going to Florida."

"It doesn't make any difference." She set the mug on his spotless workbench, next to an old clock. "What if I lose touch with everyone here?"

"That won't happen. There are letters—"

"You know I don't like writing letters. I don't even mail out cards."

"Then you'll have to come back to visit. And I'll come visit you."

She looked at him, trying to judge if he was serious. He glanced down at his mug so she couldn't read his expression. Then he looked up, smiling. "And until you move, I promise we'll spend as much time together as we can."

She shot up from the bench. "But what if it isn't enough?" she said, shoving her hands into the pockets of his coat. She wasn't cold anymore, but for some reason she didn't want to take it off. "I feel like I'm losing everything. My home. My friends . . ." She looked at him. "You."

He stood and faced her, his deep brown eyes meeting hers. "That won't happen. I promise."

The words were easy to say with only a few inches between them. With a few months and several hundred miles separating them, there was no guarantee they would stay close. "I want to believe you."

"Then do."

She kept her gaze locked on his, and for the first time since her world had been flipped over, her pulse slowed. His steady presence had that effect on her. She forced a small smile. "I should *geh*. I don't want to worry *Mamm*."

"I thought you were mad at her."

"I am."

He half-smiled. "You know how contradictory you sound?"

She shrugged. "That's me, one big contradiction."

"*Nee*, you're not." He moved toward her. "I'll take you home. You'll feel better tomorrow."

She shook her head. "I'll walk. I need to clear *mei* head before I get home."

He pulled open a drawer underneath his worktable and gave her a flashlight. "Then at least take this. And keep *mei* coat. I'll get it from you later."

She nodded and took the flashlight. She spied the clock again. "This is unusual," she said, examining the tarnished silver. She loved old things. Every scratch, dent, and imperfection carried a memory. "It's very *schee*."

"You think?" He picked it up. "Looks neglected to me."

"Not neglected. Full of history." She glanced at him. "Are you restoring it?"

He nodded and placed the clock back on the bench.

"Then it will be even more beautiful when you're finished." Able to genuinely smile now, she ran her hand down his arm and linked her pinkie with his. "Thanks again, Nathaniel. You're always here when I need you."

"It's what friends are for, *ya?*"

"*Ya.*" Her smile dimmed as she released his finger. A thick lump formed in her throat. She couldn't believe that in less than a month they would be saying good-bye. Before the tears started and she embarrassed herself, she turned to leave.

"Anne Marie?"

The softness in his voice stopped her. When she saw his outstretched arms, she didn't hesitate to walk into them. How did he know she needed this? *Because he knows me better than anyone.*

"We'll figure this out." He rubbed his hand over her back. "Promise."

She closed her eyes and leaned against him, hearing the beat of his heart through his home-knitted sweater, waiting for the steady rhythm to comfort her. But despite his promises and the comfort of his strong embrace, she couldn't be hopeful. After tonight, nothing would ever be the same—including their friendship.

Almost an hour later, chilled to the inside of her bones, Anne Marie walked into her house. Through the darkness, a pale yellow gaslight shone from the kitchen.

She paused, weary but steeling herself for the scolding. But when she entered the kitchen, *Mamm* jumped up and ran to her. "I was just about to send Jonah and Christopher to find you." Her mom hugged her. "Please, Anne Marie. Don't do that again."

Anne Marie plopped down in the chair and nodded, snuggling into Nathaniel's coat, relieved that her mother wasn't angry, even though she deserved to be. Anne Marie inhaled, breathing in his scent that infused the wool and remembering the hug they'd shared.

"Do you want *kaffee?*" *Mamm* asked. "Maybe some chamomile tea?"

"You're not mad at me?"

Mamm joined her at the table, shaking her head. "I understand why you left."

"I shouldn't have been gone so long."

"You were at Nathaniel's, *ya?*"

She nodded.

"That's why I wasn't that worried." Her mother laid her hands in her lap and looked down at the table. "I told Jonah and Christopher about Thomas."

Anne Marie fingered an empty peppermint candy wrapper in Nathaniel's coat, not saying anything.

"Christopher seems okay with it, but you know him. He's always been easygoing. Jonah, on the other hand . . ." She looked up at Anne Marie and sighed.

Anne Marie didn't know what to say. Had she expected all of them to be happy to leave the only home they'd ever known? "Where's Jonah?"

"In the barn. He needs some time, just like you." Her mother looked tired. "I know you all are upset. But I really want you to give Thomas a chance. You don't understand what it's been like . . . I've been lonely since your *daed* died. Thomas has brought a light to *mei* life that I thought was snuffed out long ago. He's an answer to prayer. Not the way I expected because I never thought I'd leave Paradise. But God doesn't work according to our plans."

What about my plans? Why do I have to give up everything?
Guilt stabbed at her again for being so selfish. Yet she couldn't
help it. She stood. "I'm going to bed."

Her mother gave her one last look, then nodded.

Anne Marie went upstairs to her room and lay down on the
bed, not bothering to take off her *kapp* or Nathaniel's coat. She
fingered the wool lapels, drawing them closer to her face. Her
mother was right about so many things. Anne Marie could have
her candle business in Walnut Creek. She could come back and
visit her aunt Miriam and her other friends. Her life wouldn't end
if she left Paradise. She knew that to be true.

So then why did it feel that way?

Nathaniel tried to concentrate on repairing the simple alarm
clock in front of him, but he couldn't focus. He kept remembering the way Anne Marie felt in his arms—fragile, vulnerable,
yet comforting. He gripped a small screwdriver. He had tried to
cheer her up by talking about letters and visits. But he'd lied. The
idea of her leaving, of her not being a part of his life . . . how was
he supposed to accept that?

The alarm clock went off in his hands, the shrill noise making him jump. He searched for the switch to turn it off. When
that didn't work, he pried the batteries out—something he should
have done beforehand.

"Nathaniel? Are you all right?"

He glanced over his shoulder at his father and forced a nod.

"You seem distracted."

"I'm fine."

"Does it have something to do with Anne Marie being here last night?"

Nathaniel turned to face his dad. "How did you know she was here?"

"*Yer mamm* told me. Somehow she manages to know everything." His father stood, slowly straightening his back. He slid a thumb underneath one of his suspender straps. "Why didn't you invite her inside?"

Nathaniel turned his attention back to the alarm clock. "We needed to talk."

"How about you? Do you need to talk?"

Nathaniel stared at the alarm clock. What good would it do to talk about it? Anne Marie was leaving. Nothing he could say would change that. And nothing could fill the emptiness that started to grow inside him the moment Anne Marie told him she was moving.

"Let me know if you do." The tread of his father's work boots thumped on the floor as he left the workshop.

Nathaniel went back to fixing the clock. After the third time the screwdriver slipped off the screw, he gave up and shoved the alarm clock away.

Chapter 7

I'm sorry," *Aenti* Miriam said over her daughter's squalling. "The *boppli* is always hungry. Junior's appetite was never so big." She lifted the corner of her mouth. "Nor was his cry."

"She has a strong pair of lungs." Anne Marie faced Junior in his high chair and tried to get him to eat a piece of cubed ham.

Miriam sat in a chair in her kitchen and settled into feeding the baby. When Junior finally started eating and the baby stopped crying, Anne Marie glanced at her aunt.

"You didn't come over here to feed *mei sohn*," Miriam said.

"I need to spend as much time with him as possible. And with you." She looked at her tiny cousin. "I don't even know her," she whispered.

"Anne Marie." Miriam touched her hand. "It will be all right."

"That's what everyone tells me." She sighed. "Did you know about Thomas?"

"*Nee*. Lydia has always been a private person. We didn't know she was dating your *daed* until they announced their engagement."

Anne Marie nudged the sippy cup toward Junior. Keeping an engagement secret wasn't all that unusual in their community.

The reminder made her mother's secretive behavior make more sense. But it didn't make the situation any easier to accept. Junior picked up the sippy cup full of milk and started to drink. "*Mamm* says you're fine with us moving," Anne Marie said.

Her aunt frowned. "I wouldn't say *fine*. I understand, though." She looked at Anne Marie, her expression sympathetic. "I'll miss all of you. But we can write to each other—"

"And visit. I know." She turned to her cousin and touched the brown hair that flipped up from Junior's bangs. He shoved a cheese-flavored cracker in his mouth. "It won't be the same."

"True, it won't. But I haven't seen your *mamm* this happy in a long time."

Neither had Anne Marie. Since telling them about Thomas, her mother was more productive and chattier than ever, even humming while she was putting the bindings on her cookbooks.

Anne Marie couldn't say the same thing for herself. She had stacks of Christmas candle orders to fill, a few for specialty carved candles that took extra time to make. Yet instead of working on them, she was here with her aunt. She had to cherish every minute she had left in Paradise.

She had thought she would have seen Nathaniel over the past couple of days, but he hadn't been able to come to their usual Sunday game night and he hadn't stopped by. She still had his coat, although she knew he had another one. Still, she should have dropped it off at his house but she'd taken to snuggling with it at night. Part of her felt foolish for doing something so sentimental. Yet she couldn't bear not to have something of his with her as she tried to sort out her feelings.

She would miss Aunt Miriam and her family. She would miss Ruth and her other friends. But the ache in her heart that appeared every time she thought of leaving Nathaniel . . . that was new, and more painful than anything else.

"Anne Marie?"

She turned to look at her aunt again. "Sorry."

"Are you okay?"

"Just distracted, thinking about everything."

"There's a lot to think about." She removed the blanket covering the baby. Little Leah was sound asleep, her pink, heart-shaped mouth still puckered in a tiny *O* shape. "Your grandparents are happy living in Indiana. They say it's a new chapter in their lives."

"I don't want a new chapter." She sighed. One look from Aunt Miriam confirmed what Anne Marie already felt—she was being immature. "I do want *Mamm* to be happy. I just don't want to leave Paradise."

"I understand."

Everyone kept saying that, but Anne Marie had her doubts. She started to bite her fingernail, caught herself, and put her hands in her lap. "If you had moved away, you wouldn't have married Seth."

She adjusted the baby in her arms. "*Ya*. But I would have trusted that God had someone else for me."

"So it's that simple?"

Miriam paused. "*Nee*," she said softly. "I would be lying if I said it was." Her aunt's eyes grew wistful. "I wasn't sure I'd ever get married. I never thought I would be with someone as wonderful as Seth."

"But why? You and *Onkel* Seth are perfect for each other."

"I know that now, but at the time I didn't think so." She glanced down at her infant daughter. "I didn't think I deserved him, or anyone else." She looked back at Anne Marie. "But that was *mei* own insecurity, *mei* own lack of trust and belief. So, *nee*, I wouldn't have trusted God. Not that easily, not at that time."

Anne Marie wiped the crumbs off Junior's face, feeling touched by Miriam's admission. At least her aunt was being honest.

"Are you upset about leaving Nathaniel?" Aunt Miriam asked.

"Nathaniel?" Anne Marie lifted Junior out of the high chair. For some strange reason heat crept up her neck. "Why would you bring him up?"

"We were talking about Seth and I just assumed . . ." She shook her head. "Never mind." Aunt Miriam smiled. "I know you can't see it now, but this might be part of God's plan. I'm sure he has *gut* things in store for you in Ohio. Maybe you'll meet your future husband there."

Anne Marie frowned. "I'm not looking for a husband."

Miriam leaned closer, her gaze intense. "Maybe because Nathaniel's in the way?"

Anne Marie settled Junior in her lap, not looking at her aunt. "What do you mean?"

"It's one thing that you were friends with Nathaniel when you were children. But you're adults now. And if there's nothing romantic between you, then it's time to let each other *geh*."

She smoothed a wrinkle out of Junior's shirt. "It's not like I have a choice anymore."

"That could be God's point."

Anne Marie's head snapped up. "He wants to break up a life-long friendship? How is that *gut* for me?"

"To make you move from childhood to adulthood. You need to put childish things behind you. Nathaniel, nice *mann* that he is, is part of that. It's time to grow up, Anne Marie."

Anne Marie rested her chin on Junior's head. Was her aunt right? No one could argue she'd been acting like a child about the move, and she was ashamed of that. She was twenty years old. An adult. Yet she couldn't see how sacrificing her friendship with Nathaniel was in God's plan. How could she give up the most important person in her life?

That evening, Anne Marie helped *Mamm* with supper. Neither one spoke as they prepared the pork chops, creamy noodles, and sweet potatoes. When the pork chops were almost done, her mother finally said, "Did you have a nice visit with Miriam?" She began to slice a half loaf of bread.

Anne Marie tensed, her mind still filled with her aunt's advice. "*Ya.*"

"Leah is doing well?"

"Everyone is fine." She continued scrubbing the bowl she'd mashed the sweet potatoes in.

"Anne Marie." Her mother put her hand on her daughter's shoulder. "You're going to clean the finish right off that bowl."

"What? Oh, sorry." She rinsed it and put it in the drainer to dry.

Mamm stepped to the side, picked up the bowl, and ran a dry towel over the outside. "Christmas is in less than a week. Could you at least pretend to enjoy the holiday? I can't have both you and Jonah moping around."

A heavy weight pressed against her chest. Miriam and *Mamm* were right. She had to accept the wedding, the move, everything. She handed her mother a large metal spoon. "Don't worry. I won't put a damper on Christmas." She managed a smile. "You know it's my favorite holiday."

Her mother set down the dish and hugged her. She stepped back and wiped the tears from her eyes.

"Why are you crying?"

"I'm happy, Anne Marie. It tore *mei* heart out that you were so upset."

Anne Marie was surprised. Her mother hadn't seemed upset the past couple of days. Then again, lately she'd hidden her feelings well. A lot better than Anne Marie had.

"I'm so glad to have your support. And I know Jonah will come around." *Mamm* smiled through her tears. "You'll come to love Thomas. He's a wonderful *mann*."

Anne Marie hugged her *mamm*. "If you love him, he must be."

Later that night, Anne Marie entered her room to prepare for bed. She removed her *kapp*, unclipped her hair, and let her braid fall over her shoulder. She turned and saw Nathaniel's coat lying on her bed. She'd slept with it for the past couple of nights, drawing warmth and comfort from it. She picked up the garment and ran her fingers over the stitching. She noticed the small dark stain on the edge of one cuff, and realized the elbows were starting to wear a little thin. She squeezed the fabric one more time before taking a breath, then hung the coat up in her closet and shut the door. Tomorrow she would make sure Nathaniel got it back.

It was time to move on.

CHAPTER 8

The next morning, Anne Marie had just finished cleaning up the breakfast dishes when she heard a knock on the back kitchen door. She opened it to see Nathaniel standing there. "Can I come in?" he asked.

Her body tensed. What was wrong with her? She'd prayed last night for God to help her let go of the past, her close friendship with Nathaniel at the top of the list. She asked him to help her see the move as a fresh start. An adventure, like *Aenti* Miriam said. She thought she'd succeeded. But seeing him after they'd been apart for a couple of days brought unexpected feelings—both old and new—flooding over her.

There was no denying he was attractive. He always had been, even as a little boy. And he'd grown into a cute—no, make that handsome—*mann*. Yet Nathaniel's looks were the last thing she noticed about him—until now. Her heart fluttered as she looked at his lips. She glanced away, her face heating.

"I, uh, came to get *mei* coat," he said. He shifted from one foot to the other, not looking at her.

He was acting as awkward as she felt. So this was how it was going to be between them? She already missed their closeness, and she hadn't even moved away yet. "I'm sorry. I shouldn't have kept it so long."

"It's okay. I have this one." He tugged on his jacket, which was a thinner version of the one she was borrowing. "You know the real cold weather doesn't set in around here until January anyway."

She wouldn't be here in January. The frown on his face showed that he was thinking the same thing.

"Anne Marie, I'm sorry—"

"I'll get your coat." She fled the kitchen and ran to her room, opening the closet door where she'd left the coat last night. She didn't linger over it. She grabbed it off the hanger and dashed back to the kitchen.

"Here," she said, thrusting the garment at him.

"Danki." He took it from her but didn't move. A moment later he sat down at the kitchen table. She threaded her fingers together and rocked back and forth on her heels.

"Can we talk for a minute?" he asked.

She sat down across from him. "What about?"

He leaned forward. "I didn't come here just to get *mei* coat. I wanted to see how you were doing."

"I'm fine." She straightened and forced a smile. "I'm seeing this move as an adventure." She gritted out the last word.

"Oh. *Gut.*" He rubbed the palm of his hand back and forth on the table. "I'm glad you're okay with it."

"Ya."

"And like I said, our friendship isn't going to change."

But it already had, and they both knew it.

"I'll write to you, even if you don't write back," he added. "And I promise I'll visit."

Until he forgot about her. She nearly choked on the bitter thought.

"I'm also serious about spending more time together. I took the *daag* off from work."

Her eyes widened. "Your *daed* let you do that?"

"When I told him I was coming to see you, he didn't have a problem with it."

Anne Marie's heart tripped a beat. She'd never known him to put anything ahead of work. That he would set it aside to spend time with her . . .

But she had vowed to let him go. She grabbed a dishrag from the sink and started rubbing down the already clean counter. "I'm really behind on work. I have a lot of candles to make."

"I can help you."

She glanced over her shoulder at him. "It's pretty boring work."

"You don't seem to think so. You love it."

True. She paused. What would it hurt for them to make a few candles together? It wasn't like she could refuse the help. "All right. As long as you don't mind."

"I never mind being with you, Anne Marie."

She turned and put her hand over her quickening heart. Letting him slip out of her life wasn't going to be easy.

"Nathaniel, you're a terrible candlemaker."

Anne Marie thought she'd given him the simplest job, dipping red tapers, but he dipped them either too fast or too slow. The last ten he made were lopsided and had drips down the sides. She glanced at him, his brow furrowed in concentration. At least his terrible candlemaking had made her finally relax around him. "For all the delicate work you do on watches and clocks, I'm surprised."

"Watches and clocks are easier to deal with, trust me." He smirked as he looked at her, holding a hoop of candles over the wax-dipping can. "You should give me a break. This is *mei* first time, remember?"

Anne Marie took the warped candles from him and set them on the counter. Two years ago when she'd taken over the candle-making business from her mother, she converted a small garden shed into her own workshop. A gas-powered heater kept the workshop warm, along with several metal tubs of colored, melted wax warming over three camping stoves. She'd recycle the wax later and make proper candles, but right now she needed to give Nathaniel a different job.

She looked up at the two fancy carved candles on a shelf by the door. She used them as samples of her more intricate work, which she made for *Englisch* customers. She'd just made a red-and-white-layered cylinder candle. It was warm and pliable and ready to be carved. With his skilled hands, maybe he'd do better with a more complex job.

She picked up the sample candle and set it on the small round table in the middle of the workshop. Then she pulled out the chair. "Have a seat."

"For what?"

"To carve this." She put the freshly dipped candle next to the sample and handed him three carving tools. "Make this plain one look like the fancy one."

"You're kidding." He eyed the sample. "I can't do this. I messed up your simple candles."

"Nathaniel, I know how well you draw. I've also seen the nice work you do on those wooden clock cases. I think you can handle carving the candle. It doesn't have to look exactly like that one. Just make it pretty."

"Pretty." He sat down, still looking dubious.

"All right, then. Make it nice."

"Nice I can do." He studied the sample, picked up a round-tipped tool, and started to carve.

"You have to work quickly," she said, watching him cut and pull down thin strips of the candle, revealing the stacked red and white layers beneath. "If the candle cools it will be hard to work with."

"That won't be a problem." He wiped beads of perspiration from his forehead with the back of his hand.

"If it is, tell me, and I'll warm it—" But she could see he had already tuned her out. She should have had him do this to begin with. The candle was already looking better than pretty, with curlicues that surpassed her sample.

She turned to the pots of wax and started working on more red tapers.

"This is a nice workshop," he said from behind her. "I should have come in here before."

"Uncle Seth helped me fix it up. It was easier to work out here while *Mamm* perfected her recipes in the kitchen."

"Smells pretty *gut* too. Like . . ."

"Vanilla and cinnamon?"

"*Ya.*"

"Those are the most popular scents for Christmas." She forced the wicks out of the candles he'd ruined and folded the soft wax in her hand. "I make scented ones for the candle jars. They're already finished, thank goodness, or I'd be really behind." She dropped the ball of wax in the red wax can.

When he didn't say anything, she turned and checked his progress. Her eyes widened. The candle was beautiful, better than she could have ever made, even with years of practice. Nathaniel had put his own design on the candle. The base was a solid red, which would be shiny after she dipped it in the final setting wax. The strips of wax were curled over and under each other, with some rolled at the top to resemble tiny candy canes. The top of the candle was pure white, with small hearts carved in a wavy pattern a few inches from the rim.

"Oh, Nathaniel." She sat perched on the edge of his chair. "It's so *schee*." She carefully touched one of the delicate candy canes. The wax was still warm, but hard enough that it didn't give under the light pressure of her finger.

"You think so?" He peered at the candle, turning his head to look at it from different angles. "I think the hearts are crooked."

"The hearts are stunning. Mrs. Potter will love this candle."

He looked at her, his chin nearly touching her shoulder. They were so close she could see the light shadow of dark-brown stubble on his face. "We make a pretty *gut* team, *ya*?" he said, smiling.

But she couldn't speak. All she could do was stare at him, taking in his golden eyes. Why had she never noticed they were the color of honey before? Or that his breath smelled sweet, like the peppermints he was fond of chewing when the weather turned cold? They reminded him of Christmas, he always said.

And why hadn't she ever noticed how badly she wanted to kiss him?

"Anne Marie—"

"Nathaniel—"

They both stopped speaking. She thought his mouth was moving closer to hers. Or maybe she was hoping it was. It didn't matter, because her heart was certain that in a few seconds, she would know for sure.

A moment ago, Nathaniel wanted to bite off his tongue. He shouldn't have told Anne Marie what a good team they made. Just like he shouldn't be sitting this close to her.

But when she sat down on his same chair, he couldn't bear to move. It didn't matter that there was only one chair in the room and she had nowhere else to sit. He liked it. He liked everything about her—the way her lips pursed, the rosy color appearing on her cheeks, her pale-blue eyes that were so clear and vulnerable, his pulse thrummed. His heart ached at the thought of her leaving. He knew letters and visits wouldn't be enough for him.

Things had changed between them. He could feel it, and he didn't want to resist. Unable to stop himself, he leaned forward, closer . . . closer . . .

"Knock, knock!" said a female voice.

His head jerked from Anne Marie's. He looked over her shoulder and swallowed. Ruth Troyer walked inside.

CHAPTER 9

"There you are!"

Anne Marie shot up from the chair and turned around, almost knocking over Nathaniel's perfect candle. "Ruth?" She struggled to catch her breath. "What are you doing here?"

"Trying to find you." She walked farther inside and pulled a piece of paper out of the pocket of her coat. "I know it's late notice, but *Grossmutter* decided she needed more candles to put in the windows for Christmas. I told her it might be better if she got them at the store, but she wouldn't think of it."

Anne Marie took the paper from Ruth, hoping her friend didn't see the flames of embarrassment rising in her cheeks. "She's always been a loyal customer."

"*Ya.*" But Ruth wasn't looking at Anne Marie. Her gaze was planted on Nathaniel, who was putting finishing touches on the carved candle, his hand as steady as ever, while Anne Marie's insides were quaking.

Maybe she'd imagined the whole thing. And the thought of kissing Nathaniel never should have entered her mind. But now she couldn't think about anything else.

Ruth leaned close to Anne Marie. "What's Nathaniel doing here?" she whispered.

"Helping me. I'm behind on my orders."

"Oh." She kept staring at Nathaniel, but he didn't seem to notice. "Did you tell him?"

"What?"

"About . . . you know." Ruth tilted her head in his direction.

"I think I'm done." Nathaniel put down the tool and leaned back.

"My goodness!" Ruth clasped her hands together and walked over to the table. "Nathaniel, I had no idea you were so talented. It's the most *perfekt* candle I've ever seen."

Anne Marie rolled her eyes. Then she realized she had said almost the same thing. But hearing it from Ruth irritated her.

Nathaniel looked at Ruth. "I'm glad it turned out all right."

"It's better than all right." She bent down, as if she was inspecting the candle with great concentration. She leaned over a bit too far and put her hand on Nathaniel's shoulder.

"Sorry. Lost *mei* balance." But she didn't remove her hand.

"It's fine." He glanced at her, and didn't move either.

Anne Marie crumpled the piece of paper in her hand.

"Is this candle for sale?" Ruth asked Nathaniel. "I'd like to buy it."

"Nee." Anne Marie swooped up the candle and put it on her workbench. "It's already spoken for."

"Oh. Well, maybe I can order another one. As long as Nathaniel carves it."

He shrugged. "I don't know, I'm just helping Anne Marie out for a little while."

"Actually, I don't need any more help." She glared at him. He seemed to be enjoying Ruth's touch a little more than necessary.

Just a few days ago she was encouraging him to ask Ruth out. Now the thought of them together made her sick.

But it was for the best, wasn't it? Hadn't she come to that conclusion herself last night?

"I don't know about you, but I'm hungry," Ruth said. "We should have some lunch." She looked at Anne Marie. "Don't you think so?"

Anne Marie didn't miss the pleading message in her friend's eyes. She couldn't be mad at Ruth, who didn't know about the turmoil going on inside of Anne Marie. "I'm not really hungry. But you and Nathaniel can get something to eat."

He finally moved from underneath Ruth's grasp. "That's okay, Anne Marie," Nathaniel said. "I can stay and help."

"Like I said, I don't need any help." She stared at him, crossing her arms.

"But I thought you were behind on your orders."

"I just got caught up."

Ruth moved in between them. "She said she wasn't hungry, Nathaniel. But I'm starving. Do you mind sharing lunch with me?"

Bewildered, Nathaniel looked at Ruth, her light-brown eyes practically begging him to say yes, and Anne Marie, whose pale-blue eyes seemed colder than chipped ice. What was wrong with her? She'd gone from being her usual happy self to being snappish. No, not just snappy. She was angry. Was she mad that he tried to kiss her? Or did he do something else wrong?

"Going to lunch with Ruth is a great idea," Anne Marie said, unfolding her arms and going to the door. When she opened it, a welcome blast of cool air swept through the small workshop. Sweat rolled down his back as Anne Marie's cold gaze landed on him. "You two *geh* have lunch."

His brows pulled in. Usually he could figure out what she was thinking. Anne Marie wasn't exactly a closed book. But she'd shut herself off from him, and he didn't like it.

"Come on, Nathaniel," Ruth said. "We'll *geh* to *mei haus*. I'll make you the most *appeldicht* roast beef sandwich you've ever had. Plus apple pie for dessert."

"You don't have to *geh* to so much trouble." He kept his gaze on Anne Marie. She looked away, then finally turned her back on him and started dipping candles, as if both he and Ruth were invisible.

Fine. If she wanted to play games, so be it. She could be so childish it drove him *ab im kopp*.

But she was also funny. Talented. Intelligent. Beautiful.

"Nathaniel?" Ruth was already halfway out the door.

He paused, then turned. "Coming." He walked out the door with Ruth, but his mind was still on Anne Marie.

"Ouch!" Anne Marie peeled off a small splash of melted wax from the back of her hand. She'd been careless since Nathaniel and Ruth left a short while ago. Her last batch of tapers looked worse than his. She put her hands against the edge of the counter and closed her eyes, praying for focus and patience.

The door opened, and for a second, her heart flipped over,

thinking Nathaniel had returned. But it was only her brother. "What do you want, Jonah?"

He held up his hands. "What are you snapping at me for?"

"Sorry." She squeezed the bridge of her nose with her fingertips. "I shouldn't have done that."

"It's okay." Jonah came over to her workstation. "The candles look great."

"Liar." She picked up the warped tapers and held them in front of him.

"I didn't mean those." He pointed to Nathaniel's candle. "That's the best one you've done."

"It's not mine. It's Nathaniel's."

"Ah."

She looked at him. "Okay, Jonah. Why are you here? You never come in the workshop." He'd always complained it was too hot, smelly, and cramped.

"Just checking on you. We haven't had much time to talk about . . . you know."

She sat down. Jonah was rarely in a talking mood, and she could see he needed her undivided attention. "How do you feel about it?"

He shrugged. "I think I'm okay with it now."

"You sure?"

"*Ya. Mamm*'s happy. That's what I want." He picked at the bumpy dots of hardened wax on her worktable. "How about you?"

She tossed the useless candles to the side, not in the mood to fix them. "I've already told *Mamm* I'm happy for her. The rest will work itself out."

"Ah."

"Would you stop that!" She faced him. "Jonah, I'm okay

with *Mamm* getting married, I'm okay with moving to Ohio. Everything is absolutely fantastic. Couldn't be better."

"Now look who's lying."

She hunched her shoulders. When did her brother suddenly grow up? He was acting like an older brother, not a younger one. "Okay, maybe not fantastic. But it's well enough." She picked up a candle rack. "If you're done drilling me with questions, I have to get back to work."

"Your sour mood wouldn't have anything to do with Nathaniel leaving with Ruth Troyer?"

She kept her head down. "Why would I care if Nathaniel is with Ruth?"

"I don't know. Do you?"

This sibling chitchat was making her head pound. "Jonah, I'm the one who suggested he *geh* out with her. It was a coincidence that they were both here at the same time, and she invited him for lunch. End of story."

"Okay. As long as you're not upset or anything."

"I'm not! Now get out of here so I can finish these candles!"

Jonah backed away. Then he paused, as if wanting to say something.

Her patience was paper-thin. "What now?"

"*Nix.*" He shook his head and hurried out the door.

She put her head into her hands, frustrated. She'd been rude to her brother, she was upset with Ruth, and she resented Nathaniel. "*Ya*, everything is just perfect," she muttered.

She lifted her head and took in a deep breath. Her face heated, and not because of the hot wax in the pots on the camper stoves. How could she have been so foolish to think Nathaniel would want to kiss her? And why, after all these years of friendship, was the thought of him being with Ruth almost unbearable? So much had changed between them in such a short time. She'd never been so confused.

She stepped away from her workbench and closed her eyes. *Lord, help me.*

"I hope you like the pie." Ruth set a plate in front of Nathaniel, filled with the largest piece of pie he'd ever seen. She must have given him almost half of it. But after a huge lunch of an open roast beef sandwich smothered in gravy, pickled eggs, and cabbage slaw, he wasn't sure he could eat another bite. For sure, Ruth could cook.

She could also talk. And talk and talk and talk. Sitting in front of her, he could see her mouth moving but had no idea what she was saying. He'd tuned her out halfway through the meal. Apparently she'd never heard the old saying that silence was golden.

He and Anne Marie could spend hours together. Fishing, playing checkers, sitting on the grass at the edge of a pond—it didn't matter where they were. Neither of them ever felt the need to fill the silence between them.

He frowned. If Ruth hadn't walked in, he would have kissed Anne Marie. The thought of kissing his best friend should unnerve him. Instead, he was irritated he didn't get the chance.

But clearly she had a different idea. She couldn't wait to shove him out the door with Ruth.

"Is there something wrong with the pie?" Ruth asked.

He blinked, her face coming into focus. "*Nee.* Why?"

"You haven't tried it yet." She folded her hands on the table and smiled, her posture as straight as a fence post. "I picked the apples myself, from the Bakers' orchard. I know they're an *Englisch familye*, but they grow the best apples in the area. Do you like their apples?"

"I guess." He took a bite of the pie. The flaky crust dissolved in his mouth. Wow. He could probably choke this down, even with his full stomach.

"Are you going to the singing at the Keims' on Sunday? It's the last one before Christmas."

"*Nee*. I'll be at Anne Marie's."

Her bottom lip poked out slightly. "Why?"

"I always *geh* over there on Sundays."

"Don't you think it's time you stopped?"

He put down his fork and looked at her, dumbfounded.

She unclasped her hands. "Nathaniel, she's leaving."

"Which is why I'm going over there on Sunday." He ran his hand across the back of his neck. They wouldn't have too many Sundays left.

Ruth tapped her fingernail against the edge of her plate. "You're spending too much time with her. You always have."

He clenched his hand. "You're not one to judge how I spend *mei* time. Or who I spend it with."

"I don't mean it that way." She sighed softly and reached for his hand. He wanted to pull away, but she held onto it with a tight grip. "I care about you, Nathaniel. A lot." She smiled and squeezed his hand.

He leaned back. When Anne Marie had encouraged him to ask Ruth out, he'd briefly considered it. But so much had changed in a few short days.

"I know you and Anne Marie are *gut* friends," she continued, her voice sticky sweet, like the pie he couldn't finish. "But you have to be realistic. Your relationship with Anne Marie can't last forever. You can't spend your Sundays playing games, pretending you're still *kinner*. You're a *mann* now." She leaned forward and licked her bottom lip. "You need to be thinking about the future. Maybe one with me."

He squirmed, finally able to pull his hand away from hers. "Ruth—"

"If you're worried about Anne Marie, she told me she doesn't think about you that way."

"You don't know that." The words flew out of his mouth.

Ruth folded her hands in her lap, her smile tightening. "I see."

"See what?"

"That you have feelings for her." She shook her head, as if she felt sorry for him. "I can't say I'm surprised. You wouldn't be with her so much if you didn't."

Her superior tone irritated him. "You don't know what you're talking about."

She tilted her head. "It's okay. I've talked to Anne Marie about us." Ruth stood and walked around the table. She moved close to him, then leaned against the table edge. "She's already given us her blessing." She touched his shoulder, then bent over and whispered in his ear. "I can help you get over her, Nathaniel. What you feel for her will fade in time."

He looked up at Ruth but didn't move beneath her touch. He didn't appreciate the way she acted like she knew him. She was too pushy, and bolder than he was comfortable with. Yet he could see she was genuine.

And she was right. Anne Marie would always think of him as part of her childhood. Not part of her future.

Ruth reached out her hand. Nathaniel looked at it. Paused. Then hesitantly put his hand in hers.

CHAPTER 10

On Sunday evening, Anne Marie paced the living room. She kept peeking out the window looking for Nathaniel. An hour after his usual arrival time, she decided he wasn't coming.

She turned to the coffee table in the living room. She'd already set up the game. Life on the Farm, his favorite. She knelt down and started gathering up the pieces, trying to stem the despair welling up inside. She hadn't seen him since he'd left with Ruth a few days ago. Today they didn't have church, so she hadn't expected to see him until tonight. Hadn't he promised they'd spend as much time together as possible?

But that was before she'd pushed him and Ruth together. Before she decided to let him go. Before she realized her feelings for him ran deeper than friendship.

Still, she had hoped he would come. Even though she pushed him away, tried to get him out of her mind and heart, she had wanted to see him tonight.

"Why are you putting up the game?" Her mother walked into the living room, holding several white taper candles in plain brass candleholders. She went to the window and placed one on the sill. "Where's Nathaniel?"

"He's not coming."

"Oh?" She turned around. "Did something happen?"

"I guess he couldn't make it tonight."

"That's strange. He never misses game night." She crossed over to the other window in the living room and put a candle in it. Tomorrow she would tie back the curtains, and in the evening, she and Anne Marie would light the candles for the few nights leading up to Christmas.

"I'm going to Miriam's tomorrow to talk about wedding preparations." Her mother smiled, her eyes sparkling. "Would you like to join us?"

Anne Marie fiddled with the lid of the board game. She had promised to be supportive. And she wanted to be. But she couldn't take discussing wedding plans, especially right now. "I'll let you know."

"Oh. Okay." Her mother's smile faded a bit.

Anne Marie stood, chastising herself for being selfish. "I'm sorry. Of course I'll *geh*."

"Miriam and I can take care of it."

"I know, but I want to help. I wasn't thinking straight when I answered the first time."

Her mother touched her arm. "*Danki*, Anne Marie. I'm glad you want to be a part of this." She started to leave the room.

"*Mamm?*"

She turned around. "*Ya?*"

"How did you know you were in love with Thomas?" The question wrested free from her thoughts, like a bird escaping its cage. She hadn't meant to voice the words or to pry. But suddenly she really wanted an answer.

Her mother sat down on the couch. "I'm not sure how it

happened. I can't really pinpoint a moment when I realized I loved him."

Anne Marie sat on the floor at her mother's feet. She wrapped her arms around her knees, the skirt of her dress touching the tops of her stocking-covered feet. "What if you change your mind?"

"What do you mean?"

"When he gets here. What if you regret saying you'll marry him?"

Mamm crossed her legs at the ankles. "Anne Marie, even though this is sudden to you, it's not to me and Thomas. We've prayed about this. I've never been more sure about anything in my life . . . except when I married your *daed*." She touched her knees and leaned forward. "Remember, Thomas and I were friends when we were younger. We rekindled that friendship when we started writing each other. One thing I've learned is that friends are life's treasures. But sometimes when you least expect it, a friendship blossoms into love." Her mother stood. "I hope that eases your mind."

Anne Marie nodded. It did about *Mamm* and Thomas, but confused her further about Nathaniel.

"I still have a couple of cookbooks to finish binding. Nothing like doing things at the last minute."

Popping up to her feet, Anne Marie said, "I'll help you."

"I can do them." She looked at the game on the table. "You shouldn't put that on the shelf just yet. Nathaniel is sure to come."

She nodded, but didn't agree.

After her mother left, Anne Marie sat down on the couch and stared at the game, willing Nathaniel to come as the minutes ticked away. Half an hour later she gave up and put the board game away.

Her mother's friendship with Thomas started a new beginning, but it appeared that Anne Marie and Nathaniel's friendship was coming to an end.

Nathaniel stood outside Anne Marie's house on the edge of the yard by the road. Instead of driving, he had walked, hoping the cold air and exercise would straighten his thoughts. They didn't, and the closer he got, the more confused and nervous he became. When he arrived, he couldn't bring himself to go inside.

For the first time in his life, he had no idea what to say to Anne Marie. Should he tell her about his changing feelings toward her? Or follow Ruth's advice and end their friendship? The thought pained him. Still, he couldn't deny they both needed to be free of each other in order to move on.

The problem was, he wasn't sure he wanted to move on.

The light in the window disappeared. Nathaniel exhaled, his breath hanging in cloudy puffs in front of him. A full moon filled the clear sky. He pushed his hat lower on his head, shoved his hands in the pockets of his coat, and headed for home.

"Nathaniel."

He turned at the sound of Jonah's voice. The kid was walking toward him from the barn. He didn't stop until he was a few feet away, close enough that Nathaniel could see the spark of anger in his eyes. "What are you doing?" Jonah asked.

"Leaving." He hated the dejection in his voice. "Anne Marie's gone to bed already."

"Because you didn't show up for your game." Jonah put his hands on his hips. He wasn't wearing a coat, and his stance emphasized his broad shoulders. "I don't know what's going on with you two," Jonah said. "Normally I stay out of things. But when *mei schwester* is upset, then it becomes *mei* business."

Nathaniel faced him. "She's upset?"

"Of course she is. You left with Ruth Troyer the other day. Then you don't show up for your weekly game night that's been going on forever." He frowned. "Except you did, but you didn't tell her you were here. I don't get that at all."

"It's complicated."

"I don't care." He stepped forward and looked Nathaniel in the eye, the straight, serious line of his brow illuminated by the silvery moonlight. "If you have something to say to Anne Marie, you need to say it. If not, stop wasting her time." Jonah turned and started to walk away. "Don't be a coward, Nathaniel. You're better than that."

His ego stinging, Nathaniel opened his mouth to rebuke him. He didn't have to take advice from Anne Marie's little brother. Or from Ruth Troyer, for that matter. He could make his own decisions. And it was time he did just that.

CHAPTER 11

"Anne Marie, did you polish the furniture in the living room?" Anne Marie stilled the broom she was holding and rolled her eyes at the sound of her mother's frantic voice from the other end of the house. She'd been like this for the past two days, fluttering around, making sure everything was ideal for Thomas's first supper with them tonight. "*Ya, Mamm.* I polished it."

"All of it?"

"*Ya.*" She went back to sweeping the kitchen as her mother rushed in. Anne Marie looked up and saw the gleam in her eyes, the rosy tint of her cheeks. She put her hand on her mother's arm. "Everything is fine, *Mamm.* Don't worry."

"I'm not worried." *Mamm* hurried to the stove, wiping her hands on her clean apron. She opened the oven, releasing the scent of garlic and peppercorns into the air. "Almost done," she said, closing the door.

"*Gut.*" Christopher looked out the kitchen window. "Because he's coming up the driveway."

"He's what?" Her mother turned to Anne Marie. "But supper's not ready, the table isn't set—"

"Christopher can set the table," Anne Marie said.

His jaw slacked. "What? That's a *frau*'s job."

Anne Marie shot him a glare before turning back to her mother. "*Geh* ahead and let Thomas in. Once you're settled in the living room, I'll bring you both a glass of tea."

"Okay." Her mother nodded, but seemed anything but okay. Anne Marie smiled. She wasn't used to seeing her *mamm* this flustered. She turned her mother by the shoulders and shooed her out of the kitchen.

"Jonah doesn't have to set the table," Christopher grumbled.

"I'm sure he's helping Thomas with his horse." Anne Marie tasted the mashed potatoes, which were warming on top of the stove. Scrumptious, as usual. She hoped Thomas knew how lucky he was to be marrying a good cook. If he didn't know, he was about to find out.

A plate landed on the table with a clatter. Anne Marie left the stove and took the rest of the dishes from her brother. "Never mind, I'll do it."

Christopher grinned and retreated from the kitchen.

She tried to focus on setting a pretty table, not on the nerve-wracking fact that her mother was in the living room with her future stepfather. As she placed the last plate on the table, she guided her mind elsewhere. It immediately went to Nathaniel, as it had done since Sunday, despite trying to keep herself busy making her candles.

She gripped the edge of the table at the image of Nathaniel and Ruth. Jealousy twisted inside her like an ugly weed winding around her heart. She'd never had a reason to be jealous, and she didn't like the feeling. For the first time she was looking forward to the move. She couldn't bear the thought of seeing Nathaniel and Ruth together.

She finished setting the table, calming her frayed nerves with a silent prayer. She set the candle Nathaniel had carved in the middle of the table. Her customer had canceled her order, and Anne Marie decided to keep the beautiful wax creation. Just then her mother walked in the kitchen.

"That's lovely." She put her hand on Anne Marie's shoulder, her face glowing. "Your skills have improved."

"Danki." She didn't bother to explain the truth. It didn't matter anymore. "Where is Thomas?"

"Talking to Jonah outside. That *bu* is giving him a thorough questioning."

"I'm not surprised." She felt a little sorry for Thomas.

The distant thud of heels against wood sounded right outside the kitchen. "They're coming. Are you sure everything is okay, Anne Marie?"

She nodded and gave her mother a quick hug. "It is. I promise."

Jonah and Christopher walked in the kitchen first, followed by a stocky man with a mop of ginger-red hair threaded with gray. His blue eyes were wide set, and he held onto his hat, gripping it by the brim as if it were his lifeline. He looked nothing like her father, who had been taller, thinner, and darker. But he was handsome in his own way.

She glanced at her mother, who couldn't keep her eyes off him. They both seemed frozen in their own moment. Watching them, Anne Marie realized how deeply her mother loved him, and that he truly loved her.

She relaxed and gave Thomas a genuine smile, beckoning him into the kitchen. "I hope you're hungry," she said, pulling out the chair at the head of the table. *"Mamm* made a feast."

Anne Marie put away the last clean pot, then drained the dirty dishwater from the sink. Her mother and Thomas had disappeared into the living room after eating. Jonah and Christopher went to the barn, leaving her to clean the kitchen alone.

She wiped down the counter, then turned to the table. The candle was still in the center, unlit. She walked to it, touching one of the delicate white and red curls. The empty kitchen instantly felt too small. She grabbed her coat off the peg by the back door and went outside.

The light of a lantern shone from the barn, where her brothers were probably taking care of the animals for the night. She breathed in the cold air, crossing her arms over her chest. It still hadn't snowed, unusual for this time of year.

"You're not too cold out here?"

She turned to see Thomas approach. He had his hat on but wasn't wearing his coat. "Sure you're not?" she asked as he arrived at her side.

"I'm a human heater." He smiled. She could see his slightly crooked teeth gleaming in the darkness. "That's what my late wife told me." He paused. "She would have liked you."

Anne Marie tilted her head and looked at him. *"Ya?"*

"She appreciated hardworking people. Lydia told me about your candlemaking business. How successful it is. You don't have success without hard work."

A knot formed in her throat. It felt good to have someone acknowledge her efforts.

"I know the move will be tough, Anne Marie. I wish it could be different."

"It's as God wills." She turned to him, a sense of peace slipping over her. "I never thought I'd leave Paradise. But that seems to be what God wants of me. Of our family."

Thomas's shoulders relaxed. "There's a busy tourist business in Holmes County," he said, his deep voice sounding less tentative. "You won't have any problem finding customers for your candles."

"That's *gut*." She turned to him and gave him her warmest smile. "We should *geh* back inside. I'm sure *Mamm* is waiting for you."

He faced her and swallowed. "Your *Mamm* said you were something special. She was right."

"She was right about you too."

As they walked back inside, Anne Marie realized everything would be okay. While she was still unsure about Nathaniel and the part he would play in her life in the future, she was sure about one thing. Thomas Nissley was a *gut* man who made her mother happy. She couldn't ask for more.

CHAPTER 12

While Christmas Day was a time of contemplation and quiet celebration of Christ's birth, the day after Christmas was anything but.

The Smucker house was filled to bursting with people. Jonah and Christopher were playing Dutch Blitz against Seth and Thomas, who in a few short days had fit seamlessly into the family. *Mamm* was holding a sleeping Leah while *Aenti* Miriam played blocks with Junior on the floor. Anne Marie watched her mom and Thomas sneaking sweet glances at each other when they thought no one was looking.

Anne Marie stood to the side, breathing in the scent of fresh popped corn, buttered and seasoned to mouthwatering perfection. Flames flickered on several of her vanilla and cinnamon candles, their sweetly spiced aroma mixing with the mugs of warm apple cider. She heard the laughter, saw the smiles. And wished she could share in their happiness, instead of being on the sidelines.

She hadn't forgotten that Nathaniel had a standing invitation for Second Christmas, but apparently he had. He was probably with Ruth and her family today. Or maybe with his own.

She went in the kitchen to fix herself a cup of hot cocoa. Her mind wandered back in time, to all the memories she held close over the years. She thought about when she and Nathaniel were eight and they'd lie in the grass, counting the stars, only to end up covered in mosquito bites. When she was twelve and he and her brothers had hidden in the loft of the barn and dumped a bucket of cold water on her head when she walked in. But she had gotten him back when she stuck a frog in his coat pocket before he went home.

She peered out the kitchen window. Large, fluffy flakes of snow floated down from the dark sky. A white Christmas after all. She took her hot chocolate and stepped out on the back porch. Stuck her tongue out and caught a snowflake. Another memory with Nathaniel. She'd never realized until now that most of her sweetest memories included him.

She didn't know how long she stood outside, sipping luke-warm hot chocolate, wrapped in a cloak of the past, until she noticed her own shivering and the snow that had blanketed the ground.

When she went back into the kitchen, her aunt was putting two mugs in the sink. She looked up at Anne Marie. "I wondered where you went off to." She grimaced. "Have you been outside long? You must be freezing."

Anne Marie set the half-full mug in the sink. "I just needed some fresh air."

"I'm pleased with how you're handling this, Anne Marie. I know you were troubled at first, but I'm glad you've come to terms with everything."

Not everything. She exhaled. "I'm sorry for the way I acted when I first found out. I should have been more supportive."

"You don't need to apologize. Everyone understands,

especially *yer mamm*." Aunt Miriam walked toward the mudroom off the kitchen. "Seth and I are heading home before the snow gets too deep." She disappeared for a moment and returned with coats, hats, and her black bonnet. "Merry Christmas, Anne Marie."

She hugged her aunt. "Merry Christmas."

Thomas left shortly afterward, also not wanting to get stuck in the snow. Her brothers were already upstairs and her *mamm* had started tidying up the living room. "I'll get that," Anne Marie said.

"You sure?" Although her mother looked happy, she also seemed tired.

"I'm sure. Get some rest. *Gut nacht, Mamm*."

Moments later Anne Marie put the card game in the drawer of the side table. She cleaned out the popcorn bowl and the corn popper and put them away. Folded the green-and-red quilt Aunt Miriam had given them for Christmas ten years earlier and laid it over the back of the couch. And tried not to cry.

She looked around the living room. The wedding was planned for two weeks from today, and a couple of days later she would be on her way to Ohio. *God, help me. One minute I think I'm okay with moving, and the next I'm not. I think I'm okay with Nathaniel not being in my life, and then I'm not. I can't get through this without your help, Lord.*

She blew out the candles in the windows, then walked to Nathaniel's candle, the flame dancing and illuminating his exquisite carving. Her mother had wanted to light it, still not knowing Anne Marie hadn't carved it. She watched red wax drip down the side, altering the curves and curlicues, changing it forever. The candle, like her life and her relationship with Nathaniel, would never be the same.

She leaned over to blow it out when she heard a knock at the back door. Who would be coming over this late and with heavy snow falling? When she answered the door, she froze. "Nathaniel?"

"I . . ." Snow covered his black hat, the shoulders of his coat. The coat she'd slept with for several nights. She leaned against the doorjamb, weary of being confused, upset, hurt. She was tired of it all.

"It's late, Nathaniel. Christmas is over." She started to close the door when he stopped her.

"Don't." He locked his gaze on hers. "Don't send me away . . . even though I deserve it."

Nathaniel's knees buckled at the pain in Anne Marie's eyes. Pain he'd caused. He shouldn't have stayed away so long. He shouldn't have waited until now to see her. To let her know how he felt.

Before she could push him away, he walked inside. He set down the paper bag he was carrying and put his arms around her. He heard her gasp as he pressed her against him, burying his face in her neck.

Yes, he should have done this a long time ago.

When she relaxed against him, he closed his eyes. When he heard her sob, he looked at her. "I'm sorry," he whispered.

She pulled away and wiped the tears from her face. "We need to talk."

He nodded as she turned on the gas lamp near the window. He followed her to the couch and sat down. She rubbed her hand over her eyes one more time before looking away.

He'd practiced the words all the way over here, hurrying his horse through the newly fallen snow that had turned to slush on the roads. But now that he was here, the words wouldn't come. He couldn't tell her how he'd spent the past few days in prayer, had talked to his father, and had told Ruth that they were over before they'd even started. He didn't doubt his decision. But he did doubt his ability to convince Anne Marie.

"I'm glad you're here," she finally said. "I have something to tell you." She took a deep breath. "Nathaniel, it's time we both moved on."

His breath hitched. "What?"

"I know we talked about writing letters and visiting, but that won't last."

"Anne Marie—"

"And I'm glad you and Ruth found each other." Tears pooled in her eyes again. "You'll both be very happy together."

He couldn't stand to listen to this anymore.

"Maybe I can come for the wedd—"

He took her face in his hands and kissed her.

Anne Marie couldn't stop Nathaniel from kissing her, and she didn't want to. The kiss was sweet and gentle and he parted from her too fast. When he drew away, she fought for words. "What about Ruth?" she asked when she was able to catch her breath.

He shook his head. "There's nothing between me and Ruth." He took her hand.

Her palm tingled in his. Then she came to her senses. "Wait a minute." She pulled out of his grasp. "You stood me up on Sunday."

He rubbed his right temple. "About that—"

"And then you're late tonight." She crossed her arms over her white apron. "Now you're kissing me. What's going on, Nathaniel?"

"I'm sorry about last Sunday and about being late tonight. But I needed time."

"Away from me?"

He cupped her chin in his hand. "I had to sort things out. Most important, I had to pray about us. I've always cared about you, Anne Marie. You're *mei* best friend. I didn't want to do anything to ruin that. But I knew things couldn't stay the same between us."

"Because I'm moving." She looked away.

He tilted her face toward him. "*Nee*. Because I love you."

She stilled, letting his words wash over her in a warm wave. "You do?"

He chuckled and let his hand drop to his side. "That shouldn't be a surprise. Everyone else has known. Even before I did. And I think from the way you kissed me back, you do too."

She couldn't deny it. "So? We love each other." It felt strange and right at the same time to say the words out loud. "There's not much we can do about it now."

"We could get married."

Her eyes widened. "Are you serious?"

"Very. I don't want you to leave. I don't want to be separated from you. I know I said letters and visits would be enough." He drew her to him. She laid her cheek against his chest, feeling him rest his chin on top of her head. "But we both know it won't."

He was right. Being in his arms, feeling his heart beating in time with hers . . . how could she be apart from him? "*Ya.*"

"Does that mean . . . ?"

She looked up at him. "It means I'll marry you."

He pulled her to him and held her. A moment later, he sat back. He grinned, his expression holding a mixture of happiness and relief. He stood, went to the door, and picked up the brown paper bag. He opened it and pulled out the antique mantel clock she'd admired in his workshop. "Merry Christmas."

She took it from him, touching the polished silver decorations, every trace of tarnish removed. The smooth blue box that encased the simple clock looked fresh, but still showed its age. "It's beautiful."

He sat down next to her. "I'm glad you like it."

She looked at him. "And all I did was make a plate of your favorite brownies."

"Can't wait to eat them." He grinned.

She looked at the clock again. "I can't believe you're giving this to me. Doesn't your *daed* want to sell it in the shop?"

"He gave it to me, to give to someone special." He took the clock from her and turned it around. A small brass plate was attached to the back. She read the engraved words: *Out of friendship grew love. Nathaniel and Anne Marie.*

Tears came to her eyes. Goodness, she'd never been this weepy in her life. But they were tears of joy. "You were that sure I would say *ya*?"

"I was pretty sure." He rubbed his thumb over her knuckle. "Okay, I was praying. Really hard."

She leaned over and kissed his cheek.

"It's about time."

Anne Marie pulled away from Nathaniel and found Jonah standing on the steps. "How long have you been there?" she asked, cutting her eyes at him.

He waved her off and continued down the stairs. "Don't mind me, I'm just getting a brownie."

"Those are Nathaniel's."

"Okay, some pie, then." He headed toward the kitchen. "So when's the wedding?" he asked over his shoulder.

Her mouth dropped open. "How did you know?"

He gave her a wily grin. "Like I said, it's about time."

CHAPTER 13

I wish I wasn't so nervous."

Anne Marie smiled at her mother. She straightened the shoulders of *Mamm*'s wedding dress, the dark-blue fabric complementing her deep brown eyes. "You look *schee*, *Mamm*. And happy."

"So do you." She hooked her arm through Anne Marie's. They turned and looked in the mirror above the dresser. "Are we ready for this?"

Anne Marie studied the two of them in the mirror. In a few minutes their lives would be altered forever. Several weeks ago she'd fought against change. Wondered about God's plan. And along the way, fell in love with her best friend. She placed her hand over her mother's. "*Ya*. We're ready."

They walked out of *Mamm*'s bedroom and into the living room. Anne Marie instantly locked eyes with Nathaniel. He grinned, and the butterflies dancing in her stomach calmed. Her mother moved to stand next to Thomas. Anne Marie took her place next to Nathaniel. Between them, the bishop started the double wedding ceremony.

As he spoke, Anne Marie glanced around a room filled with family and close friends. Her grandparents, her aunt Miriam and uncle Seth, her brothers. Then she saw Nathaniel's mother wipe a tear. She'd been the most overjoyed of all when she heard the news. Like Jonah, she had simply said, "It's about time."

She glanced at her mother and Thomas. Soon enough she'd have to say good-bye to them and her brothers. While they started a new life in Ohio, she would start her new life as Mrs. Nathaniel Mast. The thought added a touch of bittersweetness to her heart.

But she didn't have to think about good-byes right now. Today was her wedding day, and she was rejoicing over the greatest gift she'd ever received—friendship that turned into love.

DISCUSSION QUESTIONS

For *Building Trust*

1. How do you think Vernon could have responded differently when Joel and Grace announced their engagement?
2. Have you ever held a grudge against someone who betrayed you? How were you able to forgive and move on?
3. Joel never gave up on Grace. How does his dedication remind you of God's pursuit of us?
4. Do you think Vernon and Abner could have a successful partnership? Why or why not?

For *A Heart Full of Love*

1. Do you think Edna's worry over Ellie taking care of the twins was justified? Why or why not?
2. Edna thought she had good intentions when it came to taking care of her grandbabies, but she was really acting out of fear and worry. Have there been times when fear

or worry dictated your actions? How did God help you during those times?

3. Do you think Edna would have been as worried about the babies if Ellie wasn't blind?

4. Ellie and Edna both had to learn how to let God be in control of their lives. Have you ever faced this challenge? What helped you "let go and let God"?

5. What advice would you give Ellie about how to deal with her mother?

For *Surprised by Love*

1. What advice would you give Emily about how to handle her mother?

2. Do you think Reuben was being too hard on himself? Why or why not?

3. How should Emily and Reuben have handled things differently when it came to lying about their "relationship"?

4. Do you think Louwanda will mind her own business after Emily and Reuben marry? Why or why not?

For *A Gift for Anne Marie*

1. Anne Marie knew she shouldn't have read her mother's letters. What would you have done in the same situation?

2. Do you think Nathaniel was fair to Ruth? Why or why not?

3. Anne Marie questioned God's plan when she found out she was moving. Have you ever wondered why God has led you down a certain path, especially if it caused disappointment or discomfort? How did you deal with it?

4. Do you think Anne Marie and Nathaniel would have fallen in love without the threat of her moving away?

ACKNOWLEDGMENTS

As always a huge thank you to my editors, Becky Monds and Jodi Hughes, for their help and expertise. And a big thank you to you, dear reader, for going on another reading journey with me. I hope you enjoyed visiting with more characters from Middlefield, and the families from *An Amish Home* and *An Amish Summer*, while visiting some old friends from *An Amish Second Christmas* and *An Amish Cradle*.

Coming Fall 2018

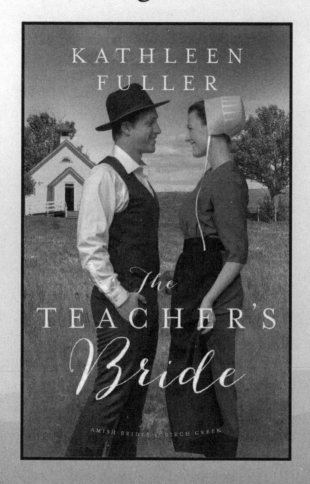

Available in print and e-book

Discover more from Kathleen Fuller!

Read more in these collections from our beloved authors!

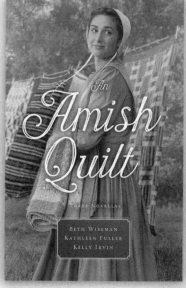

Available June 2018

Available July 2018

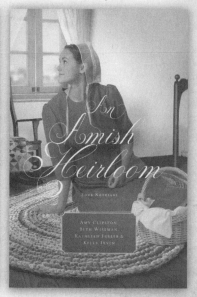

Available in print and e-book

Available in print and e-book

ABOUT THE AUTHOR

Kathleen Fuller is the author of several bestselling novels, including *A Man of His Word* and *Treasuring Emma*, as well as a middle-grade Amish series, the Mysteries of Middlefield.

Visit her online at www.kathleenfuller.com
Twitter: @TheKatJam
Facebook: Kathleen Fuller